Captivated

Annette Mori

Captivated

Annette Mori

Affinity
eBook Press
NZ
2017

Captivated
© 2017 by Annette Mori

Affinity E-Book Press NZ LTD
Canterbury, New Zealand

1st Edition

ISBN: 978-0-947528-38-6

All rights reserved.

Editor: JoSelle Vanderhooft
Proof Editor: Alexis Smith
Cover Design: Irish Dragon Designs

Acknowledgments

A huge thank you to all of my beta readers, Gail Dodge, Cathie Williamson, Ali Spooner, Carrie Camp, and my sister, who made great suggestions to improve the initial draft. Of course, once again I have to acknowledge Erin O'Reilly who is a constant support and encouragement to me. I am honored to call her a friend and have her support me in my journey. I would also like to express my gratitude to Affinity Press and the wonderful trio (JM Dragon, Erin O'Reilly and Nancy Kaufman) who continue to provide feedback to tighten up manuscripts that need assistance and publish my sometimes unconventional work.

I am eternally grateful for the opportunities they give me to let my stories see the light of day. My other family members who are also very supportive, include my nephew, Aaron and his wife, Chelsea, and my little sister, Kim and my father who struggles to read my books with one eye. I always enjoy working with the beta editor and both Kay Carney and Nancy Kaufman helped to improve my story. Thanks to Jo Selle Vanderhooft for her magic as the final editor to tighten the story even further. Inevitably there are those pesky final errors that slip through and I am thankful that the final proof editor, Alexis Smith, caught those before the book went to print. Nancy Kaufman is a rock star with her covers. Nancy is also a promoter extraordinaire.

A huge thanks to all the other readers and fellow writers who have sent personal e-mails, written reviews and posted nice things on Facebook (you know who you are). The Affinity authors are an especially supportive group and often share posts or send words of encouragement. Finally, my wife, Jody, continues her support even when it interferes with our time.

Dedication

To all the readers out there who continue to support my unconventional style of writing because without you I am sure I would never write another book. To my wife who I love dearly for her patience and her ability to take care of me when I fail to do that myself.

Table of Contents

Also by Annette Mori

The Termination

The Review

The Ultimate Betrayal

Locked Inside

Out of This World

Asset Management

The Incredibly True Adventure of Two Elves in Love

(Affinity 2014 Christmas Collection)

Love Forever, Live Forever

The True Story of Valentine's Day

Vampire Pussy...Cat

Nicky's Christmas Miracle X3

(*It's in Her Kiss*, Affinity's Charity Anthology)

Chapter One

Juliet opened her eyes and felt the cold steel lightly pressed against her forehead. She didn't want to complain about the hard, uncomfortable wood chair Tanner had secured her to—that was the least of her problems. Fortunately Tanner had used zip ties instead of duct tape. The sticky residue sometimes took an extra layer of skin and definitely most of a person's body hair when ripped off. She didn't know how she knew that—too much crime-story television, she supposed.

Her stomach grumbled, and she wasn't sure when she'd last eaten. That was probably a good thing at this particular juncture because she thought she might just vomit on top of the scuffed-up wood floor. Now she pondered the last moments of her pathetic life.

Juliet's eyes tracked to Tanner, who was smiling at her. Or was it a smirk? She wasn't sure. In all the time Tanner had been in their little town, she couldn't remember seeing her smile much. Juliet thought she'd caught her one day, but when she did a double take, that same stoic expression returned to her face. It was a damn shame in her opinion, because in that brief moment the smile transformed Tanner's face.

"I was wondering when you would waken from dreamland," Tanner said. "I had to assist you a little. Sorry about that. You present a major problem for me. Normally I'd just kill you and be done with it, but you don't meet the code." Her gun remained pushed against Juliet's head.

She wisely decided to keep her mouth shut. It wasn't her best attribute since she spoke her mind and snooped too much. *Isn't that what led me to this crossroad in my life?*

"Not that you have any voice in the decision, but I'd be interested to know what you think I should do with you. What would you do if you were in my shoes?" Tanner asked.

This might be her only chance to save her life. "I promise I'll just forget everything I saw. I'm sure you have a perfectly good explanation. I mean, you are the law."

Tanner shoulder-holstered her gun and looked curiously at her. Maybe Juliet would come out of this pickle alive after all, but then what would she do? *Can I really just walk away and let Tanner get away with cold-blooded murder?*

Tanner quirked her head. "You just won a twenty-four-hour reprieve while I consider my options. Since your stomach has been growling for the last twenty minutes, I suppose I ought to feed you. I'll run to the deli and get us both a sandwich. What kind would you like?"

A benevolent captor. That was a novel notion. Something in the way Tanner asked that question allowed her to relax. She didn't really believe Tanner wanted to kill her, and she was depending on her instincts to get her out of this life-threatening situation.

"Turkey, if it's not too much trouble. I don't suppose you would be willing to cut the zip ties from my hands. This position isn't the most comfortable."

"Don't push your luck, Juliet. One thing I am not is stupid."

Tanner spun on her heel and exited the deserted cabin.

Juliet looked around and tried to find something, anything, that would help cut through her bindings. Nothing, nada, zip. Well, she thought, she might as well start contemplating how to con her way out of this mess. She didn't think the fact she knew all the town's secrets, due to her incessant snooping, would help her get out of her current predicament. She wondered if knowing that Tanner was a lesbian, like herself, might buy her additional time, being family and all. It wasn't much to work with, but it was all she had.

✝

Juliet continued to take in her surroundings while Tanner was out getting lunch. At least she thought it was lunch. Time was a bit elusive at this point. She wasn't sure how long she'd been in la-la land. The last thing she remembered was a tiny prick on her neck.

The moment she'd witnessed the crime, she made a beeline for her grandmother's remote cabin in the mountains. Granny was off on one of her backwoods camping adventures with her best friend, Sally, so Juliet thought she could hide out there for a few days to consider her options.

She wasn't thinking clearly because she hadn't held much hope that anyone would believe her. Being the town snoop didn't endear you to the right people. Perhaps if she'd been more rational at the time, she might have tried to contact the FBI or some other law enforcement agency. There had to be evidence of the crime that would back up her story, but Tanner had somehow tracked her down and she never got the chance to tell anyone.

She looked around the room and thought she might be in an old, abandoned hunting cabin. She stretched her neck to the side and tried to look out the dirt-encrusted windows. Juliet shuddered as she focused on all that dirt. It made her skin crawl. Trees, trees, and more trees were all she saw as she peered through the glass. She suspected she was still somewhere in the mountains, maybe not far from her grandmother's place, and her heart sank. With so many secluded cabins located around the Cascade Mountains, hiding someone was a piece of cake. It was a hermit's paradise. Most of them didn't show up on any map or census document, which was how the local folks wanted it. *Mind your own f-ing business* was the motto around here. She'd heard her grandmother say it often enough for her to recognize the ingrained philosophy of the mountainfolk.

Juliet started to squirm as she realized she needed to go to the bathroom and glumly noted that once that thought was in her head, she wouldn't be able to erase it, unable to think of anything but her need to urinate.

She tilted her head, looked up at the ceiling, and in an effort to sidetrack her brain, started singing an old song from one of her all-time favorite musicals. The light, airy sound of her alto voice floated in the room.

A loud guffaw filled the small cabin as Juliet heard a creaking sound. She turned her head to the door and found Tanner's laughing eyes.

"You're singing 'I Whistle a Happy Tune' from the *King and I*? How cliché." Tanner continued to laugh. "Nice voice, by the way."

"Thanks. I think. Um…do you think I could use the washroom? I really have to pee."

Tanner blushed. "Oh…uh…yeah…um…shoot, I didn't think about that. Look, if I cut off your zip ties and let you use the washroom, will you be compliant and come back? I would sincerely hate having to hunt you down like a wild animal. I'm still considering my options, and if you take away my other alternatives, I will have no choice but to kill you. I'd really rather not make that decision."

Juliet nodded so vigorously that she felt like she might be mistaken for one of those bobble heads. A part of her decided to adhere to Tanner's request because she was petrified that Tanner would track her down, and without remorse follow through with her threat. Yet a bigger part of her was curious why Tanner had killed that man in cold blood. She had to find out, even if it meant risking her life.

Tanner dumped the bag and two large drinks from the sandwich shop on the scratched and dented oak table off to the right and pulled out a lethal-looking knife. In a couple of swift movements, she'd sliced open the zip ties holding Juliet's wrists together.

When Tanner bent to undo the ties that secured each ankle to the chair, Juliet had a notion to try to kick her in the head, take her gun, and run for her life. *What the hell? I'm not some kind of badass Rambo; stop thinking like that.* She shook her head and knew she didn't want to try to escape. Something told her this entire mess might have a reasonable explanation, and she didn't want to hurt Tanner.

Tanner looked up into Juliet's face and narrowed her eyes. "Good choice, Juliet. I have a really hard head, and I doubt you'd have been able to disable me long enough to escape. Just so you know, I'm an expert in several different types of martial arts. I'd have anticipated your move well before you had a chance to execute it."

Juliet felt the bindings loosen. "Shit, Tanner, did you just cut those zip ties without looking? You could have sliced my ankle." She smacked her hand across her mouth. *Smart move, Einstein. Do not irritate your jailor.*

Tanner shrugged. "I knew where your ankles were. You only risked getting sliced if you tried some asinine move to escape. You're smarter than I suspected, or you're too much of a chickenshit to try. Either way, I'm glad you picked the right option."

"I am not a chickenshit. But I will admit to wanting to understand why," Juliet argued.

"Why what?"

Juliet couldn't help her look of incredulity.

"Oh, that little incident earlier. I have my reasons. I suppose it depends on your perspective whether they're legitimate or not."

Juliet stood and danced around a little, resisting the urge to cross her legs or grab her crotch like a two-year-old. "Um, bathroom. I really can't hold it much longer."

Tanner waved the knife in the air and pointed down the hall with the lethal instrument. "First door on the left."

Juliet spun around and hurried to the door twenty feet away.

The washroom wasn't much, but she was grateful the cabin had running water and a toilet instead of an outhouse. She noted the tiny shower with a plastic, blue curtain rimmed with black mold. She crinkled her nose and wondered who would let their bathroom get this dirty. She lifted the toilet lid with the tips of her fingers and stared into the filthy, white bowl. Clearly it hadn't been scrubbed for quite some time.

After quickly pulling down her pants, Juliet hovered above the bowl, careful not to let her butt touch the seat. She'd rather not catch whatever might be crawling on it. She didn't see anything moving, but that didn't mean a plethora of germs wasn't hiding there.

"Aahhhh." She released a stream of urine she thought would never end. *Good thing I religiously do my squats three times a week.*

While pulling up her pants, she searched for something to wash her hands with. She found a tiny nub of soap on the sink's edge. *I wonder how long that thing has been there and whose hands have touched it.* Not finding anything else, she turned on the faucet and lathered as best as she could under the cold water. She hoped the suds would remove the top layer of grime. A nurse once told her that it didn't do a lot of good to wash your hands if you only went through the motions without taking the time to do it right. She quietly sang "Happy Birthday" as she scrubbed, knowing the duration of time needed to get her hands clean. Juliet didn't trust the hand towel hanging up on a hook because it looked more like a dirty rag. She grabbed the bottom of her shirt to shut off the water and dry her hands. She knew where her shirt had been; the towel, not so much.

"Hey, you okay in there?" Tanner called from the other room.

Juliet pushed the door open to a grinning Tanner. She was careful not to touch the door handle and used her shirt again. "Did the housekeeper take a vacation or something? It's disgusting in there."

"For someone who was tied to a chair with a gun against her forehead, you sure have a smart mouth. Didn't anyone ever tell you that you don't have to express every little thought that pops into your head?"

"Trust me. I've kept a whole slew of thoughts to myself. This is me being restrained," Juliet quipped.

"Hmmm. Good to know. I recommend you working on your tact just a smidge more." Tanner held out her thumb and forefinger to demonstrate.

"Fine, but if you expect to keep me alive, I need cleaning supplies to rid this cabin of whatever harmful germs have been allowed to flourish without intervention."

"I didn't exactly have time to make it presentable for company, and just for the record, I don't normally live this way. This was a last-minute decision. Come on, let's eat."

Juliet looked at the old oak table and sighed. Although it didn't have any obvious remnants of moldy food or other repulsive items, she was distrustful.

"Stop eyeing the table like it's your enemy. The food is in a bag, wrapped tightly. Germs aren't skilled enough to burrow inside two layers of protection. God, I've kidnapped a germaphobe." Tanner shook her head and grimaced.

"I'll just take the sandwich right from the bag. No need to get out any plates or put it on the table." Juliet scrunched up her face.

Tanner rolled her eyes and pulled out the bulging sandwich wrapped in white paper. After handing it to Juliet, she dug into the sack and pulled out a bag of potato chips and a cookie. "I hope you like snickerdoodles. It was either that or chocolate chip. I took a guess."

"I never met a cookie I didn't want to devour. Thanks." Juliet reached for it and her fingers brushed against Tanner's. Tanner's face turned bright red again.

She thought it oddly charming that Tanner, who seemed so confident and self-assured, blushed so easily. Immediately after having that thought, she figuratively slapped her head. *What the hell am I thinking? Not more than an hour ago, she held a gun against my head. Nothing's charming about that.*

Juliet rewound the recent events in her mind and felt a rush of jubilation. Tanner had only been gone a short time—definitely not more than an hour, which meant this raggedy, old cabin couldn't be too far from civilization. She might be able to break away and get help. All she needed to do was bide her time and convince Tanner to trust her.

✝

Juliet's whole life before her parents died had been about cleanliness. She could remember back when she was barely three years old and how unacceptable it had been to make a mess as she used a small spoon. Her mother had incessantly wiped her mouth each time she'd taken a bite. By the time Juliet was done with her dinner, her cheeks were raw from the rough washcloth her mother used.

At six, she had looked at her mother's face and seen the absolute disgust there when Juliet had soiled her panties after vomiting in the toilet at the same time the diarrhea exploded from her body. The message was clear—she'd been bad. She knew her mother would be disappointed and she'd tried very hard to start cleaning herself, but her mother caught her washing out her underwear in the bathtub and she knew she'd committed a grave error.

Her tears fell down her cheeks as she apologized for the mess, "I'm sorry, Mama, I got sick."

Her mother had pushed her roughly aside and poured bleach over the clothes before wrapping them up in a plastic bag to discard—the revulsion evident on her face.

Her mother had rubbed every inch of Juliet raw and followed that with a thorough bleach cleaning of not only the bathroom, but her small body. The angry, red rash lasted for several weeks, long after she'd recovered from the stomach flu.

It didn't take much else for Juliet to discover what made her mother unhappy. Her father was fastidious as well, but not to the same degree. She was smart and a fast learner.

9

If you wanted to gain favor with her parents, you had to remember, cleanliness was next to godliness.

By the time she spent any amount of quality time with her grandmother, Juliet's habits were already deeply engrained. Her grandmother could do nothing to change the direction of her life. Her parents had ensured that Juliet's personality was engraved in stone.

Intellectually she knew her parents had created a monster, but that didn't make her obsessions any less difficult to overcome. She'd given up trying to change. The best she could hope for was making a few minor adjustments.

Unfortunately her obsession with cleanliness wasn't her only character flaw. She also had to stick her nose where it didn't belong. Juliet hadn't at all followed her grandmother's advice to mind her own business.

She thought back to how she'd gotten herself into this pickle. Two days ago she'd followed Tanner because she just had to know what Tanner was up to….

Chapter Two

One problem with the town was the slim pickings of potential date material. When Juliet had first laid eyes on the new police officer, she'd classified her as positively scrumptious, but the vibe about her clearly said *stay away*. She hadn't needed to snoop to know she played for the same team, because Tanner Sullivan's demeanor screamed *lesbian*.

She didn't know what the big flippin' deal was, but Tanner didn't appear to want anyone to know about her sexual orientation. The town might be small, but no one seemed to care that Juliet was a lesbian.

Tanner had recently moved from Seattle to join the small police department, making her its third officer. Juliet couldn't figure out why she'd taken the job in South Riverville. She desperately wanted to know more about Tanner, but so far hadn't been able to uncover a single thing about the enigmatic woman. Her dumpster-diving had only revealed Tanner's penchant for expensive ice cream. She wanted more information, which was the primary reason she'd decided to follow Tanner that evening.

Juliet Lewis had on her snooping outfit—or rather, what she thought of as her snooping outfit. It wasn't anything special. In fact, it was suspiciously close to what the main character in her favorite children's book, *Harriet the Spy*, wore—rolled-up jeans, purple high-top tennis shoes, a wide, black belt adorned with various surveillance tools, and her well-worn black hoodie. Of course, she suspected that one difference was that her jeans were freshly ironed and had a crisp crease. It didn't matter if other people judged her outfit as "age-inappropriate." She knew some of the townies considered her an oddball.

Juliet rationalized that her attire and the way she viewed the world retained her childlike curiosity, and that was a good thing. In her opinion, adults socialized out of children all the simple joys in life, which in turn stifled creativity. She didn't feel the same way about her anomalous obsession with cleanliness. The therapist informed her that although she didn't have enough symptoms for a diagnosis of Obsessive Compulsive Disorder, she had enough to cause her distress and was about as close to the edge as anyone she'd ever met without crossing to the other side.

Juliet had updated gadgets because the 1960s versions of those tools were definitely outdated. As a child, she'd purchased the first spy kit with her measly allowance right after reading *Harriet the Spy* for the first time. Her tool belt contained the latest smartphone, complete with various handy apps, a flashlight, her Swisschamp XLT, a folding water bottle, and her belt bag for snacks and a small set of binoculars. She knew she looked like a dork, but that didn't matter because she had everything she needed to roam her neighborhood and ferret out information for the novel she'd been writing since age sixteen. It would be an epic story about her tiny town and its interesting characters.

Juliet was an expert on secrets, and nobody's skeletons stayed buried forever. Even if they didn't surface organically, it wouldn't take a rocket scientist to figure who was banging whom when her novel was published. She almost felt sorry for some of the people in South Riverville

Juliet shuffled down the street, heading for her favorite clandestine spying location. From the special indent in the wall of the combination bar and casino, she could watch not only the bar, but the comings and goings of the library, most of the shops on Main Street, and the combination Riverville police and fire station. She counted her blessings because this particular location gave her hidden access to practically the whole town.

South Riverville was only a village but did have a police department. Riverville, the sister town adjacent to the small community, had a much larger population, a police force, fire department, and a downtown. In the 1920s, two prominent businessmen got into a dispute, and one of them decided to form their own city to spite the other. This marked the evolution of the town and the village that was barely big enough to be its own entity. Riverville had about two thousand people, and South Riverville had a little more than five hundred. The locals started calling South Riverville S-ville, and somehow the nickname stuck.

Sometimes Tanner would visit the sister police department. Juliet assumed she did it to keep the goodwill between the two law enforcement units so the silly feud that started long ago would never have a chance to reignite.

Tonight seemed like a relatively quiet evening until she saw Tanner emerge from the brick building before ducking into another secluded alley that led to the back door of the Baptist church. Juliet always thought it was odd that a place of worship sat right next to the rowdy casino, but the congregation insisted they were there first and weren't moving just because a "bunch of heathens" moved next door. The preacher thought it was the perfect opportunity to convert a few lost lambs. Of course, he seemed to focus all his energy on the adrift female souls, especially if they were attractive.

Juliet thought this might be her lucky night. She was determined to follow Tanner and finally learn the big secret she knew Tanner was hiding. As Tanner made her way past the church to a small house, Juliet wondered if she was entering an empty home because she'd heard about the vandals who had plagued some of the vacant houses. Ever since the housing market's bubble burst, it seemed like there was an abandoned house on every street.

Juliet listened as the wind whipped through the trees. Other than the rustling of the leaves, the night was uncharacteristically quiet. Even the casino was relatively tame as she passed the front entrance. She imagined that most of the patrons were glued to their seats gambling away their weekly earnings. It was sad really. Juliet knew they would forego some of their basic necessities, like food and utilities, as they waited patiently for their ship to finally come in.

She had an uncle with a gambling addiction, and he would call on occasion asking for money. He always paid it back—not that she ever expected him to—but he was a proud man. Juliet had decided long ago that if she loaned money to anyone, she would consider it a gift. That way she would never be disappointed if they didn't repay it. Not having actual or imaginary strings to a loan felt good. When the money came back, it felt like a windfall or pleasant surprise, and she liked that.

The soft soles of her shoes allowed her to sneak up to the house to try to discover why in the world Tanner was there at this time of night. As she got closer, she thought she heard angry voices. Juliet almost decided it might not be a great idea to spy on Tanner and whomever she was arguing with, but curiosity got the better of her.

"You need to mind your own fucking business. You have no idea who you're dealing with. Nosy cops have accidents all the time," the man shouted. "Didn't you learn something when your partner got herself killed?" he hissed.

"Bingo. Confirmed guilt, and I didn't even have to torture it out of you. You are a pathetic piece of shit, Aiden, and the world will be a much better place without you," Tanner declared.

"What the fuck are you talking about? You ain't got shit. Go ahead and arrest me. I'll have my lawyer chew you a new asshole and I'll be out in thirty minutes. You wasted your time following me to this little shithole, but I will say it's the perfect place to set up operations. There are lots of empty houses to temporarily utilize. Now if you don't mind, I need to meet up with my *girlfriend* and you need to fuck off."

Juliet couldn't help herself; the conversation was getting too interesting. She inched forward and carefully stepped into the house to take a peek. The scene in front of her was straight out of Hollywood. Tanner stood immobile with a gun pressed to Aiden's forehead. A long tube extended from the barrel, and Juliet suspected it was a silencer. Tanner had a satisfied smirk on her face.

Aiden was the local bad boy, and Juliet had snooped around enough to learn a little about him. She wasn't certain what he did for a living, except a side business selling drugs. He seemed to hang out at the casino a lot, so she reasoned he must have money.

For such a small town, a whole lot of infidelity was going on. When she'd discovered Aiden was having an affair with Margie, a successful, married realtor, she had a hard time understanding what Aiden saw in her. Margie was a dowdy, middle-aged woman who was married to the local undertaker, Harold. It made sense she would want to have an affair, because Harold creeped out everyone but Juliet. She thought he was odd, but very sweet, and felt bad for him because he clearly loved his wife. She didn't want to know what Harold would do if, and when, he found out. It was always the quiet ones who reacted so violently.

Juliet also knew that this wasn't the normal way the police dealt with people who broke the law.

"Say good night, Aiden. See you in hell." Tanner pulled the trigger.

Juliet was surprised to hear the small popping sound. She always thought guns with suppressors hid the sound completely. The noise startled her and she gasped, taking a step back and running right into a coat rack. The sound of her foot connecting with the iron monstrosity caught Tanner's attention, and she turned around. Looking straight at Juliet, she narrowed her eyes, and Juliet felt like the prey on the bottom of the food chain.

"Shit," Juliet muttered.

Aiden was slumped on the floor, and Juliet didn't need to take a closer look to know he was dead. A few seconds passed as Juliet remained glued to the spot, but when her shock finally shook loose, she decided it was time to get the hell out of Dodge. She had definitely witnessed something Tanner had not intended anyone, much less her, to see.

Juliet turned and ran as fast as she could out of the house and down the street. She didn't know exactly where she was going, but anywhere was better than sticking around to discover the consequences of her ill-fated snooping.

She wasn't sure if she was paranoid or not, but she thought she heard footsteps behind her, so she just kept on running. If only she could get to the edge of town where she might be able to weave her way through the thick forest and hide out in her granny's old hunting cabin. She could regroup and think of what to do next when she got there.

Chapter Three

Juliet gingerly pulled back the covers on the only bed in her grandma's cabin. She was hoping not to find any unwelcome guests there. She suspected a few spiders or even a mouse may be lurking around the corners, just waiting for her to uncover their hiding place. She cringed as she looked around the bedroom and discovered a fine layer of dirt on just about everything. Her grandmother didn't use the cabin very often and wasn't all that particular about its cleanliness when she did.

"I'll just find the number for the FBI or some other law enforcement agency," she muttered.

Juliet reached for the smartphone secured to her belt and discovered the holster was empty. *Shit, shit, shit. It must have fallen off when I was running through the forest. Okay, think, think, think, is it better to wait until morning to backtrack and try to find the phone, or take a chance at night?*

Even though she didn't relish the thought of crashing in the dirty hunting cabin, she knew her chances of finding the lost phone in the middle of the night were somewhere

18

between nothing to zilch. She shuddered as she imagined creepy, crawly things traversing her body as she slept in her grandma's bed.

"Tea. I need hot tea," Juliet announced to the empty cabin. "Now I'm talking to myself. Not a good sign."

She walked back to the main part of the cabin and poked inside the dusty cabinets, looking for tea and, if she was lucky, some honey to go with it. All she found was a jar of freeze-dried instant coffee.

"Oh that is just so wrong." She sat down heavily at the battered wood table, ruminating about her current dilemma and began to question why she always felt the need to stick her nose in everyone else's business. Her grandmother had not so kindly warned her years ago that no good would come of it.

"Juliet, keep sticking your nose in everyone else's business and you're gonna lose your own sense of smell," she'd said.

"Where in the world did you come up with that little pearl of wisdom, and what exactly is it supposed to mean?" Juliet had asked.

"It means you're so busy looking into everyone's else's life, you don't have a proper life of your own. You don't hardly date, you have acquaintances but no real friends, and your own family hides from you."

"Hmmf. I need to take notice of things to be able to write my novel. It's the little things that matter, Grandma," Juliet insisted.

She shook her head as she remembered that conversation. Well, at least she wouldn't start dating a cold-blooded killer. Because of her propensity toward snooping, she'd eliminated every possible single gay woman from her nonexistent dating pool. They all had issues. Of course, it wasn't like there was a whole passel of single lesbians in S-ville or Riverville, so not finding acceptable dating material wasn't really her fault. She also hated to admit that even when one did pass muster, she didn't exactly embrace Juliet's unique qualities. Dating had been hard for her, so she'd given up a long time ago and preferred to spend her time observing everyone else's life.

A faint crunch of leaves startled Juliet and she strained her ears to listen. She wasn't really the outdoorsy type like her grandmother, so she prayed that some wild animal hadn't found its way to the front door. Maybe the cabin was dusty and far from the Ritz, but surely it would protect her from a stray bear looking for a tasty treat. She scrambled to the door and secured the lock as if that would keep out the hairy beasts.

"Aw hell. I might as well try to get some sleep and figure this mess out in the morning."

Juliet lumbered back to the bed, inspected the sheets, and decided it would be okay to sleep in for one night. She wasn't about to take off her clothes, though—they provided an additional layer of protection—just in case. She pulled the hoodie over her head because getting germs in her hair was the worst feeling.

Juliet's discovery earlier that evening had caused her to expend an inordinate amount of emotional energy, so even with the stress of climbing into a less than pristine bed, she surrendered to sleep.

She didn't know how long she'd been dozing when her eyes opened, and with her face turned in the direction of the window, she noticed how the full moon was shining brightly, creating a small patch of light on the floor. The hairs on the back of her neck sprung to life, and just as she was about to jump into action, she sensed another person in the cabin. She turned her head and locked eyes with the very person she was trying to avoid. Before she could react, she felt the prick to her neck. Good night, Juliet. Lights out.

✝

Tanner didn't think the cabin fit Juliet at all. From everything she'd observed of the quirky woman, Tanner was surprised she'd set one foot in there, much less accepted the rough accommodations. Juliet was such a priss. Tanner chuckled to herself as she noted that the crease in Juliet's jeans surely meant she neatly pressed them every night.

When Tanner didn't hear any sounds from inside the cabin, she assumed Juliet had done the unthinkable and settled in for the night. Tanner snuck around to the window and peeked into the bedroom. The slumbering woman's curly, blond hair fanned out across the pillow, and the moon cast a soft glow on her face. Tanner studied Juliet while she slept. Her full, rosy lips curved up, reminding Tanner of someone who'd just heard a private joke and thought it slightly amusing. Tanner remembered how Juliet's long lashes curled—a perfect outline for her sparkling, emerald eyes. The green was an unusual shade most anyone would notice right away—Tanner had. It just seemed to fit that she also had a perfect nose centered between two impossibly high cheekbones. Why did Juliet have to be so beautiful and so vulnerable? Tanner did not relish the thought of eliminating this problem. Juliet may be a pain-in-the-ass snoop, but Tanner wasn't so sure she deserved what was about to happen to her.

Tanner sighed. She pulled out the hypodermic needle and crept to the other side of the cabin. She needed to enter without disturbing Juliet's sleep. Picking locks had been a useful skill her older brother taught her while they were growing up. He wasn't really a bad kid, just mischievous.

21

The thought of doing something forbidden was enough to pique his interest. He never graduated to theft, but he could get into nearly every house, car, business, or anything else that had a lock on it. Within a matter of seconds, she'd picked the old cabin's rusted, ancient lock and entered, leaving the door ajar.

As she crept to the bedroom, she paused to look again at Juliet's beautiful face framed in the moonlight. Tanner was startled when she stirred, turned her face to the door, and those unusual green eyes opened, registering her surprise and fear. Tanner plunged the needle into Juliet's neck. Her reaction to the drugs was instantaneous.

Tanner pulled the blankets back and tenderly placed her arm under Juliet's neck while slipping her other arm under the bend in her knees. Tanner was relieved Juliet was such a slight thing. She was able to easily lift her from the bed.

Tanner carried the unconscious woman out of the cabin and down the path to her waiting vehicle, which she'd retrieved earlier in the evening after following Juliet. She'd had to park a fair distance away since she didn't want to chance waking Juliet in case she was a light sleeper. The old shack she needed to take her captor to was in a secluded area not far from town, but definitely not within walking distance.

Juliet's head flopped against her shoulder in an oddly intimate way. Under completely different circumstances, Tanner could imagine Juliet resting her head on her shoulder in front of a roaring fire. It was a stupid fantasy. One that would never come true—especially after drugging, kidnapping, and God knows what else she might be forced to do.

"Damn," Tanner hissed. She was having a particularly shitty day. She hadn't had time to properly dispose of Aiden. She didn't necessarily fear discovery of her crime, she just didn't want Margie to have to come across Aiden's lifeless body, and she knew that was exactly what would happen. She'd left Aiden in one of Margie's empty houses. Most of the vacant houses had signs with Margie's name plastered across the bottom in big black letters because she was the most successful real estate agent in town. She wasn't sure if Margie had scheduled an open house or not, but Tanner suspected she would most likely be the one to find her lover's body. That was an unavoidable consequence of the need to deal with Juliet.

Tanner resolved to continue with what she knew she had to do.

Chapter Four

Ralph narrowed his eyes at the combination fire-and-police station. He was already second-guessing his decision to take this job. It was supposed to be an easy in—snuff the target, get out, and disappear without a trace—but the nosy bitch hadn't shown up to work today and Ralph had no idea where she'd disappeared to. Her routines were very specific and she never deviated from them. She always showed up at the post office by seven forty-five in the morning, and then she would walk down to the coffee shop and get her morning beverage. Except this morning, she'd never showed.

He ran his hand through his greasy, thinning hair and moved the toothpick from the right side of his mouth to the left. The three-day stubble left an untidy shadow on his face, adding to his unsightly appearance. Most people would find his bulbous nose, pockmarked face, sallow skin, squinty eyes, thin lips, and beige, crooked teeth a combination that made him several levels beyond repulsive. Soon enough, someone would notice him and be able to describe him down to the shape and color of his eyes. Ralph wasn't the kind of man who could disappear in a crowd, and it was a significant disadvantage in his chosen occupation. Ralph's success depended on his ability to swoop in and complete a job in less than eight hours. He'd been in town now in excess of forty-eight hours, which was forty more hours than was safe. Ralph noticed the surly cop from S-ville at the local deli buying more food than one person needed. Even in the short time he'd staked out this shithole, he'd pegged her for a loner. He concluded she was connected to his mark's absence. He didn't know how she found out the person he was after, and that bothered him. He was a professional and he couldn't afford to have the police poking around in his business. She didn't look like a federal marshal, but he couldn't discount that possibility.

Deciding it was time to cut his losses, he grabbed his cell phone and punched in the number for the man who was expecting resolution—yesterday. "I don't like how this job is turning out. You need to hire someone else. I've already wasted two days, and I'm not particularly fond of the idea that some fucking marshal is on the scene.... I don't know how they found out, but my gut says the authorities are definitely involved.... Don't you threaten me, you slimy little pissant. Piss me off and you'll be my next mark."

Ralph ended his call and peeled off, leaving the tiny town and the aggravation of two lost days behind. He wanted his forty-eight hours of life back, but at least he didn't think anyone had spotted him and he could go on to other jobs with far fewer complications.

†

Margie prided herself on noticing the little things. It was what made her good at her job. She was able to decipher when a prospective buyer really wanted a particular house, but never let on, hoping to lower the asking price. Normally the men were the ones who tried not to reveal their feelings, but, on occasion, a woman would attempt to put something over on her by acting nonchalant.

Margie wasn't fooled one bit by Aiden's unusual interest in her work and the houses she was showing. He asked a lot of questions and gave her his undivided attention as she described each listing. He encouraged her when she lamented about the white elephants that remained vacant for months on end and how she wished she'd never taken those particular listings. She would admit to not spending any time on those difficult sales, leaving the houses empty and unattended for months. He understood how busy she was and how she had to spend her time on the listings she knew would move quickly. Margie thought she knew one reason for his fixation on her job, but that didn't matter much to her. He was a nice distraction, nothing more. If her husband, Harold, wasn't so boring, she might not have accepted Aiden's overtures, but he was handsome and attentive. What could having a little sugar on the side possibly hurt? They were using each other, and it was a match made in heaven with plenty of uncomplicated sex.

She'd given up on having kids a long time ago, and the news the doctor had shared with them about Harold's low sperm count had driven him deeper into his work. She'd gotten to the point where his lack of attention to his personal grooming bothered her when compared to Aiden's. Everyone in S-Ville thought Harold's creepy looks fit his vocation as the only undertaker in town. She'd started to agree with them, especially when she contrasted Harold's appearance to Aiden's rugged good looks. The fact he'd begun to pull in on himself even more in the last several years added to Margie's sense of isolation. She grudgingly admitted he still loved her and tried very hard to show her in little ways.

Margie squinted as she looked at the black car she'd seen several times in the last two days. The ugly man with the toothpick hanging out of his mouth left her with a cold feeling. The hairs on the back of her neck stood up every time she saw him, and she just knew he was up to no good. Although she would be uncomfortable talking to Tanner about her gut feelings regarding the stranger, she felt it was her civic duty to report him.

Tanner was always so surly. Margie had never once seen her smile. She supposed Tanner was good at her job because, after all, she'd heard she was some big shot from Seattle. Of all the police in S-ville or Riverville, Tanner was by far the most competent. Margie just wished she were a little friendlier with the locals.

When the dark sedan screeched away, leaving a long, black mark on the street, Margie tsked. She pulled out a notepad and pen from her enormous purse, clicked open her favorite pen, and copied down the license plate number. The ink rolled smoothly across the paper.

Margie sighed when Clark peered out the window of his store and begin waving madly at her. She often wondered why she stayed in the tiny town where everyone poked their noses into everyone else's business.

Mr. Clark Gable didn't look anything like his namesake, the famed thirties actor, but he sure acted as if he were God's gift to women. He was attractive enough in his youth, but age and alcohol had not been his friends. His thinning, gray hair and obvious paunch had turned him into another middle-aged, average Joe. He tried to hide his alcoholism, and she thought he'd made a decent attempt at maintaining control.

Margie knew he was a regular two years ago at the local AA meetings, but his sobriety had only lasted a couple of months. Margie thought that was sad and speculated it was the reason his ex-wife had left him. Clark and Nancy were the golden couple in high school and had married young. It hadn't lasted long because he'd chased every skirt in town. After making his way through most of the town's single women, he'd recently started a clandestine affair with the preacher's wife, Scarlet. Margie didn't blame her for stepping out on Hugo, because he was a disgustingly overweight blowhard who constantly berated her in public. The irony that her name was Scarlet wasn't lost on Margie.

You just can't make that shit up. Clark Gable and Scarlet—Margaret Mitchell was undoubtedly rolling over in her grave right now.

When she didn't respond right away, he stepped out, hiked up his pants, and called out, "Hey, Margie, whatcha doing?"

"Hi, Clark. Did you notice that black car hanging around town lately?"

"Yeah. I did. Do you think something's happening? Maybe there's some big undercover operation going down. It looked like a government car."

"The guy didn't look like a government man to me. He had shifty eyes. I wrote the license plate number down because I didn't like the looks of him. Mark my words, he was up to no good, and when Tanner runs his plates, I'll bet she gets a hit on him."

"Since when did you become so friendly with the big-city cop? I don't think she's said more than five words to me since she moved here," Clark spat out.

"Ooh, got your boxers in a bunch. I'll bet you tried to hit on her, huh? Don't you know she's a lesbian? I can spot 'em a mile away. Not that I'm interested or anything. I'm just open-minded about stuff like that. She's all right. Just 'cause she's not all up in everyone's business doesn't mean she isn't a good cop," Margie defended.

She didn't like when people talked ill about others, even if the object of their chatter was a woman who couldn't find a smile while surrounded by a bunch of adorable kittens. She knew how most people in town gossiped, and she was sure her affair with Aiden was fodder for their flapping mouths. At least she'd stood up for Tanner after outing her to Clark. Given how hard tongues wagged in S-Ville, she was surprised that everyone but Harold knew about her affair.

"Hmmf, I did no such thing. Tanner's way too young for me. I like my women a bit more mature," Clark insisted.

"And married," Margie whispered. It was common knowledge that Clark hadn't taken the loss of his wife, Nancy, very well at all. He'd grown up as a big grouper in a pool of minnows, and now he wasn't the star athlete and prom king anymore.

"What was that?" Clark asked.

Margie didn't know why she'd made that jab, because she certainly had no room to talk. "Oh, nothing. So have you seen Tanner today? I really want to give her this license plate number."

"She looked like she was in some big hurry earlier when she got her sandwiches from the deli. I'm not sure where she was headed, but I know she's not at the station. I think Harley's on duty now."

"How do you know all the work schedules of the S-Ville police? Never mind. Well, crap. Harley couldn't find his ass with both hands. The boy's sweet, but I think Tanner is better suited for this," Margie grumbled.

After waving good-bye to him, she sauntered down the street while stuffing the paper in her purse. She was late for an open house and didn't have time to chitchat with Clark, who could have an hour-long conversation about absolutely nothing.

Chapter Five

Tanner leaned back in her chair and stared at her captive. She had to admit Juliet was a beautiful woman. Tanner even found her attractive in that ridiculous snooping outfit. If she hadn't focused so much on taking care of business and eliminating that scumbag, she might have tried to ask Juliet out when she first came to town. Who was she kidding? She wasn't asking anyone out these days because she hadn't gotten over Faith yet. That wound was still seeping—putrid and oozing, and Aiden's death had only managed to close it a tiny bit.

Tanner hadn't planned to spend as much time as she had in the small town, but she had to be sure. The code demanded she have proof.

Juliet was funny, kind of like Faith. Tanner liked that about her, but she couldn't start comparing the two. That wouldn't be smart at all—no siree Bob, definitely not an intelligent thing to do in light of her current situation.

"What to do, what to do. I really wish you hadn't been snooping last night." Tanner sighed. "I hate to leave you tied up while I attend to some errands, but the only other alternative...well, let's just say you won't like that option."

"Maybe there's a third option," Juliet offered.

"Like what?"

"Well, you seem like a reasonably sane person, except for the 'executing a man in cold blood' thing. Why don't you tell me your side of the story? Help me understand why you decided to go all vigilante on Aiden. I mean, the guy was an asshole for sure. I knew he wasn't having an affair with Margie because she's irresistible. I know all about the drugs."

"If you know all about his little drug-distribution business, how come you never reported it to the police?" Tanner asked.

"Been there, done that. Aiden is somehow connected to some very nasty characters. Don't be fooled by Harley's back-home, dumbass routine. He's thick as thieves with Aiden and definitely involved."

"And you know this how?"

Juliet blew out a gigantic puff of air. "Oh please. You know I'm the town snoop. I root through garbage, slink around at night, and just plain observe more than the average bear."

"You root through garbage?"

"I wear gloves of course. You can find out a lot about a person through their trash."

Tanner crossed her arms and raised an eyebrow. "So what have you deduced about me?"

"Besides you being a crazy-ass Uma Thurman...you kind of look like her...she *was* kickass in *Kill Bill*...um...I don't know a whole lot about you, Tanner. You are an enigma, and I've been dying—oops wrong verbiage...uh...to unlock all your secrets."

"I can't really tell if that was a compliment or not."

"Oh the part about you looking like Uma was definitely a compliment, but the crazy-ass part not so much."

"You don't really have a filter, do you? I do still have a gun here." Tanner waved it in the air.

Juliet's eyes widened. "Is it still really an option for you to kill me? Here I thought we were getting along so well."

"You just called me a crazy ass. I'm not so sure that qualifies as a friendly gesture." Tanner grinned.

"Sorry. I don't really think you're crazy, but I am trying to get my head around what happened. You can see things from my perspective, can't you?"

Tanner shrugged. She supposed her actions did look bad from Juliet's viewpoint. She had a decision to make as she narrowed her vision at her captive, wondering if she could possibly trust Juliet. Would Juliet comprehend her moral code, or would she see Tanner as a sociopath? Tanner couldn't bring herself to kill Juliet, so she supposed her only option was to try to help her grasp the subtleties surrounding her complicated beliefs.

"I'm going to tell you everything and hope you understand, because I can't justify…you know…."

"Um, yes, I'm all too familiar with my predicament, and I promise to listen without judgment."

✝

Margie walked up to the small A-frame and frowned as she noticed the door ajar.

"Damn hoodlums," she murmured. This was the third time one of her listings was open, and every single time she'd discovered evidence that kids had used the house for God knows what. She'd even found a used condom once.

This was getting out of hand. When she reported the license plate of the stranger hanging around, she'd make sure Tanner knew about the activity in the empty houses. She was tired of picking up after those kids.

Margie pushed open the front door, then slapped her hand over her mouth as she took in the gruesome sight of Aiden sprawled out on the floor. His eyes were open and staring ahead as if he were watching a riveting baseball game, but their blue-white haze made him look like an alien. A neat, round hole in the middle of his head made it clear he'd been shot—executed by the looks of it. She watched all the police shows, so she knew an execution when she saw one.

Margie backed out of the house, then bent and vomited. Her hand shook as she located her cell phone and dialed 911. She wanted to talk to Tanner, but reporting the death was her first priority.

So much for a successful open house. It would take months to unload this beast now.

"Um…hello…yes, I'd like to report a murder. Well, at least I think it's a murder…." Her voice quivered. "Six oh one Main Street…. No, I didn't touch anything…. Yes, I'm sure he's dead…. Yes, I'll be out front waiting."

Margie couldn't muster up any emotion besides shock at finding a dead body. She suspected most people in town thought she was madly in love with Aiden. In reality she knew Aiden was using her for information on which houses were empty. Margie wasn't as stupid as some of the townsfolk imagined. Aiden was eye candy and good in bed, but that was all. She looked the other way when he peddled his drugs, preferring to stay out of his business. As long as he didn't leave any evidence in the houses, she didn't care. She was more hacked off about the kids who left their nasty trash for her to clean up.

As she ended the call, a young couple crawled out of their older-model Toyota Camry, parked across the street.

"Shit," Margie muttered.

The young woman glanced at her husband, who shrugged. "Are you the real estate agent or the owner?"

"I'm afraid the open house has been canceled. I'm terribly sorry to cause you any inconvenience." Margie was always polite, especially to someone who might be a prospective client in the future.

"You look like you've just seen a ghost," the woman remarked.

Margie was relieved that she wouldn't have to answer the woman as the police cruiser screeched to a stop behind the Camry. She wondered how Harley knew about this already. He must have been listening to the police scanner.

Harley jumped out of the vehicle and walked swiftly toward Margie and the young couple.

"Wow, Margie. I didn't know you were the one who called it in." He glanced at the strangers. "Who are they?"

"They came to see the house, but of course we have to cancel that now. You'll probably need to call Tanner, because I think you'll have to have someone keeping people who come to see the house from getting nosy and trampling all over the evidence. Tanner probably knows more about the proper procedure than the Riverville police." Margie was relieved she had an excuse to get Tanner involved right away because Tanner had the intelligence and skills to handle unusual circumstances. She didn't think Riverville or S-Ville had ever had a murder before. Tanner had worked in Seattle, and Margie thought that level of experience might come in handy now. She wondered if the two police departments would band together on this one. Tanner seemed to get along better with the Riverville police than with Harley, her own colleague.

Harley hitched up his pants and seemed to grow taller. "You folks need to move on. This is official police business now."

The man grumbled, "No skin off my back. I wasn't all that excited about this house anyway."

The young couple stalked off as Harley pushed his way inside.

Margie followed and was just about to remind him that he probably shouldn't enter and contaminate the crime scene any more than she already had, when he mumbled, "Aw shit, Aiden, you stupid motherfucker. Guess they decided it was easier to off you than the nosy bitch."

Margie held her breath, not wanting Harley to know she'd overheard. She waited a few seconds before purposely running into the coatrack so she could announce her presence. She wanted to report the strange comment to Tanner as soon as she arrived.

Harley turned and narrowed his eyes. "What the hell, Margie? You need to wait outside."

"I just thought you'd want to talk to me and get my statement. Aren't you going to call Tanner?"

"Yeah, yeah. I was just getting ready to do that. You should wait outside in case you have more buyers that come by for the open house. I just want to take a quick look here first. I know what I'm doing because I'm a trained professional."

Margie turned around and rolled her eyes. She'd be sure to add that to the list of things she would report to Tanner. Margie hadn't disturbed the body, but Tanner's idiot colleague might have.

The Riverville police were sure taking their sweet-ass time to get here too.

†

Tanner's cell phone vibrated against her belt buckle. "Shit, what now." She yanked the phone from its holster. "Sullivan. This better be good, Harley. It's my day off, and that means time off where I don't need to deal with petty small-town crap.... Hmmm, interesting. Okay, I can come back for that.... Sit tight and don't touch anything.... Yeah, I do have to remind you because I'll bet you walked all over the crime scene by now. I'll be there in fifteen minutes. How come the Riverville police or sheriff's office hasn't arrived yet?.... Okay."

The phone call had definitely sparked Juliet's curious nature. "That sounds interesting." She let the comment hang in the air, hoping Tanner would fill in the blanks.

"Sorry, Juliet, I have to go back into town now, so we won't get to finish our chat just yet. I hate to do this to you, but I'm going to have to tie you up again. I'll try not to be too long, but I might not be able to return for a few hours. I am truly sorry."

Juliet was relieved to see that Tanner honestly looked remorseful. She wasn't afraid anymore that Tanner would kill her, but that didn't mean she was happy about being tied up. "I don't suppose you'd want to trust that I'm so curious about your motives that I'll stay put without you securing me to that very uncomfortable chair with those plastic restraints that cut into my wrists."

"Sorry, no can do."

"Can you at least tie my hands in front? I really won't try to get away because I do wish to finish our talk."

"Sure. I can do that. I'll even get you a seat cushion from my car that will hopefully make your wait a little more comfortable."

"Is there any chance you have an e-reader? I think I should be able to advance the pages even with my hands tied together."

Tanner laughed. "You know, you're in luck because I do have my e-reader in the car. I hope you like mysteries, because that's all I purchase."

"Are the main characters lesbians?" Juliet grinned.

"Of course. I'm not even going to deny that I'm gay because you've probably already done your snooping to learn all about me."

Juliet looked down. For some reason she regretted snooping on Tanner now. Even though Tanner didn't seem to be upset by it, maybe invading someone's privacy wasn't a very nice thing to do. That was a sobering thought. "Sorry."

Tanner removed a handful of zip ties from her back pocket and gently brought Juliet's wrists together, leaving enough wiggle room for her to open her hands to hold the e-reader without the risk of her breaking free. After she had secured Juliet's wrists, she attached each ankle to a leg on the wood chair.

"I'll be right back with the cushion and the e-reader." Tanner walked briskly out of the cabin.

Juliet wasn't looking forward to another two hours or more in the uncomfortable wooden chair, but she supposed if the shoe was on the other foot, she might have done the same thing. Of course, she couldn't ever imagine that shoe fitting because there was no way in hell she would ever take another person's life. It just wasn't in her nature. She doubted she would be able to shoot a gun in self-defense, much less carry out some kind of execution. She didn't know why she was beginning to trust that Tanner had a good reason for what she'd done, even though she hadn't heard it yet. Something about Tanner evoked a sense of justice. Juliet desperately wanted to believe Tanner wasn't some crazed, cold-blooded murderer, but she would have to wait patiently for that explanation now.

Tanner returned with some kind of lower back cushion and a small pillow. Juliet wondered what on earth possessed her to carry those around in her car. It was odd that she conveniently had them with her. *Does she routinely kidnap people and then make sure they're comfortable?*

"I probably shouldn't ask this, but why do you have those things?"

"The pillows?" Tanner asked.

"Uh, yeah."

"I have a bad back, and when I used to do stakeouts, the pillow and cushion made things a little more comfortable for me. I guess I never removed them from my car when I moved here."

"I suppose I should count my blessings, then."

Tanner walked across the room and helped Juliet lift up from the chair while she slid the cushion behind her back and shoved the pillow under her rear end. "How's that? Better?"

"Yeah, thanks. How long do you think you'll be?"

Tanner shrugged. "At least a couple of hours. When I come back, I promise to explain things a bit, and then I suppose it will be time to decide what to do with you."

Juliet really hoped she would understand and agree with Tanner's rationale, because she didn't think she had the acting skills to fake her reaction.

Chapter Six

Tanner's dusty Jeep rolled to a controlled stop in front of the small house with the white picket fence. She chuckled as she thought, *A dead body doesn't really go with a symbol of the middle-class American dream.* Tanner watched as Margie paced the front yard, looking a little lost and slightly green around the gills.

"Showtime," Tanner whispered before exiting her vehicle.

Margie hurried across the grass to Tanner and met her well before she had a chance to enter the yard. "Oh thank goodness you're here, Tanner. This is the worst thing I've ever seen, and I think I know who might have done this. I got his license plate, but I was waiting to give it to you because Harley is such a nincompoop."

Tanner arched her eyebrow. "Whoa, Margie. You better slow down and start from the beginning. What about the guys from the Riverville Police Department?"

"I don't know. They haven't arrived yet."

The screen door slammed, and Tanner looked up as Harley approached. Tanner nodded at her colleague.

"Aiden managed to catch a slug in his head. I told Margie to wait out here while I took a look. I've never seen a murder before. Finally, some action in this town." Harley looped his thumbs in his belt and grinned.

"What the shit, Harley? You're celebrating someone's untimely death." Tanner shook her head. "Go call the sheriff's office, and where the hell are the Riverville police? We're going to need some help here."

"You don't think we can handle this on our own?"

"No, Harley, I don't." Tanner glared at him.

"I thought you were some big-city detective," Harley sneered.

"Just make the damn call. It's protocol." Tanner couldn't believe how ignorant he was.

"Arrogant dyke," Harley mumbled as he ambled to his police cruiser.

"Asshole." Tanner made sure she spoke loud enough for both Harley and Margie to hear.

Margie snorted. "He is a dumbass, isn't he?"

"So tell me what it is you think you know about this situation." Tanner looked at her with what she hoped gave the impression of genuine concern.

"Earlier today I saw a strange man in a car, and he was just watching, right here on Main Street. I've never seen him before yesterday, and I have to say, he was the creepiest person I think I've ever laid my eyes on. I got a bad vibe right away the very first time I saw him slinking around. I'm telling you, Tanner, he was up to no good, and now sweet Aiden is dead. I got the license plate number right here in my bag." She patted her purse.

Tanner had to refrain from reacting to Margie describing Aiden as "sweet." If she had been particularly vicious, she would have castrated the bastard before putting the hole in his head. She didn't believe in coincidences, so when Margie mentioned the man stalking around S-ville, her senses went on high alert, especially since she'd picked up on her comment about the first time she'd seen him, which suggested he'd been here on multiple occasions.

"Can you describe this man?"

"I sure can. I don't know how tall he was because he was in a car, but he was a slight man with greasy, brown hair. It was thinning at the top. He had these beady, little eyes and a big, bulbous nose. His lips were very thin, and I'll bet he had a bad case of acne as a teenager because his face was full of pockmarks in between all the stubble. I don't think he'd had a proper shower in a week."

"Okay. How about you give me the number you wrote down."

"Sure thing, Tanner. I just knew it would come in handy." Margie unsnapped her purse and rooted around inside. She plucked out a small piece of paper and handed it to Tanner. "Here you go."

"I'll check this out. I appreciate how observant you are, Margie."

"Oh and one more thing. Harley stomped all over the crime scene, and I don't think he realized I was right behind him, but he said something really odd," Margie whispered.

Tanner quirked her eyebrow. "Go on."

"Well, he said something about Aiden being stupid and getting himself killed instead of some nosy person. Do you think he was talking about Juliet?"

Tanner shook her head.

Flashing red-and-blue lights reflected off the front of the house, and Tanner turned around to see the Riverville cruiser pull up.

"They're on their way," Harley shouted. "Arrogant pricks had the nerve to tell me not to touch anything."

Tanner breathed a sigh of relief. Between the sheriff's department and the Riverville police, she'd be able to keep a low profile. She wanted to have as little to do with this case as possible. She had more pressing issues to attend to—like what to do with Juliet and tracking down the man in the car whom Margie had observed. If her instincts were on target, someone had sent him to eliminate a problem. Tanner had a bad feeling about it. The comment Margie overheard Harley make also weighed heavily on her.

Is Juliet unknowingly involved in this mess? Aiden was knee-deep in some very nasty business and his associates did not screw around. When something got in their way or posed a risk, they eliminated that person. Aiden had already proved how ruthless he was, and compared to his associates, he was a choirboy. Tanner needed to know who was in their line of sight, and she hoped and prayed it wasn't Juliet.

†

Tanner eased into the parking lot outside the police station. The office didn't have any of the latest equipment she'd had in Seattle, but it would have to do for right now. She'd left the sheriff and Riverville police with Harley, and no one blinked an eye when she announced that since they seemed to have everything under control, she would be leaving and salvaging what was left of her day off. Playing into their macho argument over who should take control, she easily extricated herself from the case. This was probably the one time in her life that preconceived notions about female police officers worked to her advantage. It was just as well, because now that she'd taken care of Aiden, she had no need to hang around the little backwater town for much longer.

She slipped into the worn leather chair and swiveled around to the computer, where she entered the license plate number into the database. She wasn't hopeful that she would learn anything earth-shattering about the man, but it was worth a try. She suspected he was using a rental car, and she was right. He was also likely using an alias when he rented it. She would need a much better computer, or she would have to call in a favor if she were to have any hope of getting anything useful out of the information Margie had provided.

Tanner hesitated before calling Cisco. He would gloat about the fact that she needed him and never let her forget any favor he ever did for her. Cisco was the closest thing to a brother she had, and they shared a similar philosophy regarding drug dealers, pedophiles, kiddie pornographers, and rapists. He was a crazy fucker, even nuttier than she was, or so she rationalized.

She had met Cisco when they attended the police academy, and they became instant friends. Sharing the same taste in women had created a healthy competition between them, and Tanner appreciated his acceptance of her sexual orientation.

When he'd casually mentioned at the bar one night that, "I wish we could just shoot the fuckers and save the taxpayers a boatload of money," she knew she'd found a kindred spirit.

They'd both been disciplined in the past for excessive force, but Cisco had still managed to get himself assigned to some secret special unit. He'd let slip one night that his new division allowed him carte blanche to do whatever the hell he wanted. At the time, her own undercover unit hadn't offered her the same luxury, and she was still pissed about it. Cisco had gone to bat for her, and the big brass later amended their position and made her an offer, but by then it was too late. She went off on her own, taking the law into her own hands, and Cisco and Faith were the only two people who knew about her extracurricular activities.

Tanner frowned at the information on the screen. "Well, this was a big fat waste of my precious time."

She sighed as she retrieved her phone from her pants pocket. She had Cisco on speed dial, so all she had to do was press the Power button on her smartphone and then hit it again to activate Siri.

"Call Cisco," she commanded. "Hey, C…. Yeah, yeah, I need something, and yes, I know I'll owe you…. Stop gloating. I know I have two favors in my repayment column and you're all caught up with your debts…. There's some suspicious character that's been hanging around S-Ville. I don't have a lot to go on, but I have a description and a license plate number…. Yeah, I already ran the number, and as suspected, it belongs to a rental car…. Nope, nothing on the name of the person who rented it…. Skinny guy with small eyes, pockmarked face, thinning, greasy, brown hair, and a big, bulbous nose… Rental place is Hertz, and the guy who rented the vehicle is Tom Jones…. I know, crooks have absolutely no imagination these days. You couldn't get a more boring name."

Tanner picked up a pen on the desk and began tapping as she waited for Cisco to search his more extensive database. "No shit…. Okay, that's interesting. Hmmm, I'll check this Ralph guy out. You don't by any chance have a photo you can send to me, do you?…. Aw crap, C, that is not worth adding another favor to the 'I owe you' list. Just send me the damn photo before I drive three hours and kick your ass." Tanner laughed. "Thanks, C. I do owe you…. No, I think I can handle this, but I am curious about why Ralphie would be hanging around this area. If you have any intel you can shift my way, that would be great. I think he might be tied to Aiden Carmichael…. Shit, one more thing, see what you can drag up about a Harley Thompson.... How about giving me a special two-for-one deal on the favors?.... Spoilsport." Tanner ended the call without saying good-bye. She knew he wouldn't be offended because that's just the way they were with each other.

Tanner leaned back in the leather chair and grinned. If anyone could find out more details about this sudden turn of events, it was Cisco. She was happy to have that crazy son of a bitch on her side, but she wasn't too thrilled about his initial thought that Ralph Hardgrove, one of the Mob's go-to hit men, was the suspicious man Margie had seen hanging around.

Tanner smacked her thighs and stood up. "Time to get back to the lovely Juliet. She might be getting a little stiff right about now, and I sure hope she hasn't needed to use the bathroom—that would be a total bitch. I know how much I hate having to hold it in when I really have to go."

Tanner often talked to herself. She didn't find that odd at all. Other people talked to their pets, so why couldn't she have a conversation with herself, rather than have her thoughts clunk around in her head like gym shoes in a dryer? She didn't have any pets to talk to because she hadn't planned on staying that long in S-ville, but she had managed to make friends with all the feral cats hanging around her house. One of them even let her pet him once.

Chapter Seven

Juliet was way past uncomfortable sitting in the hard chair and the cushions hadn't helped one bit. The pain had progressed to unbearable over the last hour. Her hands were cramping as she continued to hang on to the e-reader Tanner had given her. It didn't make the time go any faster, because before the day ended, she was sure her butt would fall asleep never to awaken again. She'd tried to concentrate on everything but her full bladder. Gulping down the entire twenty-four-ounce drink Tanner had brought her for lunch probably wasn't the brightest thing she'd ever done. Now she was at the point where she almost didn't care if she wet her jeans. The relief would outweigh the smell. That was saying a lot since she knew that her tendency toward OCD was epic.

When the door to the cabin swung open with force, Juliet exhaled in relief.

"Honey, I'm home. Did you miss me?" Tanner grinned.

Juliet grimaced. "Bathroom. Quick."

She was amazed at the speed with which Tanner was able to retrieve the wickedly dangerous knife and slice through the zip ties without touching her vulnerable skin. When Tanner stepped back, Juliet rushed to the simple bathroom and didn't bother to close the door as she whipped down her jeans and let it rip.

"Ahhhhh. Just in the nick of time." From her squatting position, Juliet looked up to see Tanner look away in embarrassment.

"Uh, sorry." Tanner closed the door.

"I didn't have time to worry about you catching a glimpse of my bare ass, and under the circumstances that is the least of my concerns," Juliet called out.

She pulled her jeans up, turned the faucet, and attempted to clean her hands under the distinctly yellow water flowing into the sink. The soap in the dish looked crusty again. She'd been so distracted by her current predicament that she hadn't remembered she was most likely the last person to use it. It didn't matter anyway because she rationalized again that handling soap that God knows who had used before, was better than not washing at all. Mumbling the mantra that "handwashing is the best way to prevent the spread of infection," she replaced the sudsy lump back in the dirty soap dish. She wasn't able to control her shudder.

She looked into the old, tarnished mirror and frowned at her reflection. Suddenly remembering she hadn't taken a shower in more than twenty-four hours, she lamented the lack of that simple pleasure. Maybe Tanner would let her take one undisturbed. Behind her, the old shower with the moldy curtain mocked her. She only saw mold at the very bottom of the curtain, but she was one hundred percent positive it was all over the bloody thing.

As Juliet pondered her situation, she was surprised that she didn't really want to escape. There was a story here, and Tanner had been almost ready to share it with her before having to run off after she suspected they had found Aiden dead. She wasn't afraid of Tanner any more, but she really wanted to understand what brought Tanner to the place where she felt she had no option but an emotionless execution of another human being. Juliet didn't think she would ever get to the point where that would be the acceptable choice for her.

She threw back her shoulders and mustered all the confidence she could to ask a favor of Tanner. She really needed to remove all the dirt and grime from her body. Once again, she grabbed her shirt to act as a barrier between her and the germs clinging to the doorknob, turned it, and pushed open the door.

"Um…Tanner…do you think it would be possible for me to take a quick shower? My skin is crawling, and it feels like a nest of insects invaded my hair. I'm about to rip my scalp off." Juliet raised her hand and scratched her head.

Tanner narrowed her eyes but nodded.

"I don't suppose you have an extra pair of clean underwear hanging around, or maybe a clean T-shirt and pair of pants. I'm not too picky as long as you can assure me they're clean."

Tanner guffawed. "Yeah, right. I suppose you'll want them pressed neatly for you."

Juliet's face reddened. "I'd be happy if they were just free of dirt and grime. I can live with a few wrinkles."

"Well, this must be your lucky day because I have an overnight duffle with a few of those items. I even have a clean pair of socks." Tanner moved her eyes up and down Juliet's body. "They should fit just fine. You look about the same size—maybe a few inches shorter, but you can roll up the jeans. I'm going to trust that you aren't ready to try to make a break for it while I retrieve the bag. Don't make me hunt you down, because I get impulsive when anyone puts me in a foul mood."

Juliet crossed her heart with her index finger. "I promise not to run. Besides, I'm too curious now to leave without hearing your story, and you know how nosiness is an integral part of my DNA."

Tanner brusquely exited the cabin.

Juliet's quandary created a host of conflicting feelings. She thought she might be able to think more clearly after she took care of her obsessive need to shower. She would force herself not to consider what might reside in Tanner's clean clothes. They were preferable to what she was currently wearing, considering her jeans had made contact with every filthy part of the dirty cabin.

When Tanner returned with the duffle, she dug into the muted-green bag and pulled out a pair of jeans, a T-shirt, black bikini briefs, and a pair of black socks. She handed the items to Juliet, who greedily pulled them to her chest.

"Um, I hate to be an ingrate, but you wouldn't happen to have a towel in your magic bag?"

Tanner frowned. "Sorry, I don't have a towel." She pulled out a thick sweatshirt and handed it to Juliet. "Here, use this."

"I'd guess if you don't have a towel, you probably don't have a new toothbrush or toothpaste."

"Oh ye of little faith. You shouldn't make assumptions, Juliet. When you assume, you make an ass out of you and me." Tanner laughed without restraint and plucked from the bag a trial-sized tube of toothpaste and a toothbrush.

"Ha-ha. That is a very old saying and not at all humorous." Juliet scrutinized the toothbrush, noting the absence of packaging that would indicate its newness.

"Don't look at me like that. I assure you the toothbrush hasn't been used. It's one of those that my dental hygienist gave me. I keep tossing them in my glove compartment, so I rescued this one and put it in the duffel. For some reason I just knew you would be the type to start whining about your grooming needs."

"It's what might be in your glove compartment that has me worried. I don't want to stick that in my mouth if something disgusting managed to cling to the brush while it was innocently hanging out in your little hidey-hole."

"God, you are an obsessive-compulsive germaphobe. Just take the damn toothbrush or don't. It makes no difference to me."

Juliet pondered her situation for a few seconds and decided she'd rather take her chances with the toothbrush than go without brushing.

"Just for the record, there is absolutely nothing wrong with having good hygiene. I recommend it to everyone."

Tanner stuck her nose in her armpit and sniffed. "I hope you aren't suggesting that I stink."

"If the shoe fits." Juliet smirked.

"Don't forget, I still have a gun and I might just shoot you for being a royal pain in the ass."

"I don't think you will. Your bark is worse than your bite, Miss Badass Cop." Juliet clutched the items and strolled into the bathroom, shaking her ass. She turned her head and glanced back at Tanner and smiled when she caught Tanner looking at her rear. She couldn't help feeling pleased that Tanner might be as attracted to her as she was to Tanner. She wondered if maybe she was experiencing Stockholm syndrome. Nah, she was attracted to Tanner well before this unfortunate incident. Juliet was willing to give her the opportunity to explain herself, because outer packages weren't always what they appeared to be and sometimes a person had to peel the onion to get to the innermost layers.

✝

Tanner frowned and sniffed her armpit again. "I do not smell, and there is nothing wrong with my personal hygiene," she announced to the empty room.

She chuckled as she thought about Juliet catching her watching as Juliet had wiggled her ass. She'd done that deliberately, and Tanner couldn't help enjoying the banter between them. She hated women who hung on her every word or weren't willing to give as good as they got. Juliet was different from the two women she'd attempted to date since losing Faith, and she wasn't sure if that was a good thing or not.

Tanner was beginning to accept her decision to tell Juliet everything in hopes that she would understand and accept her point of view. Although Juliet was a sticky problem that needed resolving, a more pressing issue was the fact that Ralph Hardgrove might be hanging around ready to eliminate a threat. She needed to know who was Ralph's target and she needed that information, like yesterday.

When her phone vibrated in her pocket, Tanner glanced at the screen and was relieved to see Cisco's picture pop up.

"Whadya find out?... Shit.... Are you sure?... Okay, don't get your knickers in a twist.... Yeah, I know you wouldn't tell me that unless you were ninety percent positive about the validity of the information.... Yeah, I know her.... No, I am not sleeping with her, but I feel compelled to do something now. I guess I'll have to go to plan C.... No, I can't afford to owe you for another favor. Besides, I think I can handle this on my own.... Yeah, I don't think she has a

51

clue about how dangerous her snooping has been.... Okay, talk to you later.... Sure, I promise to call if I need something.... Thanks, Cisco, you really came through for me, and, seriously, I do owe you big-time."

Tanner began pacing the cabin like a caged tiger. The latest update from Cisco put a whole new spin on the situation. Juliet might think Tanner's sense of right and wrong had taken a left turn down the alley of evil, but Tanner wasn't about to let Juliet out of her sight until she figured this whole mess out. Unintended victims were at the top of her list to protect, and Juliet might be a pain in the ass, but she was innocent.

Juliet wasn't going to like it, but now she had no choice but to keep her at the cabin. Tanner looked around and had to admit it was kind of dingy and had a questionable level of sanitation. She would have to go into town and obtain cleaning supplies. She hoped the sundries would be enough to satisfy Juliet's persnickety nature.

The bathroom door creaked open, and Tanner glanced in the direction of the noise. Juliet grinned as she stood in the doorway, and Tanner was surprised at how attractive Juliet was without an ounce of makeup to hide her beautiful face.

"Here, you can share my sweatshirt." Juliet chuckled when she handed the damp, cotton, balled-up garment to Tanner.

"I already took my shower this morning, thank you very much."

"Oh, I couldn't tell." Juliet laughed.

Tanner harrumphed. "Now you're just being mean. I sniffed and I do not smell."

"You are just too easy. Like taking candy from a baby." Juliet grinned.

Captivated

Tanner waved her arm at the wooden chair. "Sit. I have some news, and I'm afraid you aren't going to like what I have to say."

Juliet walked over to it, sat, and pulled her hands through her wet hair in what looked like a feeble attempt to remove the tangles.

Tanner followed her to the old dinette set, sat down, and leaned back in her chair, contemplating how she was going to bring Juliet up to speed on the latest development.

"Do you think you could finish your explanation about Aiden? Inquiring minds...you know...I'm just dying to hear your rationale...oh wait, that didn't come out right. 'Cause I am particularly fond of staying alive right now. I may not have an exciting or fulfilling life, but the alternative, well...."

"Can you please stop babbling? I've decided not to shoot you, and I just may be the only woman who will be able to save your pathetic existence."

"Oh please. First, you drug me, and then you put a gun to my head, tie me up, make me nearly piss my pants, and leave me alone in this disgusting cabin. I'm not sure I want you to be my savior. If you're not going to shoot me, I'd appreciate a ride back to civilization, and we can forget this whole nasty business. I would like to know why I shouldn't go straight to the police about Aiden."

Tanner sighed. "I might as well tell you the whole story. Maybe you'll agree with me and maybe you won't, but I will protect you and figure this mess out. Aiden wasn't just a drug dealer. While I don't particularly like drug dealers, they don't meet the code either."

"What is it with this code of yours?"

"The code governs how I decide to handle certain situations. I only execute individuals who meet the criteria.

53

It's why I can't exterminate you even though you present a very real risk to me and my livelihood."

"So you're telling me that you are a righteous hitwoman?" Juliet raised her eyebrow.

"Exactly. Now you understand."

"Um, not really. Back that explanation train up. Tell me why Aiden was on your list."

"He was the worst kind of kiddie pornographer. Not only did he make kiddie porn, but he set in motion the kidnapping, rape, and torture of several young girls and boys. He would lure them in, film them, and convince them to perform despicable acts with other equally heinous colleagues."

Juliet gasped. "Honestly, I didn't know that about Aiden or I would have come forward."

"Kiddie porn is big business, and whenever someone got too close or if they had an inkling one of the kids would squeal, they simply eliminated them or sold them to the highest bidder. My former partner got in his way and didn't make it to her thirtieth birthday. The justice system doesn't always work, and I was not going to let that bastard walk."

"So he's your first…um…execution?" Juliet asked.

Tanner waved her hand. "Nah, he's my seventh, but who's counting." She grinned.

"You're actually proud of this?"

"Trust me, every last one of them got what they deserved. There was indisputable proof of their monstrous crimes. We saved the taxpayers a boatload of money with our special brand of justice."

"*We?*"

"Oops. I shouldn't really reveal there are others who, shall I say, share my unique perspective."

Juliet leaned back in her chair and looked up at the ceiling. "Hmmm. I guess I can't really argue with the need to get some of these really bad people off the streets. I just wish there was another, more legal way of ensuring they got what they deserved."

"Oh, they got what they deserved."

"Okay. Let's say for the sake of argument, every one of your so-called 'code' recipients did, in fact, warrant your unique brand of justice. Were you really going to kill me to protect yourself? Because the way I see it, if you were, you're no better than the people you hunt."

Tanner frowned. "Yeah, I pretty much came to the same conclusion. I guess I thought my only chance was to convince you that what I did was an acceptable choice. I didn't think you were involved in this whole mess beyond simply witnessing Aiden's unfortunate ending. If I hadn't been able to convince you, I would have disappeared and left you instructions on how to hike back to town. I might have lamented over the fact that I'd have to assume a new identity and move halfway across the world to ensure my anonymity. However, if that were my only option, I would have taken it. Now I'm glad I did kidnap you, because you, sweet Juliet, are up to your eyeballs in shit right now. Someone sent a hitman to take you out. I don't know what you saw, but it was enough to spook a very nasty character."

Juliet arched her eyebrow. "You're just trying to scare me. I don't believe you. I haven't seen anything but your gruesome handiwork."

"Look, I am many things, but a liar is not one of them. I suggest you think back carefully on what you might have observed in the last couple of weeks. Number one on that list would be Aiden's comings and goings. He's at the top of the shit heap in my opinion." Tanner narrowed her eyes at Juliet.

Tanner watched as Juliet cocked her head and appeared to have a short internal dialogue. She remained quiet while she propped her right hand under her chin. When she removed her hand and her eyes went wide, Tanner knew she'd remembered something that might shed some light on their current dilemma.

"Oh crap. I remember following Aiden one night. It was late, like midnight or close to it. I just thought he was taking care of a niece. I almost said hello, but he rounded the corner quickly with the teenager in tow. I thought it was odd at the time, but the girl didn't seem frightened. Harley was doing his rounds and saw me shortly after. We talked for a few minutes, and I may have mentioned that I'd seen Aiden and asked if he had family in town."

"Why the hell were you following Aiden? Of all people to take an interest in, why him?"

Juliet shrugged. "I don't know. He always seemed like a bit of an odd duck and an unlikely person to shack up with Margie. I was curious about him."

"Why don't you tell me a little more about Harley and how you figured out that he and Aiden were in the drug business together?"

"Illegal drugs aren't really the primary market in Riverville—it's the prescription drugs that bring the most money. I guess there's a lot of tolerance for Miss Maribel and her debilitating arthritis. Everyone knows she buys from Aiden. Strike that—bought from Aiden. Hell, half the old-timers got their *medicines* from Aiden. I saw Aiden and Harley hanging out with one another, engaging in heated arguments that stopped anytime I got close. Also, Harley's sister is a pharmacist—I just put two and two together and got four."

"But you really don't have any proof, do you?" Tanner asked.

"Um...I sort of looked in Harley's windows one night and saw him hand Aiden a satchel full of drugs in exchange for a case of money."

"Shit, Juliet, why didn't you report this to me? I knew Harley was a douche bag, but I didn't realize how deep he was into this."

"I don't know. I guess I thought it wasn't that bad, and Miss Maribel really does have pain issues. If anyone is to blame for her oxy addiction, it's probably the doctor who kept prescribing to her until he got his license yanked, and by that time she was already addicted. The new doc wouldn't give her any more prescriptions for oxy and wanted her to try something less addictive. I felt sorry for her and didn't want to be the one to stop the flow of drugs. I hear withdrawal is especially difficult on old people."

Tanner rubbed her hand across her face. "Okay, okay. Anything else you can add to this mess? Where else have you inadvertently poked your lovely nose?"

Juliet smiled. "Lovely nose?"

Tanner had no idea why she'd said that. She didn't flirt and she certainly didn't throw out compliments about a person's appearance as naturally as they seemed to flow from her mouth to Juliet. She was in uncharted territory with her intense attraction to Juliet, and she needed to rein that in and quick.

"Don't sidetrack me. I need to know everything you know. I can't protect you unless I know who else might be gunning for you. There's a distinct possibility you're a target from multiple angles."

"I honestly haven't noticed any nefarious dealings with anyone else in town, unless you count the people involved in extracurricular activities outside of their marriage. I sure hope we don't need to include them, because honestly there are far too many to tell you about. There are more people shacking up with someone other than their wife or husband than there are devoted partners. I swear there's something in the water here. Monogamy isn't a valued trait for anyone in Riverville or S-ville."

Tanner shook her head. "Do not place me in that category. If I ever found the right person again, I would never cheat. Considering that I haven't made a commitment to anyone in over five years, you can't lump me into your assessment of this little town of debauchery. What about you, are you also of the mindset that monogamy is overrated?"

"Certainly not." Juliet glared at Tanner.

"How about that, something we agree on."

"Do you really think my life is in danger?"

"I do. Look, I know you probably don't completely trust me right now, but I'm asking you to stay put for your own safety. I need to go out and get us some supplies. When I come back, we can sit down and form a plan of action. I'll try to see if I can find out a little more. If Ralph is still around, he'll stick out like a sore thumb. We have the advantage of living in a small town—strangers get noticed."

"I live in a small town. From what I understand, you're just visiting."

"I might be tempted to stay a bit longer. This place grows on you, and certain attractions are mildly entertaining." Tanner winked.

"Can you bring back some bleach?"

"It was on my list. I know you're just clamoring to scrub the place down, and I'm going to let you." She smirked.

"Um, Tanner?"

"What now?"

"Well, I know this probably isn't on your list of high priorities, but I can't really afford to lose my job, and they must be wondering why I didn't show up at work. I've never missed a day, so don't you think they'll be curious about where I am?"

Tanner grinned. "I found your phone in the woods and used it to text your boss. You had a family emergency and I'm helping."

"I don't have family in the area anymore besides Granny, and she's out of town right now. I'm not close with anyone else."

"Yep, I guessed that, but I'm willing to bet my house that no one in town knows anything about you or your relationship with your family. Snooping appears to be a one-way direction. You dig out the stories from everyone else, but never share your own. There's plenty of speculation about you, but I've never been one to trust gossip because it's grossly inaccurate for the most part."

Juliet arched her eyebrow. "You seem to make an awful lot of assumptions about me without verifying anything."

"I pay attention. Little clues here and there are easy to spot if you know what to look for."

"Whatever. I suppose you think you have everything all worked out. Well, can you work out getting me clean clothes as long as you plan to run errands? By the way, what about your job?" Juliet asked.

"Nope. Got that all worked out too, and no, I don't have *everything* mapped out. There is still someone trying to take you out, and I think by now you know that's no longer *my* plan."

Juliet frowned. "Well, if you don't mind, I'd like you to figure that out, please."

"Everyone's a critic."

Chapter Eight

Harley tapped his hand against the steering wheel in a nervous gesture as he thought about the latest developments in Aiden's murder. Something wasn't adding up. Tanner seemed oddly disinterested in the crime and all too willing to let the Riverville police and the sheriff's office handle the situation.

He couldn't afford to have the investigation dig too deep into Aiden's affairs, because eventually it would lead directly back to him. He wasn't naïve enough to think otherwise. He'd intended on leaving some clues that would divert the focus onto someone else, but then that busybody Margie had to be the one to find Aiden and suggest he call Tanner.

Harley wasn't sure how much Juliet knew about his side business with Aiden, but when he'd learned about Aiden's other venture, Harley had told him he didn't want anything to do with that nasty business and that Aiden had better watch out because the town snoop had seen him with that young girl.

He was smart enough to know this was a professional hit, and he didn't want to be the next in line. For whatever reason, someone had decided Aiden was a bigger risk than Juliet. Harley suspected Aiden's little side drug business wasn't what got him snuffed, so maybe he was safe after all.

Juliet was an entirely different problem. He needed to think how he might throw the Riverville police and sheriff's office off his scent and in her direction. That would certainly kill two birds with one stone. Since Juliet was a known lesbian, a lover's quarrel wasn't an option; besides, everyone knew Aiden was banging Margie. Everyone also knew Juliet was squeaky-clean, so her involvement in the drug business was unlikely, but wasn't it always the person everyone least expected? He wondered if he would be able to discredit her in any way so that when the police or the sheriff asked if she knew anything, she wouldn't blab to them about his involvement with Aiden. Being an oddball wasn't enough to throw doubt on her observations. Harley guessed the town snoop probably had a pretty good idea about the illegal prescription drug business he'd arranged with the help of his sister, Darla.

He pinched the bridge of his nose. He was getting a headache from all the stress. Perhaps it was time for him and his sister to consider making a career move and venture out into the world, but not before he at least tried to set Juliet up. The news was full of stories about people who were involved in terrible things and when they were caught, their friends and neighbors swore they had no clue. A few baggies containing a variety of drugs placed in her car, her house, and if he could get to it, her ever-present belt bag would be all he'd need.

Harley gripped the steering wheel and whipped the police cruiser around. Screeching his tires and making an illegal U-turn in the middle of Main Street, he headed for the local pharmacy to talk things over with Darla.

†

Riverville was small enough to continue to have a locally owned and operated drugstore instead of one of the major chains. Old Man Garrison was the original pharmacist, and when his only son had decided to run off to California to find his own fame and fortune in the music business, Cecil Garrison finally hired Harley's sister, Darla, to take over for him.

Harley didn't really understand why everyone called him Old Man Garrison; he was barely sixty. He'd retired early and spent most of his time hunting and fishing. About a year ago, he'd come back with a brand-new trophy wife but hadn't spent much time with her. Harley suspected his first and probably only love was hunting and fishing.

Darla had an out-of-control gambling habit and needed a shitload of money to pay her debts. He'd tossed a few beers back with Aiden one night, who had talked him into the lucrative prescription drug scheme. When Harley presented his get-rich-quick plan to her, their partnership with Aiden blossomed into a robust business.

Harley screeched to a stop in front of Garrison's Pharmaceuticals. It wasn't a very creative name, but this was Riverville, so what else would Mr. Garrison name his store?

He scrambled out of the cruiser, slammed the door, and hurried inside. He breathed a sigh of relief when he found his sister alone behind the counter. Old Man Garrison was rarely there, but sometimes his wife, Barbara, was around. She was a shrewd one, and Harley got the impression she knew exactly what he and Darla were doing. He'd often wondered why she never confronted them, but decided he would just thank his lucky stars and forget about her creepy lurking.

"Hey, Darla. Aiden got his dumb ass whacked and we need to create a diversion," Harley blurted.

"What the hell are you blubbering about?" Darla looked up from her book.

"Aiden took a bullet to the head, and it won't take long for the police and the sheriff's office to trace things back to us."

"Crap. It's that little snoop Juliet, right?" Darla asked.

"Yeah, I'd bet my last dollar she's seen enough to finger us both. I thought we might be able to throw the cops off by planting drugs in her car, house, and anything else that would direct their attention to her and cause suspicion. We need a way to discredit her before she has a chance to tell them anything. Have you seen her today?"

Darla frowned. "You know, I haven't yet, and that is odd. I usually see her walk past on her way to work. Did you swing by the post office to see if she's there?"

"No, I came directly here as soon as the police and the sheriff took control of the situation. Come on, we don't have a lot of time to set things up."

"All right. Let me pull together some pills and you can place them in those strategic locations, but you need to make sure she's busy at work first. The last thing we want is Juliet catching you planting the drugs. Damn cell phones have the ability to capture everything on film and send an instantaneous picture of it to one hundred of your best friends with one click of a button." Darla began pulling bottles from the shelf and emptying pills into plastic zip bags she had stored in a drawer to her left.

"Thanks, sis. I'm sure I don't have to tell you that both our asses will be in a sling if we aren't able to send the bloodhounds in a different direction. The Riverville police and the sheriff's department are all gung ho about this murder because they don't get to see much action and this broke up their boring routine."

Harley grabbed the baggies full of drugs from the counter and stuffed them into his jacket. He waved as he pivoted on his heel and exited the store.

†

The plain brick building that housed Riverville's post office prominently displayed the red, white, and blue flag of the United States. Darrel, the postmaster, took great care with it and ensured a new flag adorned the post office every few years. He properly retired the old flag according to the United States Flag Code. Darrel was a former major in the Marines, and he ran his post office with military precision. He wasn't a bad sort, he just demanded order and efficiency, which was particularly helpful in ensuring that each piece of mail found its proper owner.

Harley strolled into the post office and nonchalantly inquired of Sallie Mae, the postal clerk, "Where's Juliet today?"

"Harrumph. Something about a family emergency. She texted Darrel. Can you believe that? She texted him. He wasn't happy about it. Didn't even recognize he'd received a text. I had to show him what it was when his phone dinged. He got himself a fancy new phone and doesn't even know how to use the damn thing," Sally Mae grumbled.

"Oh, so what's the big emergency?" Harley asked.

"How the hell should I know? Do I look like *The Enquirer* to you? Juliet's the town snoop, not me. I just mind my own business, do what I'm told, and fill in when Darrel needs me. I coulda been home with my grandkids today, but no, Juliet had an emergency. Didn't even know she had family. Knows everything about all of us, but we know nada about her." She frowned.

"So you think she's out of town or something?"

"What's it to you, Harley? She's a lesbian, so I don't think she's interested."

"There's been a murder, so I get worried about all the locals. It's my job to protect the citizens of our sister communities. I know she's a lesbian. I'm not interested in her in that way, but she's one of my charges."

"Oh please. That's the biggest bunch of malarkey I've ever heard." Sally Mae narrowed her eyes. "You got something up your sleeve, boy, I can always tell."

"Just forget about it. I got better things to do than chew the fat with you, Sally Mae. We got us a murderer in our midst. I'd be extra careful if I was you. Your nasty-ass personality might be enough of a beacon to make you his next victim."

Sally Mae waved her arm. "Oh, go play police officer and send Tanner around. She's the one I'd hang my hat on to save the day."

Harley stalked out of the post office, slammed the door, and muttered, "Fucking dykes."

"I heard that, Harley, you backwater Barney Fife."

†

Harley decided this latest piece of information was worth driving by Juliet's home to check out the lay of the land. When his police cruiser rounded the corner and rolled past Juliet's ancient VW Bug, he frowned. Why would her car still be in the driveway? If she'd gone somewhere to take care of family business, wouldn't she have taken her car?

He swiveled his head from left to right to check if anyone was around to catch him leaving the incriminating evidence in her car. The street seemed empty, and Harley thought that was a sign from God that now was his window of opportunity.

He maneuvered the car perpendicular to the Bug, and continued to look around as he emerged from the cruiser. After easing the door shut so he wouldn't alert the nosy neighbors to his presence, he crept to the vehicle. It was too much to ask for the door to be unlocked.

"Fuck. What the hell does she have to steal anyway? Fucking hunk of junk."

He walked back to the cruiser to get his slim jim. After popping the trunk, he leaned in and rooted around until he found the thin, flexible metal bar. As he pushed the trunk door shut quietly and turned around, he heard the whir of a car window.

"What the hell are you doing?" Tanner yelled out through the passenger-side window from her car parked behind his own vehicle.

Startled, Harley couldn't think up a quick reply, so he remained quiet.

"I don't see anyone on the street needing your help to unlock their car door, so I've got to wonder what you've gotten yourself into."

Harley glanced across the road and saw a fancy car parked in the street. It belonged to Nancy, Clark Gable's ex-wife, and that gave him an idea.

"Clark called and asked me to open Nancy's car. She left her keys inside it and he didn't want to come all the way to her house to unlock it."

"You even know how to use that thing without tearing up her window casing?" Tanner smirked.

"Yeah, I know how to use it, smartass. What are you doing in this neck of the woods, anyway?"

"Juliet had a family emergency, and I've been helping her out. She needed some things from her house. Since her car has been acting up, I offered to drive her."

"Oh, where's her family live?"

"None of your business, Nosy Nelly."

Harley didn't need Tanner hanging around while he fiddled with Nancy's car. Pretending to take a cell call, he raised the phone to his ear. "Hello.... Yeah, I'm in front of the house now.... Oh, okay.... No problem."

He ended the call, put his phone back on his belt, and looked over at Tanner. "She found her keys."

Tanner narrowed her eyes.

Instinctively transferring the slim jim to his left hand, he put his right hand in his jacket pocket where the drugs lay waiting. He wrapped his fingers around the contraband and slowly made his way around to the driver's-side door of his car. He pulled his hand out and quickly opened the door and slid inside. Tanner didn't seem to be in a hurry to leave, and Harley knew his window of opportunity had just slammed shut. Now that he knew Juliet was somewhere else, he might be able to make this work in a few hours. After he put his car in gear and made a U-turn, he waved good-bye to Tanner. There was no sense in putting her on alert. She was smart and it wouldn't take much to tip her off.

†

Tanner didn't like this latest development one bit. Harley was up to no good, that was a given. She rarely assessed people incorrectly, and she'd gotten the distinct impression that he had specific plans to create havoc for Juliet. Tanner wasn't about to let that happen. First, there was a hitman on the loose, and now her idiot colleague was sniffing around Juliet's place for no apparent reason.

Regardless of how on target Tanner was with the individuals she went after, her real strength was in gathering the proof so that when she delivered her unique brand of justice, she never had any question that she was doing the right thing. Checking out Harley's explanation would be simple. All she had to do was pay Nancy a visit to discredit the cock-and-bull story Harley had relayed to her.

Tanner parked her car in the spot Harley had just vacated. She wanted her presence in front of Juliet's house apparent to anyone who ventured into the neighborhood. It wasn't much, but maybe it would give whomever was after Juliet pause before acting rashly. Even the Mob was hesitant to knock off a police officer because it often caused them too much of a headache. Not that they always stuck to that rule, because Aiden sure hadn't been cautious. Tanner chuckled to herself when she thought that Aiden's bosses might just consider it their lucky day. Aiden probably caused them far more grief than he was worth.

Tanner pulled her lean body out of the car and stretched before leisurely strolling across the street to knock on Nancy's door. She had a hard time linking Nancy with Clark. He was such a putz and Nancy seemed a lot sharper than people gave her credit for. After rapping on the door three times, Tanner took a step back.

The door opened wide, and Nancy looked surprised to see her. "Tanner? Is something wrong?"

"No, no, nothing wrong. I was just checking on the call Clark made to Harley. He said you'd locked your keys in your car, and it seemed odd to me that you would call Clark. I didn't realize the two of you were friendly."

"What?" Nancy raised her voice. "That asswipe. I most certainly did not lock my keys in my car. I'm gonna show that little shithead he can't keep messing with me. Can I file some kind of harassment charge against him? That'll teach the prick to leave me alone. I don't get it. He's screwing Scarlet, why's he gotta keep messing with me?"

"Hmmm. I don't know, Nancy. Has Clark been messing with you lately?"

Nancy placed her arms across her chest and frowned. "Actually, no. So this doesn't make sense at all. We haven't talked in years. That was the biggest mistake of my life, marrying my childhood sweetheart. I was far too young to get married. I was just glad to get out of that mess early on."

"It's not like you're here all that often, anyway. Don't you travel around a lot for your job?"

Tanner was a little curious about Nancy. She seemed to be away more often than she was home. Although her house was modest, her car was not. Tanner had always wondered about that incongruity.

Nancy narrowed her eyes and Tanner got the impression that her question wasn't a welcome one.

"Thanks for checking on me, Tanner."

Tanner didn't know why she was about to tell Nancy about Aiden, but for some reason she wanted to judge her reaction.

"Harley seemed to think that with Aiden's murder, we ought to keep a closer eye on things around here."

Nancy quirked her eyebrow. "Aiden got himself killed, did he?"

"You don't sound surprised. Anything you care to share?" Tanner asked.

"Everyone knew what a little prick he was. I'll bet the suspect list is long."

"Interesting. Well, if you know anything, tell it to the Riverville police or the sheriff. They're the ones handling the case." Tanner shifted her weight to her other foot.

Nancy nodded. "Makes sense. Listen, I was just about to head out, so I don't mean to be rude, but I've really got to get going."

Tanner smiled. "No problem. Have a nice day."

Chapter Nine

The woman ran her hand absently through her hair. The recent developments were a bit surprising. She wondered whether it was judicious of her to make the call and find out more. On the one hand, things weren't adding up; on the other, her partner didn't respond well when questioned about the manner in which they chose to deal with certain problems. She could literally be committing professional suicide—with an emphasis on the "suicide" part.

That idiot Harley was going to be the biggest risk. She had to know what their plans were, because honestly she wasn't willing to hang around when everything blew up in a large mushroom cloud of totally fucked beyond repair.

She picked up her phone and made the call. It was worth the gamble.

"Yeah, it's me…. Things are interesting here with Aiden's premature demise…. What?…. So you're telling me you didn't order the hit?…. We've got other problems, because I think Harley is running scared and about to do something very stupid…. Yes, Aiden thought he might make some additional money on the side and partnered with Harley on a small-scale drug scheme.... If they dig into that, they might find other things.... No, I had no idea about that. Aiden didn't fill me in.... No, haven't seen her since yesterday, but Tanner was around. She has the license plate of the car Ralph rented, which is a complete dead end.... Yeah, I hope you carve him a new one, because that little shit left before getting the job done and now we have all this crap to contend with.... Sure, I'll keep my eyes open and let you know as soon as I get more information.... You may want to consider doubling the fee and having him take care of them both.... Don't send Ralph again, because I'm inclined to wring his scrawny neck myself if I see the whites of his eyes.... Okay."

She pushed the button to end the call and sighed. Early retirement might not be as easy as she thought. What a total cluster. It might be time to reconsider her future. She had no idea Aiden had called Miguel to tell him about Juliet seeing her with the girl. Now her ass was on the line and Juliet had to go. It wouldn't be long before Juliet or Tanner put two and two together. She never should have answered that call when Aiden needed help. That little bastard hadn't told her who the kid was, only that he was in need of assistance. Now she realized just how much of a shitstorm Aiden had created for her. At least Miguel's answer to the problem wasn't a hit on her or Aiden.

✝

Harley decided to swing by the pharmacy to give his sister an update. She wouldn't be pleased. She was constantly telling him what a fuckup he was, but that sure didn't stop her from roping him into the drug scheme. He suspected she didn't want to associate with people like

Aiden, and that left him to do all the dirty work. However, her hands were just as dirty as his were, and if he went down, so would she. He was tired of taking orders from her. *Who does she think she is, anyway?*

By the time Harley pulled into the parking space right in front of the store, he was in a major snit. He yanked open the door and the small bell tinkled, announcing his arrival.

Darla looked up and pushed aside the pills she was counting on the counter. "You're back already?"

"Don't start," Harley hissed.

"What? Geez, I just wondered why you're back so quickly. Your little errand either went really well or you have some bad news. Since it seems like someone rained on your parade, I'm guessing things didn't go as planned. It wasn't that complicated, Harley. You were the one who came up with the plan, and now it seems to have a snag in it—already. Do I have to do everything?"

"I'll take care of it. Tanner showed up, and I had to think of something quick because she caught me with the slim jim."

Darla shook her head. "Shit. What did you tell her?"

"Well, it's not like I had an abundance of options. I told her Clark called me to ask if I'd unlock Nancy's car door because she'd locked her keys inside it. I pretended to get a call and told her Nancy found her keys," Harley explained.

Darla sighed. "I suppose it never occurred to you that Tanner might find your story slightly suspicious and check things out for herself."

Harley shuffled his feet. "No. I still think it's a good plan. I'll swing back around in another couple of hours."

"What was Tanner doing hanging around Juliet's place, anyway?"

"She mentioned something about helping Juliet out with her family emergency. I didn't realize they'd gotten chummy. I suppose it makes sense since they're both dykes."

"God, Harley, no wonder people call you Barney. You can be such an ass sometimes."

"Fuck you, Darla. Just remember that if I go down, so do you. This ass will be saving yours. Don't forget that." Harley noted that the store was deserted and was thankful to not have an audience while fighting with his sister.

"I got work to do, and you need to head back to the station before people start wondering why you keep popping by."

"At least I won't see Tanner. We got that new guy— the one who also works for the Riverville police—covering for her. The boss lets her get away with murder. Never even questions her when she asks for time off. It isn't fair."

"Now you sound like a two-year-old. I can't believe you and I came from the same gene pool."

Harley clenched his fists, deciding a retort would just continue the argument, and he never seemed to win anyway. He wished he could just push his overbearing sister off a cliff and be done with it. Maybe he'd plant evidence leading in her direction, and since he was law enforcement, they might take his word over hers. That would teach her not to dis him.

He spun on his heel and pushed open the door, banging it against the brick wall, which made him feel good. As he strode out, his sister muttered, "Asshole."

Yes, planting the evidence on her was looking more and more desirable. He'd have to give it serious consideration.

†

Captivated

Nancy's evasive behavior was the least of Tanner's concerns at this particular moment. Harley might be more involved than she initially thought, and he was, in her estimation, definitely up to no good. Tanner wished she could install a camera at Juliet's place, but she just didn't have the time to deal with it now.

Walking across the street, she pulled out the keys she'd liberated from Juliet's pocket when she'd first brought her to the cabin. So far the story she'd told Juliet's boss and Harley lined up with entering her house and picking out some clean clothes.

Tanner opened the door and was not surprised to find a pristine house. Everything she knew about Juliet screamed persnickety and obsessive-compulsive. She glanced around the cozy, tidy living room and noticed a small brass hook near the light switch. After flipping on the light, she leaned in and read the white strip above the hook. *Keys.* Tanner near rolled over with laughter as she realized Juliet had labeled the hook to indicate she hung her keys there.

As much as the label tickled her funny bone, as she looked around, Juliet's home seemed lonely. Tanner didn't see any knickknacks, mementos, or personal treasures that would help her get a glimpse into Juliet's life. It was barren of all personal belongings other than the necessary items for living. The kitchen counter had nothing on top of it except for a Keurig. She suspected Juliet had a place for everything else complete with requisite labels lest anything be out of order.

She couldn't resist checking out the rest of the place to see if Juliet had labeled anything else. She guessed a variety of the miniature labels might be strategically placed inside various cabinets and closets and that the kitchen would be the most likely recipient of Juliet's excessive need for organization.

Her hypothesis was confirmed when she opened the pantry. Cans and boxes of various foods lined the shelves in alphabetical order by category. Cans of fruit in one section, cans of vegetables in another, breakfast boxes on a separate shelf—all with their own label as if the occupant was unable to determine what type of food item resided in that particular section.

Tanner shook her head. "Freak," she said fondly.

She chuckled as she made her way into the bedroom. *I wonder if she's labeled her underwear drawer.*

Tanner pulled open the first drawer of the dresser and found custom wood dividers with the same neat labels attached—*thongs, bikinis, boy shorts.* Juliet had neatly laid the underwear in the corresponding section according to color from light to dark. Tanner couldn't believe her eyes. Could anyone really be this compulsive? She plucked out one of the thongs within the front partition and fingered the silky material. She wondered what Juliet would look like in this particular garment. Would it be sexier than the other choices? The fact she had three completely different types of underwear was interesting. Tanner wasn't sure which ones to pick. Would Juliet want her to pack a variety? That thought got her laughing even harder. An underwear variety pack, like the Lay's classic potato chips her mother used to put in her lunch box.

Tanner grabbed several pairs of undergarments from each compartment and opened the next drawer to find a similar arrangement of socks. Leaving the knee-high stockings Juliet most likely had intended for dressier pants, she grabbed several pairs of casual cotton or light wool socks. After making her selections, she tossed them onto the neatly made bed.

She moved to the door in the bedroom that she suspected was a walk-in closet. She noted the white labels on each shelf marking every section that separated pants, skirts, blouses, and jackets. Juliet had arranged each one by color, starting with white and ending with black. On the opposite wall were custom-crafted shelves—also labeled—containing backpacks, luggage, duffel bags, belts, sweaters, sweatshirts, and shoes.

Tanner grabbed one of the large duffel bags and began gathering casual shirts, jeans, and sweatshirts. She carefully rolled each item, placed it in the duffel, exited the closet, and tossed the half-full bag onto the bed next to the underwear and socks. After finding the T-shirts and placing the rest of the items, including toiletries, into the bag, she decided it was time to pay Harley a visit at the station. She still needed to go to the grocery store and get food and cleaning supplies, but spooking him was a bigger priority at this point.

†

Harley's shift was almost over, so he screeched up to the station and stalked inside. A few inches of dark brown liquid remained in the coffeepot. He absently poured himself a cup and took a sip of the left-over dregs. As he tasted the burned beverage, his glower deepened and he spit it back into the cup.

His foul mood intensified as he thought about running into Tanner and the tongue-lashing his sister had given him. He slumped into the leather chair without removing his jacket. Clasping his hands behind his head, he swiveled the chair back and forth, staring into space and wondering if he should make another run at stashing the drugs in Juliet's car.

He heard the door to the station open and turned to find Tanner scowling as she entered the room.

"What do you want now? I thought you were taking the night off."

Tanner crossed her arms. "You know, it's a funny thing, Harley. I knocked on Nancy's door and she didn't know anything about misplacing her keys, and that got me wondering why you would tell me that lie. You wouldn't be petty enough to start harassing Juliet, now would you? I know you're a big homophobe, but why start hassling her now when you've left her alone before?"

"Fuck off, Tanner. I don't need shit from you, and I don't need to explain myself either. You should let this go. I'm warning you."

"Hmmm." Tanner narrowed her eyes. "Did you just grow some balls and threaten me?"

"You think you're some hotshot detective or something just because you come from Seattle. Well, you didn't seem too interested in Aiden's murder, and something about you isn't right. Why would you leave Seattle to come here? Something stinks about you, Tanner, and I'm going to uncover whatever dirty little secret you have if it's the last thing I do."

"Bring it on, Harley. Just remember that if you try to play with the big boys, you better be prepared to get a big-boy ass whipping. Trust me on this—you are way out of your league. This is your one and only warning. Stay the fuck away from Juliet." She glared at Harley for a few seconds before pivoting and marching out the door.

Tanner didn't need Harley nipping at her heels as her unease began to rise. Things seemed to, all of a sudden, stack up against her, and she wasn't prepared to deal with all of them at once.

Her fondness for Juliet was beginning to expand, and in addition to keeping the authorities from sniffing around her, Tanner felt compelled to protect Juliet. Someone with far more clout and intelligence than Harley was behind this, but her asinine colleague was also capable of adding heaping piles of stress on her already full plate.

She would take things one step at a time. Supplies first, and then she would try to fit the puzzle pieces together.

†

The woman watched as Tanner walked out of the grocery store with a cart full of groceries. She noted Tanner's posture as the officer looked left and right. She was convinced Tanner was scanning the area and assessing threats. Her rigid, almost military actions revealed a highly trained individual. She almost admired the cop's cold, calculated demeanor. In another life, they may have been good friends. She sensed Tanner would be a kindred spirit, but they were on opposite sides, and that was something she could not forget. She needed to neutralize Tanner or have someone remove her from the equation—that was a foregone conclusion. The former Seattle detective was far too intelligent to remain on the chessboard.

She wasn't concerned about her ability to follow Tanner. She was the kind of person who faded into the background—an unlikely suspect. It was what made her the perfect silent partner. However, Tanner was not a run-of-the-mill local yokel. She would have to be careful as she pursued her.

The woman had the patience of a saint. She would wait until the perfect moment to make her move. Like a lion stalking her prey, she watched as Tanner loaded her car with the groceries and slid into the driver's seat.

She smiled as she noticed her adversary look in her direction. The game was on. Did Tanner sense something about her? The woman watched as Tanner cased her surroundings and locked eyes on several others before she pulled away from the curb.

The woman wasn't a mind reader, but she got the distinct impression that Tanner's sixth sense was on high alert and she had noticed something was amiss. Tanner might recognize a fellow hunter.

The woman sprang to action and managed to follow the S-ville officer as she drove farther from town. Following someone who could easily spot a tail took tremendous skill, but she was a master at it. Following her all the way to her final destination wasn't necessary. She knew she just needed to get close enough to check out the general vicinity when the time came. She smiled because she was very familiar with this remote area. She almost wanted to be the one to resolve this situation. Tanner was the ultimate conquest, and she needed a challenge. Maybe she would call her partner and tell him not to send another person to finish the job. Yes, that's what she would do. The town was too small anyway. Strangers stuck out too much, and Ralph had certainly rung alarm bells. If you wanted something done right, well you had to do it yourself. She'd never actually killed someone before, but she looked forward to it.

†

The hairs on the back of Tanner's neck stood up. She'd been around the block a few times and knew when someone was watching her. She turned her head and saw Darla standing behind the glass door of the pharmacy. She was looking out onto the street and smiling. It was creepy.

Tanner's unease grew exponentially as she looked to her right and spied Nancy's sleek, black Mercedes idling around the corner. Puffs of smoke flowed from the tailpipe and dissipated quickly in the air. She wondered why such an expensive car would have any discernable emissions. Maybe it needed an oil change.

Margie was walking down the street, and they locked eyes. Another smile. Suddenly the whole town was smiling at her. The final entrance into the Twilight Zone was when she looked up and saw Barbara peek out of the office window situated above the drugstore. She was smiling at Tanner too. Tanner was often prone to paranoia, but this way beyond normal.

She turned her head all the way around to see if a fourth person was staring at her and felt relieved that no one was watching from behind. When she looked up again, Barbara was gone from the office window. She moved her gaze downward and found Darla had moved away from the door.

Margie, dressed in her typical realtor attire, continued to walk down the street, and Tanner wasn't in the mood to have a long, involved conversation with her, so she pulled her seat belt quickly across her chest, and with one final glance to the right, where she noted the Mercedes still hadn't moved, Tanner eased into the street.

She kept looking in her rear-view mirror because she felt sure that someone was following her, but she didn't see any familiar vehicles and they all were far enough away that she felt she could begin to let her guard down. Her shoulders were already tensed from the eerie encounter before, and she was probably going to get a horrendous migraine from her hypervigilance.

Despite all the stress, Tanner was looking forward to getting back to the cabin and Juliet. Tanner couldn't help herself—she was inexplicably drawn to Juliet. Of course, her beauty didn't hurt. Juliet had a strange combination of vulnerability and bravery that was hard to resist. She also had a warped and wicked sense of humor, and Tanner always appreciated a person who could make light of any situation. Juliet was quirky and most likely a person with diagnosed obsessive-compulsive disorder, not just persnicketiness.

She began to daydream about Juliet and making the most of their time in the rustic cabin. It probably wasn't a romantic location to Juliet because of the dust and dirt, but to Tanner, nothing compared with an isolated cabin in the woods. Before she realized it, she was almost there, and her excitement increased. For whatever reason, she trusted Juliet would still be inside when she arrived. Trust didn't come easy to Tanner, and she noted this anomaly in her thinking with interest.

Chapter Ten

At first, Juliet continued to read the e-reader that Tanner left her, but after a few hours she was bored and her overwhelming need to snoop got the better of her. Even though her tendency to stick her nose where it didn't belong had gotten her in this mess in the first place, she still couldn't resist checking things out.

Now that she was free to roam around after Tanner cut her loose from the hard, wooden chair, she took stock of her surroundings. The cabin wasn't in disrepair, exactly; it was merely dirty. Her keen eyes registered every dust ball, mold spore, water stain, and sooty footprint. She smiled when she noted the soot scattered all over the old, weathered bricks, and wondered if Tanner would start a fire in the fireplace. With a bit of scrubbing, she could turn this place into a livable space, and having a fire going would make it cozy and pleasant.

Juliet opened the pantry and found cans of peaches, corn, and baked beans. Sitting right next to them was a box of granola cereal. She shook her head and separated the items, placing the corn and beans in one area and peaches a foot to the right. She moved the box of granola to a new shelf.

"Canned peaches, yuck. Who really eats canned peaches?"

After opening a few other drawers and finding the pots, pans, dishes, cutlery, and other kitchen items intermingled in a disorganized mess, she decided the job to put everything in its proper place might take too long. It was easily a ten-hour task to do it right.

Juliet spun around and surveyed the main room, which consisted of the living room and kitchen. To its left was a short hallway where she'd found the only bathroom, and she suspected the door across from the bathroom was a bedroom. She didn't think the cabin had more than one bedroom, and that prospect both excited and disturbed her, for she had conflicted feelings about her captor.

She walked down the narrow hallway and peeked into the bedroom. It contained only a modest pine dresser and queen-sized bed with a simple log bedframe. She assumed a closet was hidden behind the sliding doors.

Juliet was curious about what might be lurking inside the closet and pulled one of the doors open. It was small but functional and contained a few flannel shirts, a pair of hiking boots, and a couple of sweaters. She was disappointed that she didn't find anything more exciting there, like a gun or a box of correspondence from a long-lost lover.

Other than what Tanner had already shared with her, Juliet didn't know much about her. Before this fiasco, she'd snooped hard to find out more about the enigmatic woman, but Tanner hadn't revealed much. At least now she knew the S-ville officer was some sort of vigilante. Juliet wasn't sure how she felt about that. If she was honest with herself, she wasn't as disturbed about Aiden's demise now that she knew the facts—or rather those truths as Tanner represented them.

She didn't think her captor had been lying to her, but that was still a possibility, and she decided to remain wary.

Juliet made her way back to the main room and glanced at the fireplace. The temperature in the cabin was dropping, and her hunger began to rise in defiance. She decided to try to start a fire as a distraction while she waited for Tanner to return.

A stack of newspapers, kindling, and a few logs haphazardly placed on the brick hearth surrounded the old fireplace. Juliet couldn't stand the disarray, so she arranged them neatly before balling up the newspaper. She made her teepee of kindling on top of the crumpled paper and looked around for matches. A box of old-fashioned ones sat on the mantel.

Once she lit the newspaper, she stood back, waiting as the fire licked around the edges of the kindling and created an orange glow. She added a log and stepped back again, watching as the flames started to consume the new source of fuel. As the smoke began to fill the cabin, she remembered she needed to open the damper and was relieved when the toxic fumes began to dissipate as soon as she did. Fortunately the metal handle hadn't heated up too much to burn her hand while opening the flue.

The fire completely mesmerized Juliet, and she almost missed the blinking red light next to the mantel. When she saw it, she panicked, thinking it was a caution light for the fireplace. Maybe she'd created some kind of fire hazard. She looked around the cabin and was about to tear open the kitchen cabinets looking for a pot big enough to fill with water, when she heard a car in the distance.

She ran to the door and yanked it open. Tanner was leaning inside her car, retrieving two bags of groceries.

"Tanner, I'm sorry, I'm sorry. I made a fire. I didn't know I wasn't supposed to," Juliet blurted.

Tanner turned around and smiled. "Hi, honey, I'm home. Now what the hell are you blubbering about?"

"The alarm. I set off the alarm. We have to put it out or I'll burn up your cabin."

Tanner started laughing. "Come on, make yourself useful and grab some of the groceries or the duffel with your clothes."

Juliet crossed her arms over her chest. "Why are you laughing at me? Haven't you heard what I said? The alarm is going off, and we need to put out the fire."

"The fire is fine. The light has nothing to do with the fireplace."

"Oh."

Tanner shifted one of the grocery bags to her right arm and plucked another bag from the backseat. "Are you going to just stand there, or can you please give me a hand?"

Juliet smirked and started clapping. "That is a mighty fine job you're doing."

"Hardy-har-har, very funny. I believe that joke ended during the Nixon administration."

Juliet smiled, then scrunched up her face, mimicking Richard Nixon. "I am not a crook."

Tanner stalked into the cabin.

Juliet scrambled to the car, pulled out the duffel bag, and slung it over her shoulder. She passed Tanner as Tanner went back to the car for a second trip. She hurried to dump the duffel bag in the bedroom and walked back out, passing Tanner again, who had two more bags of groceries in her arms.

"What did ya do, buy out the whole market? Just how long are we staying here?"

"There's only a few more bags."

Juliet headed back to the car to get the remaining items but noted that Tanner hadn't answered her question.

That worried her. She also wanted to know what that red light was about. Juliet wasn't a very patient person. When she walked back into the cabin with the remaining two bags of groceries, she started her barrage of questions.

"How long do we have to stay here? What is that red light for? Did you get cleaning supplies? What about new soap? Did you learn anything more on your reconnaissance journey?"

"Sheesh. Hold on. Can we get these groceries put away first, and then I can answer each question? One at a time, please."

"Sorry." Juliet trudged behind her and plopped the two bags she was carrying onto the counter.

Tanner began pulling the dry goods out of the bags and stuffing them into the kitchen cabinets. Juliet noted the few cans of food she'd organized earlier in the almost-bare cupboards were now sitting next to various food items that were not in the *correct* category. She was aghast that Tanner placed a box of cereal next to the cans of vegetables and beans.

"Um...don't you want to separate those?"

Tanner laughed. "Okay, Ms. Compulsive, I can see where my method of putting away the groceries is going to drive you batty. I'll put away the fresh foods. Any particular way I should do that?"

She stuck out her tongue. "You know, there's a reason certain modern-day refrigerators have labels for their drawers and shelves. How hard can it be to make sure you put everything in its proper order?"

"Sorry, this refrigerator is old and it doesn't have a cheat sheet for where things belong."

"Oh, for Christ's sake, go sit down and attend to the fire while I organize everything."

Tanner chuckled as she made her way back to the living room.

Juliet glanced over her shoulder and smiled as Tanner picked up the poker and started jabbing the log. After organizing the groceries into categories and then alphabetizing them, she began to sing the Michael Jackson song her grandma used to play when she was learning her ABCs.

Tanner's deep laugh interrupted Juliet, and she realized she was singing out loud.

"Hey, don't stop on my behalf. In fact, you can add a bit of dancing to your singing if you'd like."

"Are you laughing at me again?"

"No, absolutely not. I find your habit of breaking out in song endearing. Besides, you have a nice voice. You can get away with singing acapella."

Heat rushed to Juliet's cheeks. "I'm almost done here. Did you have something specific in mind for dinner? Because I'm starving."

"Yeah. I think your stomach is trying to sing a duet with you, and I've got to say it doesn't quite match the tempo of the song."

"Such a comedian. I'm amazed my captor has a sense of humor."

Tanner frowned. "Do you really still think of me as your captor?"

Juliet walked over and placed her hand on Tanner's shoulder before squatting in front of the fireplace. She looked directly into Tanner's eyes. "I'm sorry, no, I don't. It was insensitive of me to say that."

She realized then how true her words were. She no longer viewed Tanner as the enemy and she felt safe in her presence. Her lips were mere inches away from Tanner's, and she had the overwhelming desire to capture her very kissable-looking mouth.

Juliet took a deep breath and leaned back before she did something she would surely regret.

Tanner's pupils dilated and she cocked her head to the side but didn't make a move to close the gap. Juliet didn't know if this was a blessing or a curse. She wanted Tanner, that was a given, but this was an odd situation and she still needed answers to her other questions.

"Were you just going to kiss me?" Tanner asked.

Momentarily taken aback by her direct question, Juliet replied, coughing, "Um, I...uh...just wanted to apologize."

"That didn't exactly answer my question, but I'll let it go for now. For the record, I would have welcomed it."

"So...dinner?" Juliet knew she shouldn't encourage Tanner, but she smiled despite her trepidation.

"I'm not a great cook, so that's why I got a bunch of canned food and stuff to make sandwiches. Turkey sandwich okay with you?"

"Well, for the record, I can cook."

Tanner clapped her hands together. "Great. I think you saw that I bought some spices and a variety of meats. I hoped you had those skills."

"I'll need to organize the pots-and-pans cabinet, because I cannot work in this level of disorganization," Juliet declared.

"Of course you can't." Tanner smirked.

"Just for that snide comment, you get to make the sandwiches while I relax by the fire and imitate a lady of leisure."

Juliet walked over to the fireplace and looked for a clean pillow to place on the bricks. She grimaced as she found a dingy, cream one on the couch. "I suppose it's better than nothing." She watched as Tanner's gaze seemed to follow her every move and then shook her head and laughed. "Don't even make a comment. I'm warning you."

When she smacked the pillow and dust particles flew in every direction, she coughed and judiciously placed it on the bricks before sitting on it. "I'm going to need another shower," Juliet mumbled, "but not before I clean that disgusting thing."

Juliet fidgeted as she remembered the cleaning and bath supplies still on the kitchen counter. Leaving them unattended was driving her crazy. Finally she couldn't take it anymore and jumped up to put them away while Tanner was fixing the sandwiches. She grabbed the remaining bag, gave Tanner a *don't even think about it* look, and marched into the bathroom.

✝

Tanner was grinning as she smeared mayonnaise on the two pieces of wheat bread she had placed on one of the plates she'd retrieved from the cupboards. Knowing how much of a germaphobe Juliet was, she'd already used the dish soap to wash them and dried them with the brand-new kitchen towel she'd bought at the store.

Tanner was sure she saw desire in Juliet's eyes earlier, and even though she knew she shouldn't go there, she'd blurted out her observation. Now it was all she could think of as she watched Juliet dash defiantly into the bathroom. She was sure Juliet would scrub every single surface until they all shined to perfection.

When the red light next to the mantel blinked, her reflexes went into action, and she rushed outside and ran to the spot where she'd camouflaged the trip wire. She'd altered the system to produce a visual alarm instead of an auditory

90

Captivated

one and engineered the wire to detect long-distance movement. It had taken some time to tweak the system so random deer or other wildlife wouldn't trigger it.

Tanner valued her privacy, and if she were honest with herself, the wire silenced her tendency toward paranoia. She and Juliet would certainly make a pair—one of them with obsessive-compulsive disorder, and the other a take-charge person with a fair amount of suspicion. She didn't think her tiny fault bled into an actual disorder, but it was on the line for sure.

Breathing heavily, she finally reached the place where she'd hid the infrared trip wire and witnessed a set of taillights moving away. She tried to convince herself it was probably nothing, just someone who'd gone astray, but it wasn't working. The cabin was out in the boonies, and people didn't generally lose their way out here.

Paranoia activated. She didn't like this one bit. She decided she would sleep with her gun tonight, along with one eye open.

She took a more leisurely stride back to the cabin. She'd probably startled Juliet when she rushed outside, slamming the door open. She picked up her pace so she could settle her nervous guest.

Guest? Was that how she regarded Juliet? She couldn't blame Juliet for believing she was a prisoner. Tanner had certainly set it up that way at first. She regretted how she'd treated Juliet, but she had panicked when Juliet witnessed the execution. Something she rarely did.

Juliet was pacing the living room as Tanner walked back inside and quietly closed the door.

"Do you mind telling me what the hell that was all about?" Juliet questioned.

91

Tanner walked past her without answering and slapped a tomato and several pieces of turkey on top of the naked bread sitting opposite the slices with the mayonnaise.

"Food first. You need your strength for cleaning, which I'm sure you intend to do after I've answered all your questions."

"You're helping," Juliet grumbled.

Tanner pressed the two parts of the sandwich together and motioned with her head for Juliet to sit at the table.

"Did you wash your hands before making those sandwiches?" Juliet asked.

"Give me a fucking break. There are people out there trying to kill you, and maybe me, and you're worried about germs?"

Juliet stepped close to Tanner and grabbed her hand. "Sorry."

Juliet was too near again, and this time the urge to kiss her after looking into her eyes overwhelmed Tanner, and she crushed their lips together. At first she felt resistance, and then she felt Juliet melt into the embrace and tentatively seek out her tongue.

Their tongues entwined until Tanner almost felt like they were creating a complicated knot. She wasn't sure who moaned first, but she felt her own vocalization bubble up in her throat. It had been a long time since she'd kissed someone like this, and she panicked as she broke from it.

"Oh, God, I shouldn't have done that."

Juliet's hurt look hit Tanner squarely in the stomach, and she regretted saying those words almost immediately.

"Well, make up your damn mind. Before, you said the kiss would be welcomed, and now you tell me you shouldn't have done that. Am I that much of a freak to you? I know I can be a little obsessive and hard to handle; it's why I can't seem to keep a girlfriend. They all say it's cute at first, and then it drives them bananas. I wouldn't blame you—"

Tanner brought their lips together again, and this time she let the kiss smolder and reach a level of maturity that when she finally broke apart it didn't feel abrupt, but rather it came to a natural conclusion.

"Anyone ever tell you that you talk too much?" Tanner smiled and brushed her hand over Juliet's cheek.

"All the time," Juliet sighed.

"Grab a plate. Let's take this into the living room and we'll talk. Okay?"

Juliet nodded and grabbed one of the plates.

Tanner picked up the other dish and the bag of potato chips she'd liberated from the cupboard where the other bag resided in what appeared to be the snack section. She noted with a smile that the sour-cream-and-onion in her hand had been to the right of the bar-b-que chips and the Cheetos. Alphabetical order, of course.

She sat on the couch, placed the chips on the coffee table, and patted the spot next to her.

"The red blinking light indicates someone has come close enough to the cabin to trip the motion detector. I don't think it was a random person who got lost out here, but all I saw was taillights when I went out to check just now. Someone tripped the wire, and I'm concerned. This may not be a safe place anymore, but at the moment, I can't think of an alternative. A forewarning is helpful, and I think it would be prudent to reactivate the auditory alarm I disarmed when I installed the trip wire."

Juliet shuddered. "Okay."

"Can you please repeat your earlier questions? I might have short-term memory issues. I believe I answered the one about the light." Tanner smiled.

"Two of them have already been answered. Thanks for getting soap in a dispenser and for the comprehensive cleaning supplies. I'm not sure I could have done better. Let's start with how long will we have to stay here?" Juliet asked.

"It depends."

Juliet sat staring at Tanner for fifteen seconds. Tanner was enjoying watching her squirm and wondered how long it would take her to jump on that response.

"Jesus Christ," Juliet exploded. "*It depends* is not an answer. Can you please expound just a tad?"

Tanner grinned. "I just wanted to see how long it would take you to jump on me."

Juliet smacked her arm. "Can you please stop teasing for a few minutes while you bring me up to speed on what you have described as a life-and-death situation?"

"Sorry. I couldn't resist. You are just so easy. It really does just depend. On the one hand, I like having a built-in alarm system for when someone gets close enough to the cabin for me to take action. I hear your granny is a crack shot. What about you, can you shoot a gun?"

"Don't worry about me. I can shoot a rifle and hit my target ninety-nine percent of the time. Granny did indeed teach me well."

"Good. I have a rifle in the closet next to the bathroom."

"Damn. I never thought to check that one out."

"I knew you were gonna snoop. Didn't find anything too exciting, did you?"

Juliet shook her head.

"Okay. I'm glad I didn't rescue some helpless female."

Juliet opened her mouth to speak, and Tanner raised her hand in the universal Stop symbol. "Let me finish. On the other hand, my gut tells me the driver that paid us a visit earlier was not friendly and it might be worth finding a new location. But…I don't like going somewhere I'm unfamiliar with and can't properly defend."

"So where does that leave us?" Juliet asked.

"I think we ought to hang tight here and see how this plays out over the next few days. I suspect whoever was able to tail me undetected will make their move quickly if they've discovered you're with me. I thought someone was following me, but they were extremely good at it, so I wasn't sure."

"I think I'd feel better if the gun was beside me, but I've never shot someone before, just cans or rocks. I couldn't even bring myself to shoot an animal when Granny took me hunting; I'm not sure I could kill someone. I'm sorry." Juliet's voice quivered as she delivered the last line.

"You'd be surprised what a person can do with the right motivation. I have faith in you, Juliet."

"Thanks. Okay, the final question. What else did you learn while you were in town?"

"That Harley is a first-class prick, and I wanted to shoot him just to see the bastard's reaction. Oh, and he was hanging around your house when I got there. I think he was trying to leave a present in your car." Tanner ran her fingers through her hair. "I'll bet he wants to throw suspicion your way because he's running scared. He knows that eventually the spotlight might come back to him because he was so buddy-buddy with Aiden. It's only a matter of time before they figure out his role in the drug business. Anything else you want to know?"

"Were you and your uh…partner…lovers?" Juliet paused. "Wait, don't answer that. I'm sorry, that was rude of me to ask."

Tanner tilted her head to the side. She was curious why Juliet wondered about her relationship. Although it was a sore subject and one she wasn't eager to discuss, for some reason she wanted to be honest with Juliet. "I'll answer the question, but first I'd like to know your motivation for asking."

"Honestly I don't really know. I guess I just wanted to get to know you on a deeper level. Does that make sense?" Juliet asked.

"Yeah, I guess it does. If I answer this honestly and tell you all about her, I'll want some reciprocity. I want to know why you aren't involved with anyone."

"Deal."

"Yes, Faith was my partner in every way. We were together for five years, and I miss her every single day. It wasn't legal to get married when I first made a commitment to her, but I would have married her in a heartbeat." Tanner's eyes watered, but she wouldn't let the tears fall. "I really could not let Aiden get away with her murder. It required justice. She deserved justice. It's the least I could do for her because it's my fault she died."

"I don't believe that."

"I was the one that wanted to go after Aiden. She had a bad feeling about him and his partners. I should have listened, but I saw red every time I thought about the innocent kids he snared in his trap. The Internet is a breeding ground for these fuckers. The young girls see a handsome, older guy, who starts paying them attention, and before they know it, they're sucked into a world of depravity they never imagined. I was supposed to be the one on his tail, but I let myself get sidetracked by another person I was tracking. Faith knew the whole story about me, and God bless her, because she managed to accept my dark side. I'm a killer, plain and simple."

Juliet took one of Tanner's hands and held it, stroking her palm. "You're not a killer. You are a crusader for justice who happens to deliver a final sentence on occasion."

Tanner felt Juliet's caress and let herself lean into the gesture of support. "Faith was gentle and caring. I never understood why she chose a career in law enforcement. It didn't really suit her. She was an expert shot, but she never pulled her weapon. She always preferred talking people down. She had a gift." A tear finally escaped, and Tanner brushed it away in aggravation.

"Thank you for telling me that."

"It's your turn. No offense, but your home seems stark and lonely. Why is there no one in your life?"

"Because I'm a pathetic freak who lives vicariously through others, and my fundamental need for order drives women away before we even get to the U-Haul. I'm also a little fussy about the women I choose to date, which by the way hasn't occurred in a very long time. I've tried therapy. It didn't work. I started organizing my therapist's office one day when she was late. The magazines in the waiting room were not in alphabetical order either. It went downhill from there."

Tanner started laughing. Juliet might drive people crazy, but she was also beautiful, intelligent, witty, and a good person. She could see herself adjusting to Juliet's quirks, and that scared her. Juliet didn't seem as bothered as she was earlier by Tanner's need to deliver her own brand of justice. These were interesting thoughts. Tanner shook her head.

"See. You can't stand spending time with me either. I'll bet you rue the day you ever took me captive." Juliet turned her head away.

Tanner chuckled. "Not true, not true at all. I was shaking my head at my own internal dialogue. I don't regret taking you captive at all. I only regret how I did it and leaving you in an uncomfortable position. I'm truly sorry about that."

"Care to share that internal dialogue? Inquiring minds and all." Juliet grinned.

"Um, no, not just yet. I'm sure you noticed the bag of cookies I bought and the ice cream. What's your preference for dessert?" Tanner asked.

"Well, I am an ice cream gal and I did notice that you got a favorite of mine, but honestly I never met a cookie, pie, cake, candy bar…uh, you get the picture…that I didn't love."

Tanner wasn't comfortable talking about overly personal things, so this change of topic provided the perfect distraction.

"Ice cream it is." Tanner jumped up. "I'll get it and two spoons. You didn't happen to reorganize the drawers yet, did you? I had my own sense of order, and I don't want to go on an archeological dig just to find a few spoons."

"Funny. No, I haven't had the chance to take care of those drawers, which frankly look like something out of a hoarder house. You know that is also a disorder."

"I love a woman who can give as good as she gets." Tanner touched her index and middle finger to her head and gave Juliet a small salute.

Chapter Eleven

The woman turned her car around once she spied Tanner's car next to the cabin. She felt confident that Juliet was with Tanner. All the evidence pointed to it. The story Tanner told about Juliet having a family emergency, the amount of groceries she'd purchased, and her wary behavior were the only clues the woman needed to make an assessment of the situation. Tanner was in this whole mess up to her neck, and she would be a worthy adversary.

She pulled away quickly and headed back to town to connect with her partner and regroup. Getting her hands dirty wasn't something she wanted to do, but she was prepared to act. She was too close to getting everything she wanted. It was almost time for her to make her move and finally leave this godforsaken shithole of a town. A new identity and a pristine, white beach were calling her name. She was still young enough to enjoy her retirement. Forty was the new thirty, and she would take advantage of her good looks to find herself a boy toy or two.

Before reaching town, she pulled off to the side of the road to call Miguel. He needed to hear an update, and then they would create a plan of action.

The woman pulled out her phone and pressed the Call button. "Hello.... Yeah, I just followed Tanner, so I know where they're holing up.... That works for me, because after a bit more deliberation on the problem, I would prefer not getting personally involved.... I can tell him exactly where the cabin is, and he can take care of it as soon as he arrives in the area. How long do you think it will take him to get here?.... Hmmm, that long. Well, I suppose we don't have much choice, do we?.... All right, I'll sit tight until it is all resolved. What about Harley? Do you think we should arrange for that idiot to have an unfortunate accident?.... Okay, that makes sense. I knew Aiden was a loose cannon when the little fucker killed that cop. Something tells me her death was the spark that started this whole damn mess. I wouldn't be surprised if Tanner executed him herself. The coincidences are just too great.... Okay, I'll call if I have any more updates for you."

The woman ended the call and sat back in her lush leather seat. She closed her eyes for a moment and breathed deeply. She hoped everything would be resolved in the next few days.

✝

Harley was seething as he waited for Paul, his replacement from the Riverville police reserves. His original plan to plant drugs in Juliet's car and house had been a bust. He didn't think Tanner would let things go. She'd followed up with Nancy, which added more credence to the information she would likely provide to the sheriff's office if they found drugs in Juliet's car and home. Besides, Juliet was an obsessive-compulsive freak, and wherever he decided to plant the drugs would probably not be consistent with her pathological need to organize everything and just add to the questions. He didn't know why he thought that stupid plan would work in the first place, because there wasn't anywhere that would make sense to plant the contraband. He couldn't take that chance anymore. He needed a new plan.

The leather office chair creaked when Harley got up and moved to the window. He looked outside and scowled as Nancy's Mercedes passed by. Fucking woman ruined everything, even if the plan was half-baked to begin with. Now Tanner was on high alert.

He heard the station door open and looked over as Paul strolled inside.

"Hey, Harley. Wow, exciting day, huh? I never thought I'd be part of a murder investigation," he enthused.

"You won't be. You're only a backup cop, and the full-time Riverville police and the sheriff's office took over. They don't even want our help on this." Harley threw his hands in the air.

"Wow. Who crawled up your butthole?"

"Shut up, Paul. You're just a lowly on-call make-believe officer. I doubt you'll ever get a full-time position."

"At least they don't call me Barney."

Harley balled up his fists and barely kept himself from popping Paul in his globular nose.

"My notes on the shift are on the desk. Have a good fucking night." Harley stomped out of the station and slammed the door behind him.

✝

Darla sat at the ratty card table inside the local casino playing blackjack. Part of the reason she'd fled to this hole-in-the-wall town was its surprising nighttime entertainment. She'd needed somewhere off the beaten path, but with a casino that would feed her addiction. She couldn't believe her luck when she'd found Riverville. Who would have guessed the tiny town had an almost fully functioning casino? She didn't ask any questions but merely thanked her good fortune.

However, she hadn't had much good luck recently as her debts had begun to stack up. The side business with Harley had been her saving grace. Now with Aiden's premature demise, she wasn't sure how fortuitous said business was for her. Harley was sure to fuck things up. She needed to think up a plan to keep her out of the authorities' crosshairs, and she wasn't necessarily opposed to offering up her brother as the sacrificial lamb.

Darla was sure her idiot brother still had the drugs in his possession. A simple anonymous call to the sheriff's office should take care of it. She smiled to herself and looked down at her cards. The Six of Clubs and King of Hearts were showing on the table.

"Hit me."

The dealer placed the Queen of Hearts on her Six of Clubs. "Sorry, Darla, you just busted."

"Fuck," she muttered.

Darla scooped up her remaining chips and did the unthinkable. She left before she depleted them. She needed to make that call. It was the only solution. She couldn't help but feel a slight sense of guilt over what she was about to do to her only sibling. Still, survival of the fittest—that was the name of the game.

†

The woman watched with interest as the sheriff's vehicle pulled up to the bar Harley had stalked into half an hour ago. Harley's body language suggested he was agitated about something. He was reckless on a normal day, but when he was twitchy, he was a disaster waiting to happen.

She wasn't sure whether she should risk entering the bar, but she really wanted to know what was transpiring. She walked closer to it, debating on whether or not to go in. She glanced around to see who else was nearby. It wouldn't be good for anyone to note her interest in the goings-on at the bar.

When Sheriff Nickolas Crawford came out with Harley in tow, she smiled. Although Nick hadn't cuffed him, things clearly weren't going Harley's way. She suspected they were doing him a professional courtesy by not embarrassing him in public. At least Harley was smart enough to cooperate and follow him quietly out of the bar.

The woman's grin turned feral as she realized that someone else might have taken care of her loose end. She surmised Darla was behind this latest turn of good fortune. Cold. Very cold. If she was correct, Darla had sacrificed her own brother to save her ass.

She had grudging respect for Darla. She would have done the same thing in her position. She would forfeit anyone in her own life to save her ass, and that included Miguel. He was her business partner, nothing more. If that made her a bitch, so be it.

The woman pivoted and headed back to her observation post. It always paid to be observant. She hadn't gotten as far as she had by ignoring all the little things that provided an extra leg up. Juliet wasn't the only person who knew almost everything about this tiny town and its people. However, unlike Juliet, her motives weren't at all harmless.

Miguel had phoned him earlier and offered to pay double his usual fee. Tony didn't question the amount but figured this was an especially important job. He was the perfect hitman because he didn't have one shred of guilt about killing people and regardless of the target wouldn't blink an eye. He was also one of the few men who would take a job involving a minor. In his mind they were all just objects to be removed. Right or wrong never entered the equation for him, giving him a ruthless reputation that was well known in the industry.

Nobody knew that Tony enjoyed every job given to him. He relished looking into his target's eyes and seeing their life slowly slip away. He engineered an up-close-and-personal mode of killing in all the jobs he took. Killing made him feel powerful when his hand was the one to extinguish a person's life. Tony supposed people might label him a psychopath, and that didn't bother him one bit—it was an accurate description. He took a clinical view of others' perceptions of him. Yes, he was a psychopath who was very, very good at his vocation. Everyone should excel at his or her chosen occupation.

Tony smiled at the flight attendant as he placed his bag in the overhead bin in the first-class section. The flight attendant returned it. Tony had a disarming smile, and his attractiveness to members of both the opposite and same sex was something he took for granted. It helped him get close to his targets on many occasions. He knew it wouldn't work with the two lesbians, but that wouldn't stop him from creating a face-to-face confrontation.

He'd only been to Seattle once before, so he looked forward to visiting the city again after he completed his job. A rental car was waiting for him at the airport. It would only be a couple of hours' drive or less to his destination. The route through the mountains would provide a sense of calm and peace that was almost necessary to hold back his anticipation. A double was rare, and it spurred on an unusual amount of excitement.

The flight attendant came back around after he'd taken his seat. "I can take your drink order before we take off, if you'd like."

"Thank you. I appreciate that. I'll take a scotch, neat."

The flight attendant nodded and scurried down the narrow passageway.

Tony leaned back into the comfortable seat and thought, *Life is good.*

Chapter Twelve

An awkward silence hung in the air like a cloud that refused to move on an otherwise clear day. Juliet didn't know how to broach the subject of sleeping arrangements. She also wasn't sure whether she wanted to sleep in that musty bed when she didn't know who'd slept in there previously or if the sheets were clean. That wasn't exactly the reason for the uneasy quiet, though. The passionate kiss she'd received earlier was something neither one of them wanted to discuss.

Tanner narrowed her eyes. "I can see the wheels turning in your head. Let me guess. You aren't quite sure about the cleanliness of the sheets. They're clean. You are going to have to trust me on that."

Juliet breathed a sigh of relief. The assurance was only part of it. They would eventually have to discuss the kiss and clear the air, but she was happy for the temporary respite.

"I do trust you." As Juliet spoke the words, she instantly knew she meant them. Not only did she trust Tanner on the little things, but she trusted her with the big ones as well.

"Thank you," Tanner whispered.

It was the most subdued Juliet had seen her.

"Uh, listen...," Tanner started, her tone tentative. "There's only one bed, so if you want I can take the couch. That way if danger comes to our doorstep, I can at least slow them down and give you some time to grab the rifle, which I need to retrieve for you right now."

Juliet was silent for a second while she carefully worded her response. "If you don't mind, I would really like you to stay with me. I'll feel better if you're by my side. Whatever is out there, I'd like us to face together."

Tanner nodded.

Juliet thought she saw a hesitant smile adorn Tanner's handsome face. Tanner was a striking woman, and Juliet would need all her resolve not to let temptation take over. Her attraction was building, and she couldn't help but notice all of Tanner's attributes.

Juliet picked up the empty ice cream carton and brought it into the kitchen. She opened the cabinet below the sink, assuming this was where Tanner kept the garbage can, like most people did. She tossed the container into the empty can with the plastic liner. She was grateful to see Tanner lined her waste bucket. There was no telling what manner of germs bred in a person's trash.

Juliet grabbed the sponge sitting on the sink and tossed that into the can as well. She shuddered as she thought of all the germs trapped inside the yellow scrubber. She'd placed one package of the new sponges beneath the sink among the rest of the disarray. It had taken all her energy to avoid organizing everything under the sink, but in the end hunger won out and she hadn't had time to rearrange everything in the kitchen.

With the new sponge in her hand, she washed the plates Tanner had given her, along with the two spoons. She'd surprised herself when she allowed Tanner's spoon to dip inside the same container of ice cream Juliet was eating out of. She pushed herself not to think of all the germs they might have shared. She knew it wasn't at all logical because earlier they had certainly swapped enough spit, but her disorder defied logic. She knew that.

Tanner grabbed the clean plates and spoons and dried them with the new kitchen towel. "I'll just put these away so you don't have to look inside my cabinets and feel the compulsion to rearrange everything. We have plenty of time for you to do that tomorrow and the next day."

"Please don't think you have to do the same, but I need another shower and I don't want to step into the mold magnet without giving it a quick scrub."

"Knock yourself out. Believe it or not, even I think it's disgusting. I should have cleaned it earlier, but I haven't been here in a while and it wasn't my top priority at the time. I can work on the alarm system by reengaging the audio."

Juliet was thankful Tanner didn't make fun of her overwhelming need to clean the bathroom. That was a higher priority than the kitchen, which would be the next on her list.

"Thank you for understanding."

Tanner looked directly into her eyes and pushed a lock of hair back from Juliet's face. It was an intimate gesture and resulted in goose bumps all along her arm. "You're welcome."

Tanner pressed her lips against Juliet's, giving her a quick, chaste kiss.

Juliet thought it was sweet. She turned away and headed into the bathroom and the project that awaited her.

✝

Juliet and Faith were so different from one another. Yet in the one area that really counted, they were the same. Juliet was innocent, vulnerable, gentle, and kind, just like Faith had been. The overwhelming loneliness that permeated Juliet's demeanor got to Tanner the most. She wanted to wrap her arms around Juliet and assure her that she was loveable despite her quirks. Tanner rewound her last thought and amended it to *Juliet is loveable because of her unique qualities.* Tanner wasn't eloquent and was sure she'd never be able to communicate her perspective in a way Juliet would understand or accept.

Faith had rounded out Tanner's hard edges when she was alive. Since her death, Tanner had reverted to her former self—cold, precise, and unforgiving. Thus, she'd surprised herself when she'd kissed Juliet, especially the second time.

Faith had known everything about Tanner yet had never judged her. It was Faith who had gently nudged her in the direction of the code. Tanner was grateful she hadn't acted irrationally before Faith helped to develop the principled building blocks to Tanner's very immoral missions. She missed Faith's ability to serve as her own personal Jiminy Cricket. Without Faith, it would be only a matter of time before she would begin to relax the code and travel down that very slippery slope.

First things first. Tanner walked down the narrow hallway and opened the small hall closet to retrieve the rifle. She leaned it up against the wall on the other side of the bathroom. When Juliet was finished cleaning, she would see the gun and could check it out. Tanner hoped she would be able to familiarize herself with the weapon without Tanner needing to hover over her.

Tanner pulled out her toolbox so she would have everything she needed to reconnect the wires that would set off an audio alarm in case someone decided to interrupt their peace and quiet. She had no qualms about blowing away anyone who invaded their space. She only needed a few seconds, because previous training had taught her the skill of complete awareness within a short period. Plenty of time.

Tanner listened as Juliet sang, and she laughed again. "Juliet, really? 'Happy Working Song' from *Enchanted*?" she called out.

"Stop listening to me sing." Juliet laughed on the other side of the door.

Chuckling, Tanner returned to the living room and her task of securing the cabin. She went to work, quickly unscrewing the protective cover over the alarm. It was a simple fix. It only took her a few minutes to reconnect the wires and put back the light casing she'd engineered for an alternative alarm, providing both visual and auditory notification of a breach. Noise tended to bother her, but she'd make an exception because she wasn't the only one in peril now.

†

Juliet stopped singing and looked at her handiwork. Not every surface was gleaming, but she attributed that to the age of the bath fixtures. She quickly stripped and was thankful for the brand-new towel hanging on the rack. She wondered if the towel had touched the grimy walls at any point before she'd had the chance to wipe them down with bleach.

She shuddered before pushing the dirty walls from her mind. She was determined to enjoy every second of the shower, and then welcome the feeling of the minty toothpaste as she brushed away the leftover sugar from the ice cream, leaving her well-cared-for teeth free of the evening grime.

Juliet thought Tanner might find it odd when Juliet brushed her teeth every time she woke up to go to the bathroom. Her hygienist praised her for her compulsive dental habits, but she didn't think anyone else would appreciate this small idiosyncrasy. Of course, if Tanner kissed her in the middle of the night, maybe she would value this quirk.

Stop that, stop that right now. There might be some crazed hitman out to get you, and all you can think of is Tanner kissing you again? Juliet chastised herself, but the grin remained, and she played back the second kiss. It tingled all the way to her toes. Other women had kissed her before, but not quite like that, and, miracle of miracles, she'd completely forgotten about all the germs while she did the tongue tango with Tanner.

Juliet stepped into the warm spray and let it flow over her body, caressing every nook and cranny. She squeezed out a dollop of shower gel and began massaging the sudsy comfort over her breasts. Imaging Tanner's hands roaming freely over her body, Juliet allowed herself to fantasize about what making love with Tanner would be like. For once, she didn't let thoughts of disgusting body fluids filled with microorganisms waiting to attack her vulnerable system get in the way of her pleasure.

Her grandmother had tried to undo the unhealthy teachings of her mother, but they had already taken root by the time her parents had died when Juliet was in her teens. She often wondered how her parents could possibly have had sex often enough to conceive. They were definitely two peas in a pod. She'd loved her parents, but they'd both been bat-shit crazy and had passed a decent amount of their maladies on to her. Juliet couldn't bear to hope that Tanner might be the answer to her prayers.

Every other time she'd slept with a woman, she'd scrubbed her body raw afterward. No amount of pleasure took away the pain of knowing they suspected exactly what she was doing and would soon turn away in disgust.

She often thanked whatever higher power existed in the universe that at least she was born a lesbian, because she didn't think she'd ever be able to have sex with a man. Semen was the worst possible bodily fluid in her mind. She gagged hard whenever she envisioned sexual intercourse with a guy. Besides, that dangly thing was just plain ugly. A woman's body, on the other hand, was beautiful and sensual. Clean-shaven armpits and legs were added bonuses. She also preferred either short-clipped pubic hair or a shaved mound. She let her mind wander to what Tanner preferred or what she chose for herself.

When her hand traveled to her nether regions, her arousal surprised her. She was sure thoughts of Tanner had spurred her on. It wasn't as if she'd never pleasured herself before. Masturbation was the only way she'd ever reached orgasm, because she didn't have to worry about where her own hands had been.

Wondering about the cleanliness of the woman she was sleeping with always frustrated Juliet. Had she washed her hands before touching her? Were her fingernails free of debris? How thoroughly had she brushed before going down on Juliet? Those questions had plagued her in the middle of sex. It sucked, and she'd given up having sex at all five years ago. That was a sobering thought. She hadn't had sex or dated in five years. She was a pathetic loser with an obsessive-compulsive disorder, but Tanner brought a spark of light into the possibility that sex might be different with her. Juliet had hope now.

She finished washing her hair and made sure she completely rinsed the soap out. She pushed open the newly clean shower curtain and grabbed the new towel on the rack. A brisk rub of her hair pulled most of the water out, leaving it damp but not dripping. She quickly wrapped the towel around her body after drying her arms, torso, back, and legs.

"Damn. I forget to bring in my clean T-shirt and sweats," she announced to no one.

She wondered if Tanner was still in the living room fixing the alarm. Maybe she could sneak in and grab her clothes.

Hesitating as she opened the door, she looked to her left and then to her right. The hallway was empty. She tried to listen for where Tanner might be, but the woman was as quiet as a church mouse. She suspected Tanner had a great deal of practice at operating in stealth mode.

She tiptoed to the bedroom and was startled to see Tanner sprawled out on the bed in nothing but a tank top and boy shorts. Juliet gasped. Tanner raised an eyebrow.

"I didn't mean to startle you. I was just waiting until you were finished."

"Um, I haven't quite finished yet. I still have to brush the bucks," Juliet clarified.

Tanner chuckled. "God, I haven't heard that expression in years. My mom used to say that. She'd tell us we needed to say our prayers and brush the bucks before heading to bed every night."

"I just need to get my clothes to sleep in. Um, I'll just do that and finish off in the bathroom after I change."

"Hey, don't mind me. I'm a patient sort of person. I'll just wait until you're done. By the way, the towel looks particularly smashing on you." Tanner's grin was wolfish.

Juliet held the towel against her body with her right hand and ruffled through the duffel with her left as she pulled her favorite T-shirt and sweats from the bag. She hurried into the bathroom to change quickly and brush her teeth.

She fetched the brand-new toothbrush she'd placed next to the one she'd used earlier in the day. They both resided in a drawer she'd designated earlier for dental care. Juliet thought it was sweet of Tanner to bring her the new toothbrush after the hesitation she'd displayed earlier. Even though Tanner had assured Juliet the first toothbrush was unused, Juliet raised a mini fuss like she always did.

She was happy to use the soap dispenser since it contained fewer germs than placing her hands on a bar of soap someone else had used right before her. As she washed her hands again, she thought that maybe it wouldn't be that bad if it was Tanner's hands, because she'd imagined those same hands caressing her body and that didn't seem too awful.

Juliet laughed and started singing. The words were almost pornographic as she belted out the song from the musical comedy that had turned into a popular audience-participation sensation. A song about being touched by a hunky creation seemed appropriate right now.

"Juliet, you know I can hear you singing that song from *The Rocky Horror Picture Show*, and I really have to wonder what on earth brought that little ditty to your warped brain." Tanner laughed.

Juliet quickly dried her hands on the towel she'd used after her shower and looked around for an appropriate place to hang it. She held it in her hand and picked up her dirty clothes that she had neatly folded and placed on top of the toilet seat before she walked out of the bathroom and into the bedroom.

"Your turn. By the way, does this cabin have a washing machine?" Juliet asked.

"Nope," Tanner answered.

114

Juliet frowned. "What do you do with your dirty clothes, then?"

"What dirty clothes? If you mean the towel in your hand, I don't consider that dirty. You just had a shower, so presumably you dried off your clean body. The towel doesn't need washing. Here, let me take that back to the bathroom."

Tanner snatched the towel from Juliet's hand before she could protest.

"Um...."

"Relax. I'll let you use a new towel, but this one is perfectly fine for me to use tomorrow. I'll just drape it over the shower curtain to dry. Haven't you ever heard of being green? That means you don't wash your towels after every use. You can set your clothes on the floor in the corner, and we can figure out where to put them tomorrow. It won't kill you to have them out for one night."

Juliet walked over to the closet and opened the door to set her clothes on the top shelf because she would think about them sitting in the corner all night long. When she turned around, she glanced at the pile of clothing Tanner had balled up and tossed into the corner.

She gingerly picked them up, folded them neatly, and placed them on the shelf next to her own discarded outfit. It wasn't a perfect solution, but it would have to do.

She listened as Tanner hummed the song she'd been singing earlier. She smiled to herself.

A few minutes later she stepped into the bedroom and grinned. "Catchy little tune. Now you have me humming it. So tell me, were you singing that as an invitation?"

"In your dreams, Tanner," Juliet growled.

"Yep." Laughter filled the room again.

Changing the subject, Juliet asked, "Do you think I should get the rifle from the hallway and keep it next to my side of the bed?"

Tanner smacked her forehead. "Damn. Sorry, I meant to do that. I'll take the right side because that's where the nightstand is and I put my gun inside. I should have plenty of notice with the alarm to retrieve it if needed. I'll go get the rifle for you right now."

Her protector scrambled out of the bedroom and returned a few seconds later with the rifle in her hand. She walked over to the left side of the bed and set the gun against the wall.

"It's loaded, so all you have to do is grab it and aim. Don't hesitate. If you hear the alarm, pick it up. If someone gets by me and comes into the bedroom, blow them away because they won't be here for a friendly visit. I can guarantee you that."

Tanner lifted the blankets, pulled them down, and gestured for Juliet to crawl inside the covers.

Juliet watched as she walked around the bed to her own side, getting a good look at Tanner's well-muscled behind. She had the urge to touch it.

"I can feel your eyes on my ass."

Juliet scrambled to get under the covers as Tanner pulled her side down and slipped inside.

She settled under the sheets and turned toward Juliet. "I'd like nothing better than to ravage your body tonight, but I'm afraid that kind of distraction might get us killed. I can't afford to let my guard down. Do you understand?"

The gravity of her tone hit Juliet squarely between the eyes. "I'm scared."

Tanner opened her arms. "Come here."

Juliet folded herself into the strong woman's embrace and settled her head against Tanner's shoulder as she wrapped an arm across Tanner's stomach.

The confident cop pulled Juliet tightly against her body and placed her own arms around Juliet's back. "I won't let any harm come to you. I promise."

Chapter Thirteen

Tony lifted his arms above his head and stretched his long frame. He turned his wrist to glance at his Rolex and noted the time. He could feel the plane descend, and the sudden pressure in his ears let him know the flight to Seattle was almost over.

The flight attendants scurried down the aisle, presumably to take their seats in preparation for landing.

"Folks, we've just begun our descent into Seattle-Tacoma International Airport. The local time is nine forty-five. With only light winds out of the west, we're looking for an on-time arrival today. We should be on the ground in just a few minutes. Flight attendants, prepare for landing," a deep male voice announced.

Tony had already decided he would stay the night in Seattle, then make his way to the rural community where Miguel had informed him that his double targets were holed up. The directions to the rustic cabin were very specific, so Tony wasn't worried about getting lost.

His biggest dilemma was which up-close-and-personal method he would choose to extinguish their lives.

Knives were satisfying, especially when he got to view the lifeblood flowing from the dying body—but that was messy. Sometimes he enjoyed strangulation—it was clean and he could watch his victim's eyes as their fear registered in their last moments of life. His least preferred method was a shot to the head because it didn't prolong the death, but sometimes that was his only option. From what he'd heard, the cop wasn't stupid or careless, so unfortunately he might have to dispose of her quickly and take his time with the other.

As he pondered his options, the plane came to a complete stop and the lights came on along with the chime that signaled the passengers could unbuckle their seat belts. The ding was the same in every airplane. Tony wasn't in any hurry, so he leaned back as the other passengers jumped up and squished against one another vying for the opportunity to retrieve their bags from the overhead bins.

Tony never understood why people stood so quickly only to wait patiently as everyone before them stumbled from their seats and made their way slowly down the aisle, bag in hand. It was ridiculous, he thought, especially given that he often had the upper hand and should have been one of the first to deplane as a valued first-class customer.

When the final passenger in coach moved past Tony, he stood, reached into the overhead bin, and retrieved his small leather bag. He smiled at the flight attendant. He was too tired for fun and games tonight, so he didn't turn on the charm in an attempt to secure companionship for the evening. Sometimes it worked and other times it didn't. It was a crapshoot, but always worth a try when he was in the mood. He hated using an escort service or visiting a bar, regardless of how upscale the club was.

After he exited the gangway connecting the plane and the airport, he walked confidently to the rental car counter to pick up the keys to the vehicle Miguel had arranged for him.

Tony never chanced making those arrangements for himself. He alternated between several aliases and had asked Miguel to use Ben Larson.

The young woman at the rental car place was a perky blonde with wide-set eyes and a perfect cupid's bow. Tony smiled and hoped she was quick with the paperwork.

"Hello, I'm Ben Larson. I believe there is a car waiting for me."

Tony pulled out his wallet and removed the credit card and fake license. He handed them to the woman and waited patiently for her to pull his paperwork.

"Thank you, Mr. Larson. I just need you to sign here and initial here." She pointed to the papers she'd pushed in his direction. "May I see your driver's license? I don't need a credit card because it's all been taken care of. The shuttle to the parking lot is right outside those sliding glass doors. There's usually one every ten minutes, so you shouldn't have to wait too long. Do you have any questions?"

"No, thank you." Tony scribbled his assumed name, took a copy of the paperwork, and walked out the door.

He noticed the shuttle pulling up. *Great timing.* He was glad that so far, everything was running like clockwork, and the lack of delays or snags was a good sign in his mind. He'd be in and out within twenty-four hours, five hundred thousand dollars richer. Not bad for a day's work.

✝

Darla hadn't expected Harley to call her after Nick had taken him in for questioning. She thought for sure he would realize she'd sold him out. She viewed this as a turn of events that worked very nicely into her plan. She could play the devoted sister who would find him a good lawyer and send his ire in another direction.

Although he was the one with the incriminating drugs on him, he could always claim he'd gotten them from Darla and finger her. She wasn't prepared to defend herself. But perhaps he erroneously believed Tanner was responsible. That was perfect.

The sheriff's department hadn't exactly arrested him yet, but they were asking questions and he wasn't answering without the presence of a lawyer. She'd gotten in trouble earlier in her life and fortunately knew a good one. She would call him again because he'd been a miracle worker, managing to keep her out of jail and forcing the police to drop the charges for lack of evidence. He had used a technicality to accomplish that miracle, and Darla was grateful. He'd also been able to erase any trace of her arrest, which allowed her to return to school and complete her pharmacy degree.

Darla didn't know why she'd kept the lawyer's card, but she had. He'd written his cellphone number on the back, and she suspected his interest in her was more personal than professional, but she'd never called to explore that possibility. It wasn't that he was unattractive, she just hadn't ever bothered. A couple of years ago, she'd run into him in Seattle at Pike Place Market of all places, and they'd had a nice lunch together, but once again life had gotten in the way and neither had made a move to meet up again.

She pulled the card from her wallet and dialed the number, hoping he would answer. It was late, but this was his cellphone, and she suspected that for an extra amount of money, he'd come running. It was the least she could do for her brother, considering she was the one who had turned him in to the police.

"Hi. This is Darla Thompson. Sorry to disturb you so late at night. I wouldn't have called if it wasn't important, and I'm prepared to double your fee if you're able to come tonight to assist my brother.... Thanks. He's at the Riverville Police Station in one of the offices this backwater town uses for an interrogation room.... Okay, I'll tell them to expect you in about another hour and a half. Thanks, Cole."

✝

Harley sat in the chair with his arms crossed, glaring at Nick. He'd been humiliated when Nick had led him out of the bar like a common criminal. He would make Tanner or Juliet pay for this if it was the last thing he did on this earth. Harley was convinced one of them was responsible for his current predicament.

He had said exactly four words to the Sheriff, "I want a lawyer."

After he uttered those magic words, Nick allowed him to call his sister and arrange for legal representation. Harley knew his rights, and if they had more than supposition and the couple bags of drugs they'd found on him, they would have arrested him already.

Nick looked bored as he scrolled through his phone. *Probably checking Facebook.*

Time ticked slowly by, and without anything to occupy himself, Harley got increasingly agitated. Shifting in his seat, he finally blurted out, "Can I at least get something to read while we wait?"

The sheriff looked up from his phone. "It talks, amazing! Hmmm, care to say anything more about the drugs we found in your possession?"

"Fuck you," Harley sneered.

Nick returned his attention to his phone, seemingly ignoring him.

Finally Harley heard the outside door open. Nick stood and exited the office. A few minutes later, he returned with Darla and an attractive man in an expensive suit.

Looks like he's paid well. I sure hope he earns his fee by getting me out of this mess.

The man held out his hand. "Cole Harding. I presume you haven't said anything yet."

Harley nodded.

Cole turned his gaze on the sheriff. "I sure hope you have more than a couple of bags of drugs, because, son, after I'm through with you, you're gonna wish you'd never embarrassed this fine officer of the law."

"I'm not your son, and we just had a few simple questions to ask Harley. If he hasn't done anything wrong, I'm not sure why he isn't willing to clear things up for us," Nick responded.

"Before you begin asking any questions, I'm sure you won't mind if I confer with my client." Cole grinned.

The sheriff nodded and left the office.

"Harley, would you like your sister present or not?" Cole asked.

"She can stay."

"Got any ideas about how they knew you had those two baggies of drugs in your pocket?" Cole asked.

"I'd guess they got some kind of anonymous tip. The sheriff's office is leading the investigation into a recent murder here, and the victim was dealing prescription drugs to some of the locals."

"What's your involvement in this?"

"We were friends—sort of."

Cole raised his eyebrow. "Were you involved in this side business the guy had going?"

Harley nodded. He figured he should be honest with his lawyer, and Darla already knew about everything since she was up to her neck in this nasty business herself.

"Were you helping at all with the investigation?" Cole asked.

"Well, I did go to the murder scene when it was first called in," Harley answered.

"Good, good. Okay, here's how this is going to play out. You found the drugs in the guy's house or car and were at the bar trying to find out more information so you could help with the investigation. Maybe you didn't follow proper procedure by not logging the evidence right away, but that's not a crime."

Cole nodded and walked out of the office before Harley could agree. It didn't matter because that was a plausible explanation—one he hadn't thought of.

Nick followed Cole back into the makeshift interrogation room.

"Okay, my client is prepared to answer your questions," Cole offered.

"Just one, Harley. Where did you get the drugs?" Nick asked.

"I've been trying to help with the investigation, and when I came upon Aiden's car, I thought I'd check it out. I found these two bags in the glove compartment. I went into the bar tonight to ask around to see if any of the locals knew anything," Harley explained.

"Hmmm. That's interesting, Harley, because I already looked in Aiden's car and I didn't find any drugs in the glove compartment. We found drugs at his house, but not in the car." Nick narrowed his eyes.

"I found them shortly after you arrived on the scene and told us all to get lost. After that I got busy."

"And it took you—" Nick glanced at his watch "—
five hours to go to the bar without logging the evidence or
contacting us to tell us what you found. You expect me to
believe you didn't have any time before the end of your shift
to call us or take care of this evidence? I know they call you
Barney, but even a shit-for-brains officer like you would
have turned this in several hours ago."

Harley was seething. He wanted to throttle the
bastard, but instead he balled his fists, clenched his jaw, and
held back the retort on the tip of his tongue.

Cole interjected, "Is there a question somewhere in
that little display of harassment? Because if not, I think we're
done here. He answered your questions, now either arrest
him, which I don't think I'd recommend, or let him go
home."

Nick glared at Cole and then turned his steely gaze on
Harley. "I fucking hate crooked cops. Don't go far, Barney—
oh, I mean Harley. We may have more questions for you."

Harley pushed past Nick, bumping him on the way as
he strutted out of the office. "Thanks, sis."

Chapter Fourteen

Tanner opened her eyes after her vivid dream of Juliet insisting that Tanner had missed a spot while she was scrubbing the bathroom floor. It was such a ludicrous dream, and since her bladder was also sending her messages, she reluctantly awakened.

If felt nice having Juliet curled up in her arms, and her light snore was adorable. The light from the moon cast a soft glow on her face. Tanner inspected Juliet and smiled at the smattering of freckles across her nose. She carefully disengaged herself and padded into the bathroom, where she quickly emptied her bladder.

After slipping back into bed, she propped herself against the log headboard and wondered about the dream. Normally when she had peculiar dreams, there was something behind them—a clue to whatever mystery she was ruminating over at the moment.

Tanner smacked her forehead and gently roused Juliet. "Hey, wake up."

"Mmmff. What's wrong?" Her voice indicated she was still half-asleep.

"There's something not adding up about this hit that was ordered on you. If all you witnessed was Aiden with some young girl, that wouldn't be enough to order you killed, especially since Aiden had that unfortunate tussle with a bullet." Tanner grinned. "You mentioned you'd asked Harley about this. Did you get a strange reaction from him?"

"No. Harley just shook his head."

"There's something we're missing here."

"I only caught a glimpse of the girl that night. I got a better look the following evening when I saw her by the pharmacy, but then Aiden distracted me when he came barreling around the corner. I thought it was strange at the time that the girl wasn't with him."

"Maybe Harley is more involved than we thought, but I don't see him getting his hands dirty in that particular business. It doesn't quite compute. Something else is going on here, and I think this young girl is the key."

"I'll try to recreate my memory of that evening...." Juliet shifted her eyes toward the ceiling as if the answer might suddenly appear. "I was walking along Main Street like I normally do...."

"Hey, Mr. Gable. What's up?"

"Hi, Juliet. You're out late tonight. Got a hot date or something?" he asked.

Juliet snorted. "Yeah, right."

"I know you're a lesbian, but Petey Smith is dying to go out with you. How come you haven't accepted any of his invitations? Free dinner is free dinner," Clark said.

Juliet wanted to say that free dinner didn't make up for the fact he was the wrong sex and smelled like horse shit all the time. "I don't think his mamma would approve. She thinks women who wear jeans are direct descendants of the devil." Juliet wisely left out that Mrs. Smith would probably go into cardiac arrest if her son started dating a lesbian.

Clark laughed. "Yeah, Mrs. Smith is a bit on the conservative side."

"What about you? Any hot prospects for the evening?" She couldn't resist the evil question, knowing Clark would probably be meeting the preacher's wife later that night.

"No. Just a quiet night for me with my television and a *Special Victims Unit* marathon. That Mariska sure is sexy."

"Oh, I have to agree with you on that." Juliet grinned.

She hurried along because she had a whole evening of snooping planned, and Clark was interrupting her tight schedule.

The young girl she'd seen with Aiden was standing next to the pharmacy.

When Aiden nearly mowed her over, she'd murmured, "Excuse me." She looked back in the direction of the pharmacy, and the street was empty. She couldn't see where the teen had gone, so she continued on her predetermined route without another thought.

Juliet turned to Tanner after attempting to recreate the evening, but the details other than her conversation with Clark were frustratingly fuzzy. "I'm sorry, I don't really know what else I might have witnessed. They may have been meeting someone, but I couldn't tell you who it was. I snoop around a lot, you know. Other than strange liaisons between the locals, I'm not sure what dangerous information I possess."

"I'll figure it out, or Cisco might find something out for me."

"Cisco?"

"Yeah, a former colleague and buddy of mine who has an inside track to a lot of useful information in my line of work."

"Since I'm up, I might as well use the bathroom." Juliet pushed the covers aside and made her way there.

After several minutes passed, Tanner climbed from the bed to see what was keeping Juliet. When she heard what sounded like Juliet brushing her teeth, she couldn't contain her chuckle. "Are you actually brushing your teeth in the middle of the night?"

Tanner heard a spitting sound and then running water.

"There is nothing wrong with superior dental hygiene. Besides, I would think you would appreciate snuggling with a person who has minty-fresh breath rather than sharing close proximity to a foul-smelling mouth," Juliet answered through the closed door.

Tanner forced it open, pushed Juliet aside, and rummaged through the drawer to find her own toothbrush. "Well, I'm not going to be the only one in the bed with nasty morning or middle-of-the-night doggy breath."

Juliet smiled. "It's not the worst habit to adopt, you know."

Tanner quickly brushed her teeth, set the toothbrush on the counter, and pulled Juliet close. "Hmmm, I think we ought to take advantage of our clean, freshly brushed teeth."

Tanner locked her lips with Juliet and pushed her tongue against the soft flesh, seeking entrance to her mouth. At first, the kiss was almost desperate, but then Tanner backed off and began teasing Juliet with nibbles to her bottom lip and a tentative exploration. She felt Juliet melt into her embrace and was delighted to hear her moan first.

When she pulled back and looked into Juliet's eyes, she noticed her dilated pupils. The kiss had the desired effect on Juliet, and Tanner was particularly pleased with herself. "So, did I do an adequate job with my dental hygiene?"

"Mmm-hmmm, but I think I ought to get some additional confirming evidence. Just to be sure, you know."

Juliet leaned in, captured Tanner's lips, and sucked gently. Her tongue ventured out and caressed Tanner's bottom half. After a few more seconds, she deepened the kiss, and this time Tanner heard herself moaning in pleasure.

She needed to end this little midnight game before she became too distracted. She couldn't afford to forget about the person still out there who wanted them dead. She reluctantly stepped back.

Tanner took Juliet's arm and began to lead her back into the bedroom. "Come on, we should get some sleep and revisit this tomorrow morning. Maybe you'll remember something else that will provide an additional key to the mystery."

"Okay. I could use a few more hours of sleep. Will you hold me again?" Juliet asked.

"It would be my pleasure."

After Juliet settled in the crook of Tanner's arm, Tanner stayed awake thinking of all the possibilities. She suspected the young girl might end up being an important person and therefore someone Juliet would recognize. She made a mental note to check her tablet tomorrow. She hoped the *Seattle Times* would provide her with a clue about a missing child. It was worth a shot. That spot on the bathroom floor she was missing from her dream was just out of reach, but it was there and she would find the evidence. Her last thought before nodding off was that the pharmacy seemed to be important in this whole situation. Maybe Darla was more involved than anyone suspected. Could Aiden have been in a separate partnership with her?

†

Juliet's neck was sore. She woke up to discover that she hadn't moved during the night. With her left arm tucked against her body and her right arm draped around Tanner's stomach, her head remained against Tanner's shoulder. Tanner wasn't very cushy—not like a soft pillow—which had created the stiffness in her neck. She appreciated the fact Tanner hadn't moved from her protective embrace even though the position was probably not comfy for her either.

She carefully rolled onto her back after removing her right arm. While her head rested against the pillow, she swiveled it from side to side. She listened as Tanner grumbled at the loss of contact and then rolled over without waking.

It was still early. Juliet guessed it was probably five thirty or six, and she didn't want to rouse Tanner, who had finally fallen asleep after their rendezvous in the bathroom last night. She wondered if she could slip out of bed without disturbing her.

Juliet had a burning need to brush her teeth again, but worried Tanner would grow weary of her idiosyncrasies, and she definitely didn't want that to occur. If she could just hide a few of them from time to time, maybe Tanner might remain in her life. Juliet sighed at the possibility of having some kind of relationship with her.

She mentally smacked herself when she realized Tanner might hear her sigh as Tanner rolled back over and her eyes popped open.

"Good morning, beautiful." Tanner offered a lazy smile. It was like an exquisite daybreak gift, and Juliet felt her own smile blossom.

"Morning. It's still early if you want to go back to sleep."

"I could feel you squirming next to me. You want to brush your teeth, don't you? It's okay, you know. I still find that odd habit of yours charming, but I insist on adopting it so both of us have minty-fresh breath." Tanner chuckled.

"Are you making fun of me?" Juliet frowned.

"Absolutely not." Tanner brushed her hand across Juliet's cheek to move a wayward lock of hair. "How do you manage to look so beautiful in the morning? I like the messy-hair look."

Juliet blushed. "You're not so horrible-looking yourself."

"Ooh, such a charmer. 'Not so horrible-looking'? Was that an actual compliment?" Tanner teased.

"Sorry, I kinda suck at this...um, whatever this is...um...I don't know what I'm doing or saying, you have to know what a goddess you are...oh...ugh...I'll just stop talking right now." Juliet bounced from the bed and rushed into the bathroom.

She was amazed to see the two toothbrushes and the toothpaste carelessly sitting on the counter. She couldn't believe she hadn't put them back into the drawer in their proper place. It might be the first time she hadn't followed her routine. She smiled. Perhaps Tanner was having a therapeutic effect on her. She felt an overwhelming hope that her condition might temper itself just a little if Tanner distracted her with love.

Oh shit, love, am I falling in love? Juliet shook her head at the absurdity. That thought scared her more than never finding a way to stop her destructive habits.

Tanner's arms circled her waist, and the kiss on her neck sent goose bumps up and down her arms. Tanner reached around her and snatched her toothbrush from the counter.

Juliet carefully squeezed a ribbon of toothpaste onto her own toothbrush and turned to hand Tanner the tube.

Tanner quickly kissed her nose before taking the tube from her hand. "Thanks."

It was such an endearing thing to do; the sweet gesture completely overwhelmed Juliet. She stuck the toothbrush in her mouth and began her routine, silently counting to thirty as she ensured each section received a thirty-second brushing.

Tanner raised her right eyebrow and pulled the toothbrush out of her mouth. "You're counting, aren't you?"

Juliet nodded, not wanting to interrupt her rigid sequence.

"I'll bet you strictly adhere to the two-minute recommendation."

Juliet ignored the comment as she continued to massage her gums with the soft toothbrush.

"I suppose I should have procured electronic toothbrushes. I'll bet that's what you use. You know, one of those fancy ones that does the little buzzing thing after thirty seconds are up to ensure a precise timeframe on each area." Tanner stuck the toothbrush back in her mouth and began brushing again.

Juliet finished brushing and spat out the excess paste before thoroughly rinsing her mouth.

"It's okay. I'm just happy to have a new toothbrush. I would have worried about something getting on my electronic toothbrush during transport."

Tanner nodded, quickly finished, and startled Juliet by drawing her into a passionate kiss. "Now that's the correct way to greet the sunrise."

Juliet had to admit that Tanner's method of welcoming the day was indeed very pleasant. "I'm glad last night was uneventful. I remember putting away some eggs.

How about if I scramble up a few of them and maybe add some cheese?" she asked.

"That sounds wonderful. I can make toast. I think we have an old toaster somewhere. I'll paw around the cabinets until I find it."

"See, that's why it pays to organize everything. That's first on my list today. I simply cannot work in this level of disorganization."

"Of course you can't." Tanner smiled.

Juliet got the sense Tanner was teasing again, but not in a mean-spirited manner. She walked into the kitchen and could not force herself to ignore the inefficiency. It was still early enough that perhaps a cup of coffee would tide Tanner over until she got a handle on the kitchen.

Juliet began to sing "Whistle While You Work."

"You've got to do the whistling part properly, not just hum it," Tanner interjected.

Juliet laughed. "I don't whistle very well. You can do that part."

"Okay. I can also help, so tell me what to do."

Juliet turned her gaze on Tanner. "Um, no offense, but you'll just be in the way. You just sit there and look pretty while I whip this place into order."

"I'll feel like a slacker if I just watch you work. Not that looking at your fine swaying ass isn't pleasant, but I'm not used to sitting around."

"Really, I'd prefer that you stay out of my way. I'm kind of like a tornado when I'm in cleaning mode and it'll take much less time if you aren't in my hair. I mean that in a very loving, kind way," Juliet hastened to add.

"Okay. I'll just get my tablet and catch up on the news. Maybe I'll learn something helpful there. At least I'll be contributing."

"Okay." Juliet began her singing again as she worked on organizing the cabinets.

†

Tanner felt happy spending the morning with Juliet. She was fun—eccentric, but entertaining. She grew angry as she contemplated Juliet's previous lovers or casual dates and their low tolerance for her individualism.

How hard could it be to let Juliet clean and organize things? Besides, Juliet was cute as she swayed to the music she created. Her voice was pleasant to listen to, and her movements as she twirled around were nothing short of sensual. Tanner imagined Juliet was probably a very good dancer. Maybe someday they could go out on a real date and dance away the night. This thought made her feel warm all over.

While Juliet cleaned, Tanner nearly skipped into the bedroom to retrieve her tablet and begin reviewing the news. After turning on the device, she went to her news application and pulled up the *Seattle Times*.

Still Missing—Another Teenage Runaway or Foul Play?

The seasoned officer looked at the picture of the young girl below the headline and all the puzzle pieces shifted into place. She'd bet her last dollar this was the young girl Juliet had seen that night with Aiden. The article went on to report that the daughter of the Seattle mayor was still missing, and he continued to insist his youngest wasn't a runaway. He was incensed that the authorities wouldn't believe him after they looked at her Facebook and Instagram pages. Her contact on both platforms with some young men who appeared to be in their twenties or older suggested she'd ventured out quite a bit and her innocence was in question.

She shook her head at the media's portrayal of the girl as a promiscuous teen. That was the primary reason the Feds hadn't devoted more energy and resources to police efforts to shut down kiddie porn sites. How could anyone shift the blame to the young victims of these horrendous crimes?

Tanner hurried back to the kitchen.

"Juliet, can you take a look at this girl and tell me if she's the one you saw Aiden with?"

Juliet stood and reached for the tablet. "Sure, let me see the picture." She adjusted the screen with her thumb and index finger to zoom in on the picture. "It's a little bit grainy, but I think so. Who is she?"

"The mayor's daughter. It makes sense that whomever Aiden was working for is worried. She's high-profile, and Aiden made a fatal mistake when he lured her into his business. I'd be surprised if she's still alive. Someone wants to clean up all those loose ends, and they think you saw something more than you might have. I'd venture a guess that someone else in this town is involved in this and Aiden's accomplice doesn't want that observation uncovered. Do you remember anything else that might help? Other than seeing this girl with Aiden and then again by the pharmacy, did you see her at any other time?"

Juliet shook her head. "Not that I recall. I didn't get the impression she was frightened or I would have intervened. God, I'm so sorry. That girl might be dead and I could have saved her."

"I don't think so. All you would have managed to do was get yourself killed. I'm glad you didn't interfere with whatever was happening at the time, and maybe it's not too late for her," Tanner offered.

Juliet slumped into one of the hard wooden chairs in the kitchen. A tear rolled down her cheek. "God, I'll never forgive myself if something happened to that girl."

Tanner pulled her up and wrapped her arms around Juliet, kissing her forehead as she gently rubbed her back.

"First, we need to resolve the little problem of a contracted hit against you, and then I'll think of something. I'm sure there are a shitload of resources on the hunt for her, but I'm not willing to risk you popping your head up for some asshole to shoot at until I know it's safe. I think it's time I called my buddy Cisco again."

Chapter Fifteen

Tony hummed as he held his dick while urinating after he'd emerged from a restful sleep. The hotel he'd chosen had all the amenities he required—a pillow-top mattress, fully stocked bar, and an enormous bathroom.

He took his time in the shower, almost giddy with anticipation. He wasn't in a hurry to drive to Riverville since he didn't want to alert anyone to his arrival. Ralph was a bonehead and never should have created a stir. Tony was thankful Miguel had provided him with a specific location and that it was in a relatively remote area. This would be one of his easiest jobs to date.

Tony intended to take advantage of his visit to Seattle to sample its well-known gourmet restaurants. Perhaps he would visit Taylor Shellfish Oyster Bar today for a late breakfast or more accurately brunch since they didn't open until eleven thirty.

After his leisurely shower, Tony donned the fluffy, white robe hanging on the brass hook outside the shower door. He walked into the sitting room and opened the copy of the *Seattle Times* the hotel staff had placed outside his door and noted the article on the front page, the subject of which had prompted the need to eliminate the two women. At least Aiden was no longer a problem, but Tony would have enjoyed a third target. Only once had he been able to satisfy his dark needs with a triple hit. The high he experienced after that job had lasted nearly a month. His penis got hard just thinking about it.

Tony enjoyed reading the newspaper in every city he visited. Each paper had a slightly different feel. He knew most people read their news via their notebook computers or tablets now, but he preferred the crinkle of the paper in his hands. He would never convert to the electronic version. Sipping coffee and reading the news was relaxing for him and a way to prepare for the day. The normalcy of this routine convinced him of his sanity.

He whistled as he read the rest of the paper. He was in a good mood, and why not? He was doing work he loved—craved, even—and getting paid well for doing it.

After finishing the paper, he stretched and walked back into the bedroom to select comfortable clothes for the day. Seattle's weather was cooler than where he had come from but was still a pleasant temperature.

Tony selected a pair of worn Levi's and a cotton, button-down shirt, then dressed quickly. He would leave his overnight bag and shaving kit in the room, knowing he would return very late after finishing his job. He hadn't decided whether he would stay an additional day in Seattle or not. It depended on how much he was able to see of the city and enjoy its fine cuisine. It might be worth another day.

Tony didn't need the extra hassle of bringing along his gun, so he was glad when Miguel offered to connect him with his business partner. He planned to meet her later that evening, and she would provide the weapon—even though he hadn't yet completely decided on the method he would use.

He was smiling as he walked outside and let the rare Seattle sunshine fall on his skin. He took that as a sign that things were pointed in the right direction. God was smiling on him. Survival of the fittest.

†

The woman peered out the window. It was a sunny day. She felt calm when the sun shined. Rain irritated her. She decided that when this was over, it was time to consider moving to a warmer location. She was done. She had enough money saved now, and surely Miguel wouldn't begrudge her an early retirement. She'd been honest with him from the start. She would only partner with him for a few years, and after that her plans involved settling down in a nice remote location with sea, sand, and perpetual sunshine. She had a few possible options in mind, and some of them were outside the borders of the United States. To get there she would have to adopt another new alias, but that was easy. This suited her just fine.

Miguel had asked if she could meet Tony and provide him with a gun, and she'd reluctantly agreed. As long as he completed the job and ensured her involvement remained anonymous, she would take the risk and meet him.

She'd learned her lesson and would not rendezvous anywhere prying eyes might remember. Fortunately, multiple locations near Riverville were remote enough to conduct business. This was where she'd stored the young girl who had started this whole shitstorm.

She wasn't sure what she intended to do about that little problem. While she had no problem with Aiden luring precocious teens into the pornography business, she never actually killed any of them. It served them right for responding to the Facebook and Instagram posts Aiden had placed on social media. The little hussies wanted this kind of action. Most of them relished the notion of becoming a star. It was disgusting how they strutted in front of the camera in revealing lingerie, doing a slow striptease and loving every minute of Aiden's compliments on their beauty and how they would be shoo-ins for the big lights of Hollywood. After several years and unfulfilled promises, they all simply accepted their small degree of fame within the perverted community they serviced. On occasion, she'd heard about some of the young girls realizing what they'd stumbled into and fighting to escape the life. She didn't want to know what Miguel did about them. It wasn't her business. She provided the face of legitimacy to the girls, and they believed her soothing words that it just took the right film clip to send them to stardom. She had that polished, glamorous look to convince them of the lie.

She didn't get involved in the other side of the business either—the one that offered the girls extra money if they performed a few sexual favors in front of the camera. Most of them eventually devolved to this level of depravity. She understood the vast majority came from dysfunctional homes where sex at a young age, voluntary or not, with friends or relatives was commonplace. This notion added to her justification that her business wasn't that horrible.

The ringing cellphone startled her from her musings. She glanced at the screen and noted the number she assumed was Tony.

"Hello.... Okay.... Yes, I'll meet you at the address Miguel provided.... No, as far as I know, they haven't moved from the spot. I don't think they'll leave the cabin, and I haven't seen either of them in town. I can drive out there and make sure if you'd like…. Okay, fine. I'll see you in a few hours."

The woman ended the call and relaxed just a little. Soon everything would be resolved and she could breathe easier. She wasn't used to this kind of pressure.

†

Tony pulled up to the small A-frame house set far back in the woods. He noted the curtain flutter and suspected the woman was a little paranoid about this meeting.

He walked confidently to the front door and knocked. The woman who answered surprised him. No wonder she was able to calm the young girls. She was an attractive, middle-aged woman with a disarming smile. She was probably able to convince them that she knew the business well and could pull off being a well-connected agent.

"Hello," the pleasant alto voice greeted him. "Come on in. We can take care of business quickly and you can be on your way. Do you plan to wait until nightfall?"

Tony entered the small house. "I doubt you want to hear any of the details, so I'll just spare you."

"I need to know when this will be over. Perhaps you can call once you've finished the job."

Tony smiled at her. "You're awfully nervous for someone in this line of work."

"I don't normally get involved in this end of the business. It's not my specialty."

Tony narrowed his eyes. "You don't strike me as the squeamish type. I suspect ice runs through your veins."

"I'm not sure how to take that comment."

"Oh, you can take it as a compliment. I appreciate a strong woman."

Captivated

The woman raised her eyebrow. She turned around and picked up the Glock with a suppressor attached and handed it to Tony. "Even though the cabin is pretty far into the woods, I think it's always best not to draw unnecessary attention."

Tony grinned. "I normally use quiet methods of disposal, but since this is a double job, I might need to take care of the cop quickly, and the best method is usually a gun when I'm unable to get up close and personal. Thanks, a suppressor is a good idea."

He took the gun from her hands and spun on his heel. Then he turned back around and decided to let her know he would call after the job was complete. He didn't like the idea of a jumpy woman fucking up his perfect record.

"I'll call Miguel when the job is finished, and he can relay the good news to you."

Tony walked out of the house without another word. He had several hours to waste before he could satisfy the burning need to kill again. He hadn't decided whether he would hang out in the woods by the cabin or take a drive around the area and do a little sightseeing.

Chapter Sixteen

Tanner was pacing the floor after a surprisingly tasty lunch Juliet had prepared with the limited choice of food offerings she'd bought. She didn't do well cooped up inside a tiny cabin and was going stir-crazy after scouring all the Washington newspapers and trying to contact Cisco. Juliet, on the other hand, was perfectly content in her quest to completely dust, scrub, and polish every inch of the place.

"Would you stop pacing, please? You're making me dizzy."

"Oh, and all that whirlwind cleaning isn't the true culprit." Tanner stopped wearing a groove in the floor.

Juliet chuckled. "Come on, let's sit down on the couch and play truth or dare."

"You're kidding, right?"

"No, I'm not. Too many people grow up too quickly and forget to have fun. I either get to learn more about you or..." Juliet wiggled her eyebrows. "...I get to satisfy a few fantasies of mine."

"Hmmm, now why in the world would I select truth when I can satisfy a fantasy? I don't need to play truth or dare to do that. All you have to do is ask."

"I like playing games." Juliet grinned.

"Oooh, I like the sound of that. Can I suggest a few games of my own?" Tanner teased.

"Maybe," Juliet whispered.

"Come on, don't get shy on me now. I'll play your game, but I get to ask the first question—unless you want to take my dare."

"No, I'm not brave enough for a dare just yet. Hit me with your first question."

"Okay. Name one of those fantasies."

Juliet blushed.

"You have to be honest. That's the rule, as I recall."

"Okay, I've always wondered what it would be like to be cuffed or tied up and not be in control. Except...um, before...that wasn't a whole lotta fun, but in this situation, I might find it more appealing. You know that OCD is all about control, so for once I'd like to relinquish that control."

"Well, that fits well with my preferences. I'm kind of a top."

Juliet chuckled. "I never would have guessed that," she deadpanned. "Okay, my turn. Truth or dare?"

"Why do I think I won't get my wish for a fantasy dare?"

"Smart and sexy. I like it. Come on, stop stalling."

"Okay, truth."

"Why did you really kidnap me if you weren't going to kill me?"

"I don't know."

"Not good enough. Try again, because 'I don't know' is not an answer."

Tanner paused. She had to think about Juliet's question. Why did she kidnap Juliet and not just leave S-ville? Something about Juliet was irresistible. Tanner hadn't realized how much she intrigued her until now. She'd been watching Juliet, and she knew all about her snooping and illness. Aiden had brought her to S-ville, but Juliet had kept her there after the execution, and not because she'd witnessed it. Tanner decided Juliet deserved the truth as she understood it at that moment.

"You fascinate me, Juliet."

"Oh. Like a science experiment or something? Suddenly I feel like I'm under a microscope and you want to figure out the nutcase." Juliet looked away.

Tanner gently cupped Juliet's chin and turned Juliet's face back to look at her. "Not at all. You fascinate me in a good 'I'm wildly drawn to you' kind of way. Let me add that I think you're gorgeous, funny, intelligent, and interesting. All those other women missed out."

Tanner could almost feel Juliet's discomfort at the compliment and decided to give her a break as she moved on to the next question. "Your turn now. Truth or Dare?"

"Truth. I suspect your dares might be too outrageous for me. Besides, I'm an open book."

"Hardly. What were you like as a kid?"

"I can see through that question. You want to know if I've always been a freak."

"No, not at all. I just want to know more about you, and that seems like a common question people ask when they want to get to know a person."

"All right. I was shy. I watched people a lot. I guess I found out I was pretty good at the snooping thing because they never really noticed me since I was so quiet. I was always a neat child, but not quite so regimented as I am today. I think it got worse as I got older. My grandmother says it got worse when my parents died."

"What happened to them?"

"They died in a freak car accident. A drunk driver hit them head-on. Miraculously he lived, but my parents didn't. I was nineteen at the time and enrolled in the local community college. I was living at home because that was safe for me. After my parents died, I dropped out of school. My dad made some very bad investments and I couldn't afford to continue, so I went to live with my grandmother here in Riverville. Maybe someday I'll go back and finish my degree. Although I'm not sure how much use an English degree will be. Maybe I'll learn a few tricks to help with my writing. My turn. What were you like as a child?"

"I had a pretty normal childhood." Tanner shrugged. "I can't attribute any of my vigilante tendencies to the way I was raised. I can tell you that my mother did have a very well-developed sense of justice. I suppose I adopted those values and perhaps took them to the next level. How come you work in a post office?"

"I don't know. I guess it suits my personality and I'm good at it. All those little pieces of mail that go in very specific boxes. It's organized, and people appreciate my attention to detail. Mail never gets lost or put in the wrong box when I'm on duty."

"Do you actually know how many hands have touched the mail before it gets to you? Don't all the germ-infested parcels bother you?" Tanner smiled to show Juliet she was only kidding.

"Uh, uh, uh. My turn. You asked two questions in a row, and now you'll have to wait to ask your second question," Juliet teased. "What's going to happen to us after we manage to resolve this mess? Are you just going to move on to the next town and the next, um…I don't know what to call the people you, uh…decide should not continue to walk this earth?"

"That's two questions, but I'm a generous sort, so I'm going to answer them both. I'd like to say I have all the answers worked out, but I don't. For right now, my priority is keeping you safe. I can't really consider anything else."

"So you're just going to ride off in the sunset and I'll never see you again," Juliet choked out.

"That's not what I said. Look, I never intended to…oh, never mind."

Juliet brushed away a tear. "No, please tell me."

"I never intended to fall for you, or to hope I would have any kind of future with anyone. Ever since Faith died, I've been…well, let's just say there hasn't been anyone. Correction—there were those two disastrous dates I tried. They didn't work out so well. I'm more of a freak than you are. I'm a little paranoid at times and hunt down bad guys so I can deliver the sentence I deem appropriate for them. What kind of life is that for a partner?" Tanner hoped she would understand.

"A life I might want with someone I've come to care for a great deal," Juliet whispered.

"Do you really mean that? You would move with me where I choose to go—anywhere?" Tanner asked tentatively.

Juliet nodded, and her serious expression bored into Tanner.

"I think I just fell in love." Although she said the words in jest, she was surprised at how true they felt.

"Kiss me again already."

"Yes, ma'am."

Tanner finally decided to let go and shower her emotions on Juliet. She'd never wanted to make love with anyone as badly as she did with Juliet. It was still relatively early in the day, and she wasn't worried whoever was after them would make their move just yet, so she took Juliet's hand and gently pulled her to her feet.

Juliet wordlessly followed her into the bedroom.

Tanner noted the crisp look to the comforter and smiled to herself as she recognized Juliet's handiwork with the tightly made bed. There would never be any leftover tussled sheets after a night of making love with Juliet. Evidence of their passion would always remain a secret.

Tanner wondered how it would feel when spontaneity was lost because of Juliet's need to fold their clothes after Tanner removed them. Seductively stripping your partner and tossing their clothes to the side was an exciting part of foreplay. Not being able to do this would be an adjustment for Tanner, but she was more than willing to adapt if it made Juliet happy. Compromise. That was what loving someone was all about, and Tanner realized she was, in fact, falling in love with Juliet if she hadn't already. After the bargaining Faith had done with Tanner to get her to accept the *code*, Tanner figured making a concession with Juliet would be a walk in the park.

†

Juliet's heart beat wildly. Tanner stood in front of her smiling, and the tender look was her complete undoing. She felt Tanner's hand slowly travel up beneath her shirt. The sensation created a pool of moisture between her legs, and for once, her physical reaction to someone's touch didn't bother her. In the past, she would become anxious wondering what kind of germs lingered.

She shivered, and Tanner moved in to kiss her lips gently. Before Juliet realized what Tanner was doing, Tanner had pulled her shirt over her head and removed it in one practiced motion, then tossed the shirt on the bed. Tanner's hands caressed her sides and moved to her back, where she unclipped Juliet's bra. Her fingertips brushed down Juliet's arms as she removed her bra. It joined the shirt in a crumpled, small heap on the bed.

"Gorgeous. Just as I envisioned in my dream. You have a beautiful body, Juliet."

"Thank you. I seem to be a little underdressed now, compared to you." Juliet squirmed as she turned her head to see her clothes in a messy pile again.

Tanner chuckled. "Can we at least wait until the pile is a bit larger before we fold them? I'd prefer adding to it without interruption." Tanner ran her finger down Juliet's stomach and stopped at the top button of her jeans. "May I?"

Juliet nodded. She was almost overwhelmed by the sensations as Tanner undid the button and slowly pushed the zipper down until her jeans were completely undone.

Tanner moved her hands to Juliet's hips and pulled the jeans down, stroking each leg as she went. When she reached Juliet's ankles, she tugged the denim off and removed each sock while she lingered on Juliet's feet, stroking each one with reverence. She kissed Juliet's toes.

Juliet giggled. "Um, I'm feeling a little overexposed here in my undies while you're completely dressed."

"I just had to do that...you know, undress you. I've been thinking of it ever since I brought you to the cabin. It might have been a tad creepy to do it while you were still tied to the chair though." Tanner laughed. "Go ahead and fold your clothes now while I get undressed and add mine to the neat pile you're about to create. I still have the vision of you in front of me to tide me over until we crawl under the covers."

Juliet blushed and proceeded to gather her jeans, shirt, socks, and bra. She methodically prepared each article of clothing and then stepped out of her bikini underwear to add it to the pile on the dresser. When she turned around, Tanner had her own pile of clothes in her arms. Although they weren't as neatly folded as Juliet's were, she recognized the effort and forced herself not to refold them. As Tanner added them to her orderly pile, Juliet smiled, realizing this was another compromise on her part, and she ignored her compulsion to place the clothes in a tidy corner on the shelf in the closet.

She turned to face Tanner and took in the sight. Tanner was slender, but not skin and bones. Her flat stomach and well-muscled arms and legs indicated a body that participated in regular exercise. Juliet had an immediate desire to run her hands along the muscles and feel the tautness of Tanner's stomach. The urge was so great that she reached out and made the first tentative move.

Tanner blinked once and sighed as Juliet ran her hand down Tanner's cleavage to her stomach, then stopped her touch before reaching the soft mound of hair at the apex of her legs.

Tanner grabbed Juliet's right hand and quickly pushed back the covers, then tenderly guided her onto the bed.

They each turned on their side and lay face-to-face, soaking in the loveliness of the other. Tanner placed her fingertips on Juliet's face and lightly moved them across her skin.

Juliet accepted Tanner's tongue and twirled it inside her mouth, seeking greater pressure as the intermingling of tongues reached a crescendo of passion.

Tanner pushed Juliet on her back, moved on top, and ground against her as their desire ascended. Juliet felt each of Tanner's movements as her arousal grew. She hadn't slept with many women, so any amount of pressure on her clitoris was enough to make her excitement climb.

Juliet was surprised when her moan reverberated in the quiet cabin. "You have no idea how good that feels."

"Tell me what you want."

"I...I...don't know, because I don't have a lot of experience. Whatever you're doing is nice."

"I really want to taste you, but I don't know how you feel about that."

Juliet was feeling so good, she tried not to let her hang-ups get in the way, but the notion of Tanner's mouth down there was enough to make her body stiffen.

Tanner lifted her head and caught Juliet's eyes. "Not ready for that, are you?"

"Oh, God, I'm so sorry. I've never...I just can't stop the tape in my head...," Juliet stuttered.

"It's okay. I just want to love you, and that's only one way. A very glorious method, but it's not for everyone."

"Rain check?" Juliet whispered.

"You bet. Please tell me if I do anything that makes you feel uncomfortable."

Tanner continued to move sensually on top of her, and Juliet felt Tanner shift slightly as her hand traveled down to the dampness between Juliet's legs. The light stroking on Juliet's fine hairs as Tanner's fingers traveled down to her wet center caused Juliet to buck to meet the poignant caress.

"That's good, oh yes, please continue to do that." Juliet didn't know what alien entity entered her body as she articulated her need. As her breathing increased, she continued to encourage Tanner's expert touch.

Tanner was playing her like a fiddle. At least, that's how it felt. Juliet had never experienced an orgasm with someone else before because she'd always stopped well before that occurred. She could feel the tsunami building and felt near the edge.

"Oh, God, I'm so close."

"Just relax and let these feelings flow over you."

The additional light strokes on Juliet's clitoris forced the contractions, and she cried out in ecstasy. "Holy shit. That was amazing," she said when she could find the words again.

Tanner slowed her touch, and Juliet's orgasm subsided as Tanner left her hand on Juliet's pulsing vagina.

She pressed her lips lightly to Juliet's and gathered her in her arms.

Juliet couldn't help the tears that escaped and fell on her lover's neck.

"Shhh, it's okay."

"You're my first. Well, not the first person I've tried to sleep with, but the first person I've had an...uh...orgasm with."

"I gathered that."

"It just felt so good, and you managed to make me forget about my little quirks enough to enjoy the experience. If you can be a little patient with me, I'd really like to try to touch you too. In my dreams, I have no issues," Juliet revealed. "Can you guide me a little?"

Tanner sighed. "I'm good. There's really no need to reciprocate."

"But I really want to try. Have I mentioned I've been fantasizing about it?"

"Well, in that case, I'd hate to be an obstacle to achieving your fantasy. Grope away."

Juliet rolled to the side and lightly smacked Tanner. "No groping. I just want to feel and hear you respond."

She ran her hand over Tanner's breasts, lightly pinching the prominent nipples, which responded to her touch. Juliet felt powerful as she continued to elicit a response from her partner. The pleasured sounds that came from Tanner bolstered her confidence as she continued her journey down the tempting body, as the more experienced woman guided Juliet's hand.

"My God, woman, you are driving me mad. I think you've got the teasing technique down."

Juliet slowly swept her fingers inside the slick folds. She wasn't thinking about the bodily fluids as the sensation of her fingertips gliding through Tanner's wet center caused a surprising reaction in her own body. She felt arousal instead of disgust. Her joy threatened to overwhelm her as Tanner's movements got more insistent.

"If you want, you can go inside with two fingers."

Juliet didn't stop her ministrations as she guided her middle and index finger inside and stroked upward to feel the spongy surface. It was a glorious sensation. Her thumb remained on Tanner's clitoris, and Tanner bucked wildly.

"I'm so close, please don't stop."

She was so adrift in the pleasure Tanner generated inside her that when Tanner's walls pulsed around her fingers, she almost didn't recognize what was occurring. She reveled in the completely new sensation as the culmination of her caresses throbbed against her fingers. Her own arousal skyrocketed and the beginnings of her own orgasm burst through in harmony with Tanner's. She'd never known how splendid the feeling of mutual orgasm could be.

She collapsed on top of Tanner, satiated beyond her wildest dreams.

Tanner whispered in her ear, "You're probably going to question this, but I think I'm falling in love with you, Juliet. Can you just accept those words at face value? Don't say anything back. I just want to wallow in this magnificent afterglow."

"Okay." Juliet closed her eyes and rested against Tanner as Tanner lightly stroked her back. She wasn't prepared to fall asleep, but the emotion of the experience and Tanner's repetitive caress lulled her into dreamland.

†

It was late evening when Tanner opened her eyes. Juliet was still snuggled against her, and Tanner felt a sense of peace and contentment that had always escaped her in the past. The closest she'd ever come to it was when she was lying with Faith after they'd made love. She'd told Juliet she was falling in love and had meant every word. Something about Juliet brought out her tenderness. She wasn't sure what the future held, but she wanted Juliet to be a part of it.

Juliet shifted and her lovely green eyes opened. "Oh, God, I fell asleep on you."

"We fell asleep." Tanner chuckled when Juliet's stomach gurgled. "I think your stomach is registering a complaint. I've never met a person with a louder hunger warning. You must ignore it often enough for it to make a proclamation so vehemently."

"I don't mean to ignore her, but I am kind of hungry. How about if I whip us up a quick dinner?"

"I could eat. I think we worked up an appetite." Tanner grinned.

Juliet blushed. "I guess we did. I…um…it was incredible."

"Yes, it was," Tanner responded honestly.

"Did you really mean what you said?"

"I did. You are an amazing woman, Juliet. You need someone who will cherish everything about you."

"I felt extremely cherished."

"Good."

Tanner popped up and stalked over to the dresser without hesitation. Walking around nude in front of someone had never been an issue with her. She noted how Juliet held the covers against her body.

Tanner began to dress and watched with interest as Juliet remained in bed. "Aw, come on. Don't tell me after the afternoon we just had that you're reluctant to get dressed in front of me."

"Baby steps, Tanner, baby steps. Might I hasten to add that my first baby steps felt like giant leaps?"

"Your body is stunning, but I'll leave you alone to get dressed if that's what you need."

"Thanks. I promise I'll be out in a few minutes."

Tanner was taking bets with herself on the probability of Juliet coming out of the room in the same set of clothes. She thought the odds were sixty–forty that she would pick a new set from the duffel she'd tugged inside the closet. Tanner laughed as she guessed that Juliet probably didn't want her clean things touching the insides of the dresser drawers without a thorough cleaning. She wondered which would drive Juliet crazier, clothes remaining in the duffel or putting them in an unclean space.

As Juliet emerged from the bedroom, Tanner noted she was, in fact, wearing fresh jeans and a T-shirt.

"Damn I'm good."

"What?"

"Don't forget, we don't have a washing machine, so you're going to run out of clean clothes if you keep changing them so much."

Juliet looked down at her outfit. "I guess I didn't think about that." She frowned.

"You may just have to recycle what you wore earlier today, tomorrow."

"I think I can do that."

"I don't think you'll have a lot of choice not to, because I'm not leaving you here by yourself to make a clothes run."

"Right. That would be bad."

Tanner crossed the room and pulled Juliet into a fierce embrace. "Look, I didn't say that because I wanted to make you feel bad. I just want to be clear about my desire to keep you safe. If there was another way, I would happily accommodate your needs."

"I know. Maybe this whole experience will be good for me. It'll force me to face my compulsions and push myself a little to get beyond them. Years of therapy be damned, a life-threatening experience is the best medicine." Juliet smiled as her stomach growled again.

Tanner pulled away from the embrace. "What can I do to help with dinner?"

"Nothing. You'll just be in the way, and I say that in a loving 'I don't need the assistance' way."

"Okay, I'll just take a quick walk to the trip wire, because I want to make sure the audio alarm is still working. When I get back, I need you to give me a report on it. You should hear it activate and go through at least one cycle."

Tanner felt confident it was still early enough that leaving Juliet in the cabin alone would not be a risky proposition. She whistled as she walked into the dense woods surrounding the cabin. The sun was just starting to set on the horizon and the rainbow of colors painted the sky.

157

Chapter Seventeen

Tony decided a little bit of reconnaissance wasn't a bad idea as he made his way to the remote area where the two women had decided to hide out. He drove carefully over the backroad, bumping up and down as the wheels hit the numerous potholes.

"Fucking backwater towns with their dirt roads," he grumbled.

He looked off in the distance and thought he saw a woman walking on the path fifty to one hundred yards from the cabin camouflaged in the thick trees. Not wanting to signal his arrival in case it was the cop, Tony whipped his car around and sped down the road faster than he would have liked.

As his body bounced around despite the fact he had securely fastened his seat belt, Tony cursed loudly. This job was going to make him earn every dollar.

As soon as he reached the main road, he sat idling for a minute before pulling out his phone. A quick call to Miguel's partner to confirm the woman he'd seen in the distance was his mark might get the job done faster. He could park the car in a location where nosy neighbors wouldn't notice and then head back on foot to dispose of one of his targets while the two women were separated.

"Hey, it's Tony.... No, the job's not complete yet. I just wanted a description of the women. I think I saw one of them taking a walk in the woods.... Perfect, it sounds like I might be able to take care of the cop right now.... Yeah, I'll call when I'm done."

Tony didn't necessarily have a problem killing someone who wasn't on his hit list, but he also didn't want to bring more authorities into the mix, which killing the wrong person would surely do. Unnecessary attention wouldn't help.

He rolled his car onto the backroad, looking for a place to park his vehicle where passing cars wouldn't notice. Since the sun was setting, it wouldn't be long before darkness would hide his car. He smiled as he spied two massive trees with thick trunks surrounded by lush foliage and eased his rental between them. He climbed out of the car and stuffed the Glock into his waistband. Creeping into the forest, he moved toward the cabin, hoping to catch the cop unawares. This was a welcome turn of events.

†

Darla ended her call and looked at her brother, who had leaned back in his chair with his legs crossed in front of him. She'd led him back to the pharmacy, carefully keeping him away from her home.

"So who was that on the phone?" Harley asked.

"Never mind that. You need to think about what you're going to do about your suspension. What the hell were you thinking? Why'd you hold on to the drugs?"

"I told you. Tanner caught me hanging out at Juliet's. I didn't get a chance to plant them. I was going to swing back around later, and then the shit hit the fan. Now that plan is shot to hell. We'll have to think of something else to send the sheriff's office in a new direction."

"Don't do anything more. Let me handle this now. You'll just fuck it up again. Cole was barely able to drag your ass out of the fire, so don't do anything to mess that up."

"Do you think Cole can help with my suspension?"

"He's a criminal attorney, so you're on your own with that one."

"Maybe I'll just resign. I've had about enough of this town anyway," Harley grumbled and stood. "Okay, I'll just head out. Call me if you hear anything I need to know."

"All right." Darla was glad when he left. She laughed at how well she'd fooled him. She was the loving sister who'd helped her brother in his time of need, and nothing would point in her direction now. Harley would never finger her because he thought she was his savior. Everything was working out as planned. Her retirement was just around the corner.

†

Tanner saw the taillights flash and felt the hairs rise on the back of her neck. She hadn't even brought her gun with her. She was only one hundred yards from the cabin. Her feet pounded on the brush and leaves, and the sound reverberated in her ears. She hoped the woods muffled her quick dash back.

"The alarm blasted thirty seconds after you left," Juliet blurted as Tanner rushed inside.

"I know. We had a visitor, and I don't think he was a friendly sort. Get the rifle. I don't want either of us unarmed in the event that he decides to pay us a visit," Tanner ordered as she grabbed her gun from the table. "You stay here while I check things out. Go back to the bedroom and stay hidden. If anyone opens that bedroom door, shoot first and ask questions later."

"What if it's you?" Juliet asked.

"I won't be bursting through the bedroom door without announcing my arrival."

"Please be careful. I've kinda gotten used to you and am sorta fond of your smile."

Tanner glanced out the window and noticed the sky rapidly darkening. She wasn't sure if her night goggles would be a help or hindrance at dusk, but she decided to grab them from the closet just in case. It wasn't a bad idea to be armed with equipment that might give her an advantage against a trained killer.

She brushed past a wide-eyed Juliet and yanked open the closet door. She pushed aside the boxes, reached into the corner, and snatched the gear from its hiding place. As an afterthought, she grabbed the black sweatshirt folded neatly on the top shelf. After temporarily setting down her gun and goggles, she pulled the sweatshirt over her head before shoving the gun in her pants and picking up the night-vision glasses again.

As she swept past Juliet, she stuck her arm out. She needed to make some contact with Juliet to reassure Juliet that everything was going to be just fine. A quick squeeze on her shoulder and she was out the door.

Tanner knew these woods, and that gave her an advantage. Like a cat on the prowl, she crouched behind the thick foliage and lightly stepped over the damp leaves. Her footfalls barely made a sound as she made her way across the forest floor.

She could feel the predator and turned her head when the rustle of a branch against a hard object attracted her attention. She couldn't make him out through the thick branches, leaves, ferns, and bushes that occupied the dense woods, but she knew he was there somewhere, waiting to make his move. She was patient. She could wait him out.

Tanner kept a dual line of sight between the cabin and where she'd heard the noise. There was still enough light that her goggles were an impediment, but in another thirty minutes or more, they would prove their worth. Every one of Tanner's senses was on high alert. She'd be damned if she would let that bastard get to Juliet.

†

Tony was impressed. He'd listened intently as he creeped along while pushing branches aside. He thought he heard careful footsteps and assumed the cop was launching her own attack. She was a worthy opponent. The game was on. He figured she'd probably noted his arrival when she was out for her walk. Surprise was no longer an option.

A branch snapped against his arm with a dull thwack. He hadn't realized it was there until it was too late. Crouching, he silently progressed through the damp forest, getting closer to the flickering light of the cabin. He lifted his nose in the air and imagined he caught a whiff of her soap—lavender.

He needed to wait a little longer to let the comfort of darkness blanket the area. Tony moved well in the night, better than during the day. Darkness provided solace to him—a shelter for his chosen vocation.

Time ticked away as dusk evolved into an inky blackness. Tony remained as still as a statue while he waited for the obscurity of the night to offer protection.

He narrowed his eyes, looking all around, watching for any disturbance. There it was—off to the left of the cabin—barely a movement. He fixed his eyes on the shadow that shifted against the fading light.

Gotcha.

He inched closer to the silhouette and pulled his gun from his waistband. He could barely make out the stooping figure as he saw her stir. He took aim and fired.

†

Tanner played a mental game as she waited patiently for him to make his move. After the initial noise, she hadn't heard anything more, but she knew he was out there, waiting like she was. They were both night predators, but she smiled at the knowledge that he might erroneously believe he had the upper hand in the dark.

As the dusk faded, the night sky took over. Tanner sent up a small prayer of thanks that the half moon remained hidden behind thick clouds.

It wouldn't be long now before the inevitable confrontation. Tanner smiled. She suspected something might be terribly wrong with her because she was eagerly awaiting that moment when she could dispose of another escapee from justice. The thought was sobering. She wanted some kind of relationship with Juliet and that wouldn't be possible if she insisted on continuing her vigilante ways. Maybe she could capture this one and let the wheels of justice roll as intended—without her assistance.

Tanner looked up at the sky and decided it was time to don the goggles. Moving slowly, she carefully adjusted the strap behind her head, securing them over her eyes. When she looked through the lenses, eerie green light illuminated her surroundings. When she'd first bought the fancy equipment, the salesperson boasted they would let her clearly see objects as far as two hundred yards away. She'd doubted him, but now she was a believer.

She could distinguish distant objects as she turned her head side to side. Fear overtook her body as her eyes focused on the man bringing his gun up in front of his chest and pointing the long barrel in her direction.

Her last thought before instinct took over was that she deserved this because she was no better than the dark forces she'd given a final sentence to. Yet Juliet did not deserve the same fate.

†

Juliet heard the dull pop half a second before the loud bang.

Tanner.

She recognized the sound of a gunshot—that was one thing she was one hundred percent positive about. Her panic intensified as she grabbed the rifle. She didn't have a single clue what to do, only that she had to help Tanner. For all she knew, Tanner was dead now and she was on her own.

Wide-eyed, she stumbled outside, dramatically moving her rifle left and right without order or thought. As her booted feet crunched heavily over the ground, she ignored the sound of snapping twigs.

Juliet wasn't sure where to run to, but in her state of alarm, she charged through the woods, branches slapping at her body and stinging her cheeks. A patch of thorny brambles attacked her as she rushed into the deathlike gloom.

Her war with nature and the abuse it was doling out to her body barely registered.

A pair of hands snaked out seemingly from nowhere and yanked on Juliet's ankles, pulling her down onto a soft bed of pine needles. She struggled and managed to break her attacker's grasp as she pulled the rifle close to her body and sprang into a crouching position.

Before she could cry out, a strong hand covered her mouth. Cold metal brushed against her head and she felt the hardness of the object, which she assumed was a gun.

She deeply regretted not telling Tanner she'd fallen in love with her too as she reluctantly accepted her fate. Maybe if there were an afterlife, she'd meet up with Tanner there and could confess her feelings then. It was a ridiculous thought.

"Sshh. He's still out there, but I think I nicked his shoulder."

Juliet relaxed as Tanner's soothing voice whispered in her ear.

"Fe, fi, fo, fum, I smell the blood of a stupid one. I could hear you crashing through the forest, and now I'm coming after you. You're a dead woman, cop, and then I'm taking my time with your little friend."

Juliet shivered as Tanner removed her hand and gently pulled her downward. She realized they were in a cavernous alcove with a sizeable indent in the earth. The hole was large and deep enough to conceal their whereabouts.

She felt Tanner's finger press to her lips as they crouched down deep into the depression, which was surrounded by a small ridge. She turned to face Tanner, who was sporting what she thought were the perfect spyglasses. She wanted a pair of her own.

Why am I having such outrageous thoughts in the middle of this perilous situation?

She tried to control her breathing, because she knew her panting was a dead giveaway to their location. If she could hear her desperate attempts to breathe, surely the attacker would as well. She was going to get them both killed. She wondered why she couldn't have just stayed in the cabin and let Tanner take care of everything.

Juliet lamented that she had only one skill—cleaning and organizing her world. She wasn't even a good spy since everyone in town knew about her snooping and politely tolerated her odd behavior.

†

Tony felt lucky that the bullet had only grazed his arm. He'd underestimated her, and he would not duplicate that mistake. He still didn't quite understand how she'd managed to roll and squeeze off a shot. He was particularly irritated about the fact her bullet had managed to skim over his arm while he didn't think he'd found his mark at all.

When the other woman came crashing through the woods, he'd tracked her progress to the ridge on the right. He could hear her heavy breathing and he'd barely made out a whisper, so he suspected they were together now.

He knew taunting them wasn't the smartest thing, but he couldn't help himself. It probably gave away his position temporarily, but he would remedy that in a second.

Tony silently dropped to the forest floor and slithered along like a snake, inching his way toward the woman's heavy breathing. His progress was slow, but at least he wouldn't give away his position. He'd learned how to do this during his Navy SEAL training. It was a useful tool for a hired gun.

His left arm began to sting, reminding him of how badly he wanted to make the cop pay for his injury. He was getting closer to the women, and he thought he could feel the fear coming off them in waves. One of them lacked training. That was a weak spot he intended to use to his advantage.

Tony lifted his head and smiled as he reached the backside of the ridge. He'd managed to approach the hole without alerting them and had the backs of their heads clearly in his line of sight. He lifted his stomach and gently pulled the Glock from where it had been rubbing him as he made his way across the forest floor. He could have stored it in the back of his pants, but he felt comforted by the cold steel rubbing against his body as he inched toward his targets.

When he got close enough to make his move, he realized why the cop had managed to get the drop on him. She was wearing night goggles. *That fucking bitch.*

A quick bullet to the head and he could move on to the other woman. He undid the suppressor because he wanted the other bitch to hear the shot and realize she only had minutes left of her pitiful life.

A light wind rustled through the trees, and the sounds of the night did nothing to mask the deafening sound of the gunshot as it reverberated through the forest.

†

Tanner blocked out all the other noises in the forest and concentrated on listening to the quiet rustling as the man moved closer to their hiding place. She knew Juliet's loud, panicked breathing was a dead giveaway. Her only advantage now was to let him believe he'd found them unaware and won. She would pretend she didn't hear him approach from the rear and hope her timing was perfect when she pivoted and dropped the motherfucker.

Tanner spun around in one graceful movement and took a second to find the dark shape less than twenty feet away. She put consistent pressure on the trigger as she squeezed off one shot. The bullet found its mark like a heat-seeking missile, and the man plummeted forward.

She jumped up from the hole and clambered to the lump at the edge of the ridge. Her night vision goggles were still securely fastened around her head as she pressed her fingers against his neck. She breathed a sigh of relief as she noted the absence of a pulse. It was a clean shot through the middle of his forehead.

Tanner had wanted to keep him alive long enough to ask a few questions, but he hadn't left her that option. She wasn't willing to risk Juliet's life. It was simply too precious to her now. She'd have to find a different way to locate the mayor's daughter, provided she was still alive. Maybe she needed to bring the big guns in to take over the investigation. Tanner knew she had a little time before the enemy had an opportunity to regroup. They wouldn't expect to hear from their man until later in the evening, and by then she would have already rallied the troops.

Juliet had critical information to give the authorities, and that would bring the necessary resources to the area. Their arrival would make the situation too hot to send another outsider to the cabin, and that gave her time. Things were working out quite nicely for Tanner. Suspicion for Aiden's murder would fall on whoever was running the child pornography ring, and she would be the last person the authorities would turn their attention to.

She still had a niggling suspicion that someone in town was more connected to this mess than anyone suspected, and that still posed a risk to Juliet. She'd need to remain alert.

As Tanner hopped back into the hole, she saw Juliet's bowed head. She yanked on the strap of her goggles, anxious to remove the barrier and kneeled in front of Juliet. With her face mere inches from Juliet's, she could see her tears.

"Hey, it's okay now. He's dead. He can't hurt you." Tanner leaned forward and kissed each eyelid. She brushed her thumb against Juliet's cheek to remove the moisture. "Come on, let's get you back inside and I'll call the sheriff. Now that the immediate danger has passed, I think it's time for you to tell them everything you know about Aiden and the young girl you saw, who I'm pretty sure is the mayor's runaway daughter. I really wish I knew exactly what you may have seen that's making someone particularly nervous."

Tanner took Juliet's hand and gently tugged her to a standing position before carefully leading her out of the hole.

"I know you were just protecting me, but doesn't it bother you to kill another human being?" Juliet asked.

Tanner suddenly felt deflated thinking Juliet would never love her back. She wanted to feel guilt, if that would please Juliet, but she didn't. "No, it doesn't. I suppose that makes me a horrible human being."

"Oh, God. No. I didn't mean for my question to come out the way it did. I'm not judging you, I just wanted to understand."

"Hang on a second. I think I'd better put the goggles back on so I can lead us back to the cabin without tripping over any fallen logs or getting attacked by thorny bushes."

"I think it may be a little late for that. I'm starting to feel the aftereffects of my idiotic decision to come save you." Juliet chuckled. "I couldn't see shit."

"I have a first aid kit in the cabin. I'll get you all fixed up, and then I'd like to try to call Cisco again before I call the sheriff. I've got the distinct impression they're more prepared for this kind of thing than the Riverville police. I have no idea why Cisco hasn't answered my calls though. That's not like him."

"Are you just going to leave...uh...the body out there?"

"Yeah, they'll need to get the crime scene techs here, so it's best I leave everything undisturbed for now. I hope they can find the bullet he discharged because it'll help verify our story."

Juliet shook her head. "This is just so...so...unbelievable. I need to tell you something. I should have said something earlier. God, Tanner, I almost lost you."

"We can stay in the cabin tonight. It's probably better to delay all the hoopla anyway. Who knows, maybe I can convince them to hold off coming out tonight because they'll just have to bring in more resources. This is a small town, and they aren't going to like spending time away from their families to traipse around in the woods in the middle of the night. A well-placed suggestion might just do the trick."

Chapter Eighteen

Nick was still seething over the little prick who'd dressed him down. He hated slick attorneys with a passion. They were always defending every slimebag the police tried to get off the streets. Every bone in his body was screaming that Harley was up to his eyeballs in shit. There was a lot more to Aiden's murder than they'd uncovered, and he'd be damned if he'd let that little fucker just walk away.

Grumbling to himself, he drove by the casino and noted Harley's car occupied the handicapped space close to the door.

What an asshole. Nick wasn't interested in busting Harley's chops for a parking violation, but he couldn't pass up the opportunity to have a little chat with him.

When he entered the casino, he noted Darla at the blackjack tables and Harley cozied up to the bar. He'd heard a rumor that Darla had a gambling addiction, but hadn't given it much thought until she showed up with her fancy lawyer to help her brother. The wheels in his head began to turn as he put the pieces together. He'd already talked to some of the locals and found out Aiden had a little side

business going. He tried not to feel too bad about shutting off
the supply to some of the old ladies who genuinely believed
they needed the drugs to offset their pain.

"How's it going, Darla? Having any luck tonight? I
see your brother's bellied up to the bar. You ought to make
sure he isn't the kind of idiot to start spilling his guts after
several drinks. You never know what he might say about his
closest friends or family," Nick taunted as he walked up to
her.

Darla frowned. "Piss off, Nick. Don't you have
anything better to do than harass people? Your veiled
warnings don't mean squat. You played. You lost. As a
seasoned gambler, my advice is to know when to hold 'em
and when to fold 'em."

"Don't go too far, Darla. I may have some questions
for you."

Harley swiveled on his stool and glared at Nick. After
a few seconds, he stalked over and invaded Nick's space.

"Harassing my sister now? Maybe I'll make an
official complaint through my attorney," Harley sneered.

"Just having a friendly chat. In fact, I'd love to bury
the hatchet and buy you a drink or two, Harley." Nick
smacked him on the back and headed for the bar.

"Sure, why the hell not."

Nick looked back over his shoulder at a scowling
Darla and smiled.

†

The woman watched with interest as Nick entered the
Casino. He was still sniffing around Harley, and that
bothered her. It was getting late and Tony hadn't called to
confirm completion of the job.

Her nerves were starting to fray. She really did not want to get personally involved in resolving her problem. Miguel had assured her everything was under control, but it wasn't.

God damn it, if you want something done right, you have to do it yourself. Her self-preservation was at stake, and she would do whatever it took to make things right. She didn't like getting her hands dirty, but she was definitely capable of eliminating a threat. It was time to take another trip out to the cabin. She'd hold off until the morning, because there was still a chance Tony wanted to wait a little longer to ensure the women were asleep. That would make sense. Miguel always recommended a surprise attack, and that usually occurred in the middle of the night.

The woman closed the blinds and settled back into her chair. She decided to get some sleep and then perhaps poke around to see what kind of information Nick had uncovered. It was a small town and people gossiped. She would call her lover early in the morning and wiggle the information out of him. He had a thing for sex just before sunrise, so she knew she could get him talking. If Tony hadn't called by the time she finished her rendezvous, she would pay a visit to Tanner and Juliet. She had the whole night to think up a cover story.

She wasn't an expert on guns, but she did know how to use one. She glanced at the kitchen table where she'd laid the weapon. It was a good thing she'd decided to procure two of them—one for herself and one for Tony. They were remarkably easy to acquire through her black-market connections.

The young girl was becoming an even greater pain in the ass, and she needed to make a decision soon about what she intended to do with her. Killing the women was one thing, but she wasn't sure she had the stomach for killing the mayor's daughter. She needed to confer with Miguel on that. He was a cold-hearted bastard and wouldn't have an issue with doing whatever was required.

She was thankful she was alone that evening, because dealing with either of them now was the last thing she wanted to do. Husbands and lovers provided a good cover, but she was ready to move on.

She nestled into her down comforter and fell into a restless sleep, dreaming of palm trees and pristine, white beaches overrun with police specifically looking for her. In her subconscious, she seriously doubted she'd ever get what she wanted. Too many things had gone wrong.

†

Darla busted again at the blackjack table. She was not having a good night before Nick came in, and after he'd uttered the veiled threat, it had truly turned sour.

Harley was a dumbass, but at least his lips didn't loosen with alcohol. Instead, he was a mean drunk. He got belligerent and started fights. He'd puff up his chest and shoot off insults like a rapid-fire gun. The locals ignored his blustering, and that tended to add fuel to the fire. He wanted to one-up someone, and the barflies refused to play his game. Darla hated when one of the local drunks called her to get her brother before fists started flying. She was amazed he hadn't been fired yet. His boss had reprimanded him so many times that he was still on probation from the last incident. She felt mildly bad about reporting him, but the authorities could easily point the finger in his direction and the fact she was the one who had turned him in left her clear from suspicion.

Darla managed to pull Harley out of the bar after Nick bought him his third round. It was time to nip this impending train wreck in the bud. Leaving Nick glaring at both of them, she shoved Harley into her car and drove him home. At least Nick wasn't about to do any more snooping around that evening after throwing back three shots himself.

It was a good thing she had an alternate stream of money. She had a hard time justifying what she had to do, but she was in a pickle and it seemed like a relatively easy thing. She knew what kind of business they were in, but as long as she didn't see the evidence first-hand, she could claim ignorance. Harley had been right when he once told her that she was a first-class bitch who only cared about herself. She was amazed at her ability to play the loving sister when the need arose. Too bad she wasn't able to bluff her way through a crappy hand of poker. It's why she always stuck to blackjack, but recently her luck there had turned.

Before Darla returned home, she placed the call as promised. She still needed that stream of money until she made plans to leave this little shithole of a town. She wouldn't miss her brother in the slightest, and if that made her a cold bitch, so be it.

Chapter Nineteen

Juliet relaxed into Tanner's arms and the world tilted back onto its axis. She had to let Tanner know the depth of her feelings. When she'd asked Tanner how she felt about killing that man, she saw the profound sadness in her eyes. She hadn't meant to hurt her. It was an honest question, and she wanted to understand what made her tick.

She slowly disengaged herself and looked into Tanner's eyes, eyes that revealed unasked questions.

Juliet grabbed Tanner's hand and pulled her to the couch.

"I'm a coward," she began.

Tanner shook her head.

Juliet placed one finger on Tanner's lips. "Please let me finish. When you told me you were falling in love, I didn't say a word. I wanted to, but I got scared. I couldn't quite imagine anyone putting up with my shit. I know I don't really have the kind of obsessive-compulsive disorder that causes severe psychological problems, but it's about as close to that edge without falling over as it can be."

"It's cute. Really. It's one of the things I love about you," Tanner interrupted.

"Are you always so, oh, I don't know—dominant? You didn't let me finish. I'm trying to tell you I love you too. I realized that when I heard that gunshot. It hit me like a ton of bricks that I might lose the one person with whom I had a real chance at making a go of it."

"You had me at *dominant*." Tanner laughed. "How about I show you that dominant side? I promise to let you play too." She winked.

"I didn't mean to hurt you when I asked about killing that man. I just wanted to understand you. I want to crawl inside your skin and learn everything there is to know about you. It's a good thing. I promise."

"This, what's happening between us is definitely a good thing. Listen, hold that thought, because I still need to make that call to the sheriff. Okay?" Tanner stroked Juliet's cheek and kissed her lightly.

Tanner shifted slightly and picked up her cellphone off the coffee table. She pressed a few buttons and began to speak. "Hi, yeah, this is Tanner Sullivan. Listen, I know the sheriff's office took over the investigation into Aiden's murder and I hate to call so late, but we had an incident tonight that I'm confident is connected. A guy came after us, and I had no choice.... Sorry, Juliet Lewis. She has information to add to the investigation, but she's pretty shaken and the guy isn't going anywhere. I think it can wait until the morning. My cabin is deep in the woods, and you can get the address from the station because I left it on file for them.... No, don't come out tonight. Juliet needs a good night's rest and I'd rather everyone is fresh on this in the morning. Besides, you're going to need to bring in a lot more resources to unravel this whole mess, and I'm confident they aren't going to let the locals handle it after you hear what Juliet has to add to the investigation….

"Look, I don't really care what protocol dictates, because right now my first priority is the living, breathing person in front of me. You'll get your information and the location of the bastard's body tomorrow morning. If you come out tonight, I'll start shooting and ask questions later. People don't take kindly to folks trespassing on their property here. The last guy learned the hard way about that…. You know, Nick, you go right ahead and make your report, because I was ready to move on anyway…. Great. I knew you'd see it my way."

Tanner ended her call and Juliet giggled. "Wow, I love it when you get all dominant. I'm going to enjoy every minute of getting to know every facet of you, Tanner Sullivan."

"I'll let you inside of my deep and disturbing head, but first can we crawl in bed and let nature take its course? I'm sure you're as emotionally exhausted as I am, so can we please forego another shower? I know you can't wait to get out of your dirt-encrusted clothes because crawling around on the forest floor must have sent you into a tailspin, but for just one night I think it will be okay, unless…."

Juliet grinned. "Unless we save some water and take a shower together, huh?"

"Add mind reader to your vast set of skills. Give the woman a prize."

"I believe that is the perfect compromise, because you know I can't just crawl in bed without a shower. I can already feel the germs burrowing their little heads into my skin." Juliet shivered.

"It's a good thing we only have to stay one more day in the cabin, because I believe you're just about out of clean clothes." Tanner grinned.

"Come on, smartass, my back needs washing. I can't quite reach all the spots that need a thorough cleansing. My shower at home has a back scrubber. It's been driving me crazy not having that essential apparatus."

"Ooh, we definitely cannot have that. I can be your permanent back scrubber. In fact, I think you ought to toss the old one, because there's no telling how many disgusting germs have collected on it just waiting to attack your unsuspecting body," Tanner teased.

"Don't even joke about that." Juliet walked toward the bathroom. She really wanted to do a seductive striptease in front of Tanner, dropping her clothes along the way, but she hadn't come that far yet. So she just swayed her hips a little.

Once Juliet reached the bathroom, she began to remove her clothing. Pine needles and a few leaves fluttered to the floor as she pulled her shirt over her head. Her eyes tracked the debris and she began to bend over to pick them up.

"Stop right there. I'm sure I'm going to add to the mess, so I can help you clean up after we're out of the shower," Tanner directed.

Juliet felt indecisive as Tanner began to remove her clothes. The sight of Tanner's gorgeous body distracted her, but her eyes kept tracing all the remnants of the forest that fell to the floor. Eventually Tanner and her smoky come-hither look won out. It was probably the first time in her life that someone was able to divert her from the compulsion to tidy things up immediately.

While Tanner dropped her clothes on the bathroom floor, Juliet neatly folded hers and placed them on the toilet seat. She was folding her jeans as Tanner turned on the shower and let the water flow over her wrist.

"I think the temperature is perfect now." Tanner waved her arm. "After you, my beauty."

Juliet giggled. "That's about the corniest thing I think I've ever heard. Somehow it doesn't quite fit with your big badass-cop persona."

"Hey, I can be quite chivalrous when I want to."

Juliet stepped into the shower and let the warm water flow over her. It felt nice. She looked down and didn't see any dirt on her body as she'd envisioned, but her hands were filthy from crawling around on the ground. She pumped the soap container three times and lathered up, removing every speck of grime before placing her hands on Tanner's body. Her phobia extended to the ones she loved.

Tanner reached around and kissed her neck as she moved her mouth upward. She nibbled on Juliet's bottom lip, sending an instant message of arousal to the rest of her body. Juliet couldn't tell if the dripping between her legs was because of Tanner's devotion to her body or the water cascading down her back.

"Mmm, that feels nice," Juliet murmured.

She brought her hands down Tanner's backside and reached around to stroke her buttocks. The hard muscles were a complete turn-on to Juliet as she caressed her left cheek with her right hand.

Tanner brought her close and Juliet felt the gentle caress of Tanner's fingertips on her own ass. She felt Tanner's soft pubic hair brush against her own. Her arousal skyrocketed as Tanner slipped her hip and leg between Juliet's thighs, creating a scissor-like position.

An involuntary moan escaped from Juliet's mouth, and Tanner added to the chorus with her own sounds of pleasure. Tanner's continued movements caused Juliet to arch in ecstasy as the wave overtook her body, and her climax hit at the same time she suspected Tanner was having her own.

Tanner pressed her lips firmly against Juliet's mouth. When she broke apart, she whispered, "I love you."

"Ditto," Juliet responded.

They spent another twenty minutes soaping each other's bodies before the water turned cold and they admitted it was time to leave the shower.

"I never want to take another shower alone again." Juliet smiled.

"Don't look at the floor or my pile of clothes; just double-time it into the bed and I will take care of everything. Tomorrow you can redo my cleaning, but for right now I believe I'll be a lot quicker." Tanner wrapped the towel around Juliet and pushed her out the door.

Juliet sighed as she pulled the towel tight around her body and walked into the bedroom, completely ignoring the mess on the floor. She was looking forward to their continued lovemaking, because she knew that was exactly what would transpire over the next several hours.

†

Beep beep beep beep

The noise startled Tanner awake. She rubbed her eyes and jumped from the bed, instantly alert.

They'd only fallen asleep four hours ago, and the noise from the alarm caused her adrenalin to skyrocket. "Stay here and don't make a sound."

Juliet nodded, her eyes wide in alarm.

Tanner grabbed the sweatshirt and jeans she'd worn the day before from the corner where she'd placed them and pulled them quickly over her body. She dashed out of the bedroom and grabbed the rifle Juliet had set next to the couch the night before. She hurried back into the bedroom and saw Juliet pulling on a pair of jeans as she sat on the edge of the bed. Tanner handed her the rifle.

"Here, you keep this and don't say a word while I check things out. It's probably just Nick, but it's still early and I'm a bit paranoid. I still have an uneasy feeling about all of this and haven't had a chance to connect with Cisco to see if he's heard anything using his little street network."

Juliet took the rifle and laid it on the bed. She was naked from the waist up, and if the audio alarm hadn't worried Tanner so much, Tanner might have found the sight humorous. Regardless of the danger, she'd probably never get that image out of her brain. It was very, very, sexy.

Tanner's first thought was to arm Juliet, but now she needed to retrieve her own weapon. Juliet had inadvertently distracted Tanner last night when she sat her down to tell her what was in her heart and Tanner had to think where she'd left her gun.

A knock on the cabin door diverted her attention. She glanced back over her shoulder and saw the bedroom door close. Good. Juliet was taking her direction to remain hidden.

Tanner crossed the room and cautiously opened the front door.

"Barbara? What are you doing here?" Tanner narrowed her eyes. "How'd you find this place?" She couldn't imagine why the pharmacy owner's wife was at her cabin.

"Nick sent me. He was concerned he couldn't get here at first light and wanted me to relay the message that he would come as soon as he could. He has Harley and Darla in custody right now and is waiting for some other people to come to Riverville. I guess this is a big deal."

Tanner hesitated before she opened the door, but then decided since this was a small town, it wasn't out of the realm of possibility that Nick had sent Barbara, especially if Darla was connected and Nick had questioned Barbara. Old Man Garrison was probably still out on his hunting jaunt and had left his wife in charge of the pharmacy. Small-town amateurs were both a blessing and a curse to her at this moment.

"Come on in. I guess I can offer some tea or coffee while we wait for Nick and the rest of the circus to arrive. I'm surprised he sent you all the way out here. I don't think you really want to be involved in this mess." Tanner turned around and started to head into the kitchen.

She glanced down the hallway and was glad Juliet was remaining behind closed doors. Maybe she was letting her paranoia take control again, but her unease suddenly overwhelmed her.

Her compulsion to glance back over her shoulder stopped when she heard the click of the safety. Barbara smiling at her through the window above the pharmacy flashed before her eyes as she remembered her troubled feelings the other day in town. Everything shifted into place for her—Juliet seeing the young girl by the pharmacy and bumping into Aiden at the same time. Barbara must have thought Juliet saw her with the young girl.

Too late. She felt the barrel of the gun at the back of her head.

"Where's Juliet? I don't have a lot of time before Nick comes out here. I'm sure you called him last night after eliminating Tony."

"Fuck you, Barbara," Tanner yelled.

"Now that was really stupid, Tanner."

The gun smacked her head, and then it was lights out. Her last thought before entering dreamland was that she'd failed Juliet.

183

†

Juliet heard Tanner yell, "Fuck you, Barbara," and she knew it was a warning. She heard a thud and rustling around in the living room. Her heart beat wildly as she crept toward the bedroom door. Footsteps echoed on the wood floor in the hallway as someone approached the door.

Juliet took a step back, brought the rifle to her shoulder, and aimed at the closed door. She would follow Tanner's instructions, but she wasn't sure who would be coming through it. Tanner had told her that "anyone coming into the bedroom unannounced would not be a friend," and she depended on those instructions. The last thing she wanted to do was shoot Tanner.

The door slowly opened and Barbara's body loomed large as she pointed her gun directly at Juliet.

"Stop right there. I don't want to shoot, but I will if you don't drop your gun," Juliet warned.

Barbara blinked once. "I'm sorry, Juliet. You should have kept your nose out of things. It really is your fault that I'm forced to do this."

Juliet aimed for Barbara's left shoulder and squeezed. The bullet blasted into her body, and Barbara instinctively released her gun, grabbing her injured shoulder. The gun fell to the floor and skidded a short way across it.

Juliet kept her eyes on Barbara as she pulled back the bolt, ready to shoot again if she needed to. Barbara's gaze traveled to the gun lying innocently on the bedroom floor. It had come to a stop at the edge of the remaining T-shirt and sweatshirt neatly folded in the corner. Juliet had an absurd thought that Tanner had managed to leave the remainder of their clothes in a neat pile despite rushing to get to the door. She was deeply touched that Tanner had slipped from the bed last night and taken such care with the clothes after their shower. Sure, Juliet would have put them away neatly in the closet, ready to launder later, but the fact Tanner had attempted to feed her compulsion was terribly sweet.

Juliet returned her attention to Barbara. "You're close enough for me to put another hole in you, so I'd recommend not moving an inch. I'm a good shot at fifty yards, but in this close proximity, even a hundred-year-old woman could hit her mark. Don't test me, Barbara, because I believe I've already demonstrated my lack of hesitancy to shoot first and ask questions later."

Barbara slumped to the ground. "I have information to trade."

Juliet walked to the handgun, picked it up, and placed the cold steel in her waistband. She didn't relish having the foreign object there, but didn't want to chance Barbara scrambling over to pick it up or making a move in her direction while Juliet had both hands occupied with two weapons.

"I better find Tanner alive out there, or I might have to shoot you again for good measure."

"She's alive. She might have a helluva headache, but she's alive. The girl is alive, too, and I can tell you where she is and who I report to in exchange for a suspended sentence," Barbara pleaded.

"You know, I never saw you. Only Aiden. You could have walked away without a care in the world, but now I'm glad you thought I saw you, because maybe some good will come from this after all. You stay put while I check on Tanner. I'll call for an ambulance."

Juliet realized it wasn't very difficult to shoot another person. All she could think about was that Tanner was in danger and Barbara was the cause. Keeping the rifle close to her body, she entered the living room, scared about what she would find.

Tanner lay crumpled on the floor, and seeing her so vulnerable broke Juliet's heart. She rushed to her side and brushed a lock of hair away as she tried to determine how much damage Barbara had done. At that moment she understood how Tanner could take on the role of judge, jury, and executioner, because she was livid.

"Baby, please open those beautiful eyes of yours." Juliet pressed her fingers against Tanner's neck and confirmed that her pulse was still strong.

"Mmmf," Tanner groaned. Her eyes slowly opened. "Juliet, are you all right? I'm so sorry. I let her in. Fuck, where is she?"

"Ssh, she's nursing a shoulder injury right now. Bleeding all over your cabin. Damn, I hate blood. It leaves such an unsightly stain that you can never get out."

"You're joking, right?"

Juliet nodded. "About the stain, yes, but not about her shoulder. I shot her and was prepared to shoot again. Where's your gun?"

Tanner pointed to the coffee table. "Over there."

"Can you sit up?"

Tanner put her hand on her temple. "Damn, that's going to leave an ugly mark for a while."

Juliet pressed her lips to the place Tanner had touched. "Does this make it better?"

"Yeah. Now go a little lower."

"Um, Tanner, I hate to remind you, but a crazy woman is in the bedroom with blood leaking out of her shoulder."

Tanner sat up and groaned. "I think I might need a few drugs and a...." She leaned over and puked on the floor. "Aw shit. I think I have a concussion and that..." Tanner pointed to the floor "...is going to cause you apoplexy."

Juliet pulled Tanner into her arms. "It's okay. You bought bleach for me."

Tanner laughed. She reached her arm to the coffee table and grabbed her gun and cell phone.

The knock on the door startled them both.

"Geez, now what? It's Grand fucking Central station today," Tanner grumbled.

Juliet lifted the rifle. "Come in very carefully," she shouted.

The door slowly opened and Nick raised his eyebrow. "What the hell is going on?"

"Dead hit man about one hundred yards east of the cabin, injured accomplice in the bedroom." Tanner jerked her head in the direction of the bedroom and winced. "I believe she has a bullet in her shoulder."

"Um, I sure would appreciate it if you pointed that rifle somewhere else, Juliet. I waited until this morning, so there's no need to greet me that way. The rest of the crew will be here shortly. I recommend not welcoming them in the same manner, since they're a lot jumpier than I am."

Juliet flushed. "Sorry, it's just that we had a very...um...interesting evening and morning. Everyone who's come to visit us out here hasn't been the friendliest sort."

"Tanner, you look a little peaked. Have either of you called for the ambulance yet?" Nick asked.

Tanner shook her head. "Aw crap, I shouldn't have done that." She leaned to the side and dry-heaved.

Juliet rubbed Tanner's back. "I'm calling right now."

"I got it." Nick pressed a button on his shoulder mic. "I need an ambulance at the Sullivan cabin. I have an officer down and a gunshot victim." He continued down the hall and pushed the bedroom door open with his foot.

"Barbara?"

Small towns. Juliet knew that Nick would know Barbara and noted the genuine surprise and disappointment in his voice. She had suspected Barbara was stepping out on Old Man Garrison while he took his many hunting and fishing trips, but she hadn't yet figured out with whom. Mystery solved.

Riverville is such an incestuous place. She took comfort in knowing that at least the young girl was still alive. There was one more mystery—where Barbara had taken her. Juliet knew she wasn't going to give that up for free.

Tanner was groaning and Juliet stroked her head in a comforting manner while she laid it on Juliet's shoulder. "I'm coming with you in the ambulance. They should be here any minute. Just hang on, okay?"

"God, my head is killing me. I never imaged a smack to the noggin could hurt so much. My stomach feels like there's worms crawling around inside."

"Sheesh, you just had to put that visual in my head, didn't you? You know I see germs around every corner. It's going to take all my willpower to leave your puddle of...ick...you know, as I accompany you to the hospital. It must be true love. I sure hope you appreciate it."

Tanner smiled. "Oh I do, I really do, but I won't mind if you come back later to take care of it, because if I try to clean that..." Tanner pointed to the pile of puke. "...I'm going to hurl again right on top of it."

Chapter Twenty

Darla was idly looking out the window of the pharmacy when the Crown Victoria rolled up to the sidewalk and the tall, broad-shouldered man walked briskly toward the store. She had a sinking feeling she wasn't going to like whatever was coming her way. The man screamed law enforcement even though he was wearing a suit and tie.

She shrank back from the window and walked behind the counter, where she'd neatly lined up all the drugs on the shelves. That way there would be a protective barrier between her and the man. He stepped into the store and the bell tinkled, announcing his arrival.

He reached into the breast pocket of his jacket and pulled out his badge. "Are you Darla Thompson?" His deep, booming voice was almost soothing.

"Yes. What can I help you with?" She gave him an innocent smile.

"Ma'am, I'm Special Agent Noles, and I'm here to take you in for suspicion of drug trafficking—"

Darla sighed and waved her hand in the air. "Save your breath, I know my rights. I'll call my lawyer."

"Ma'am, I'm sorry, but you didn't let me finish. The reason I'm here instead of the local police is that we found Jessica in your basement. I sure hope you have a good attorney, because the mayor is out for blood, and since Barbara already agreed to provide information in exchange for a deal, that leaves you and her partner holding the bag. We've been working on this child pornography ring for a very long time, so you're holding a very large bag. Drug charges aren't your biggest problem now."

"I don't suppose there's anything or anyone left to offer up at this time," Darla said.

"That's not for me to decide. I'd talk with your attorney sooner rather than later if you hope to get any kind of deal out of this."

He guided her from behind the counter and they walked into the bright sunshine. Outside, Harley rushed toward them.

"Don't say a thing, sis. I'll call Cole."

Darla looked at her brother and wondered if serving him up as a sacrificial lamb would manage to reduce her sentence. She didn't have any illusions that she would do some time. It was the inevitable conclusion of her fateful decision to accept the pile of money Barbara had offered her. She'd assured Darla it would be the easiest ten grand she ever made.

Maybe I'll get some help with my addiction in prison. I've finally hit rock bottom. Sometimes a person had to reach their lowest point before they could climb out of a hole. Was she a bad person, or just someone who had a terrible disease and chose desperate measures when painted into a corner? She didn't really know, but she had certainly been capable of doing horrible things.

✝

The hospital in Vicksburg wasn't that large, but it was the only one within a forty-five-mile radius. Although they were a critical-access hospital, they were one of the best in the state, so Juliet felt satisfied Tanner would get the care she needed.

The ambulance took longer than expected, and Tanner bitched the whole way there. When they finally arrived, it took another hour for them to get her a room.

Juliet smirked as Tanner walked out of the bathroom attempting to hold the back of her hospital gown closed. "You know, I might have to snag a few of those for later because your ass is looking mighty fine in that alluring cotton ensemble."

Tanner scowled as she turned her head to speak to Juliet. "That's not even remotely funny. Keep it up and the next time I feel the urge, I'm spewing all over the front of your T-shirt. Remember those stomach worms I was talking about."

Juliet laughed. She was getting better. Baby steps. A comment like that would have sent a shiver of disgust up her spine a week ago, and today she could laugh at it. She didn't need a therapist—she needed Tanner, who was the best medicine for her at this point. Maybe, just maybe, Juliet was what Tanner needed as well.

Tanner returned to the hospital ER bed and immediately started to grumble. "I don't want to stay the night. I'm perfectly capable of taking care of myself. As soon as those x-rays come back, I want that doctor signing my release. If I hadn't been in such misery, I never would have agreed to put this flimsy cloth on my body. I know it's a conspiracy to get me to remain in the room. You can observe me as well as these yahoos."

"You know I can, and I will if the doctor says it's okay, but if she thinks you need to stay, I'll personally hold you down while the nurse shoves a hypodermic needle in your ass."

"Is it completely bonkers that what you just said makes me totally hot for you? I kinda like this little dominant side to you. Don't get too used to it though. By the way, I also find it beyond hot that you shot Barbara in the shoulder and...I didn't miss the gun that you shoved in your pants. Smokin'. Mmm-hmmm. I have a totally badass girlfriend."

Juliet couldn't help the few tears that leaked down her cheeks after hearing Tanner refer to her as her girlfriend. "You consider me your girlfriend?"

"Well, you don't think I just sleep with anybody, do you? Of course I consider you my girlfriend. It's kind of elementary, don't you think?"

"I wasn't sure where this was heading. You know, now that everything is resolved, I wondered what your future plans were going to be. Are you hanging around, or...?"

Tanner pulled her close and laid a kiss on her that left no room for interpretation. "I'm hanging around wherever you are. If it's in S-ville, fine, I'll adjust. Whither thou goest, I will go."

"Ruth, from the Bible. I love that passage. I never took you for a Bible-thumper," Juliet remarked.

"I'm not, but I read."

Juliet swiveled when a woman cleared her throat. "Hello, Tanner. I have the results of the CT scan, and you're one lucky woman. I don't see any bleeding or possible bruising of the brain, but I'd still like to keep you for observation. Vomiting is a symptom of a more serious concussion."

"Oh no, no, no, no. Please, if I promise to lay low and have someone with me who can watch over me, will you agree to release me?"

Dr. Bridges frowned. "I don't like it. It really is better—"

"Look, I'd rather have your blessing, but it doesn't really matter because I'm checking myself out against medical advice if you don't agree to spring me."

Dr. Bridges narrowed her eyes. "I'll sign you out on one condition. Juliet has to stay with you and follow my discharge instructions to a T."

Tanner grinned. "No problem, Doc. Right, Juliet?"

"Oh now, when it's convenient, my obsessive-compulsive disorder works in your favor. Oh goody, now I have something new to obsess over."

Dr. Bridges raised her eyebrow. "Come with me, Juliet. I'll give you the instructions while the sheriff visits with Tanner. He's pacing outside, and I'm getting cranky about it. I don't like the police taking over my Emergency Department."

✝

Nick shuffled into the room. "You still look like shit, Tanner."

"Whatya want, Nick? I don't have a lot of patience. I hear concussions make a person cranky and change their normally cheery disposition to a raging bitch. Since I generally don't have a cheery disposition, I'll probably become a super bitch in ten seconds flat."

Nick held up his hands. "Hey, I'm not trying to bust your chops here. I just wanted to let you know the kid's safe and back at home with Papa Mayor. The dead guy in the woods was a lowlife named Tony. A real sick fuck. From

193

what I hear, he had over a hundred kills attributed to him personally. He worked for another complete lowlife named Miguel. Miguel is already in custody, but the Feds had to make a deal with Barbara to get their names and Jessica's location, and she'll probably get probation. I still can't believe Barbara and Darla were mixed up in this whole mess. A kiddie-porn ring with a side order of drugs. Oh, and Darla gave up her brother in a last-minute attempt to save her ass."

"I'm not too surprised about Harley or Darla. She has a serious gambling problem, and when I realized Harley was involved in the drug scheme, it only made sense that Darla was too. Sorry I sniped at you. I don't like hospitals. Nothing about sitting around in a gown that shows off your ass is appealing to me."

"So….you and Juliet, huh?"

"Sheesh, it looks like Juliet isn't the only snoop around here. God, I swear this town likes to gossip more than Perez Hilton."

"Who?"

"Perez…the famous Hollywood gossip. Oh never mind. Yeah, I need a good housewife." Tanner looked up and saw a very pissed lover staring at her. She hadn't noticed when Juliet re-entered the room. "Hey, I'm kidding, honey."

"Ooh, you better start practicing your groveling right now." Nick laughed. "I think that's my cue to leave."

"Coward," Tanner muttered. "Look, I just took a major blow to the head. Sometimes people say stupid shit after that, right, Doc?" Tanner glimpsed the doctor walking by her room.

Dr. Bridges poked her head in the room for a second. "Hey, don't put me in the middle of whatever fairy tale you're spewing." And then she walked away.

"She's just pissed because I threatened to leave against medical advice," Tanner sputtered.

"Bye, Tanner, Juliet. Good luck." Nick waved as he walked out of the room.

"Oh thank God, saved by the bell." Tanner grinned.

Juliet turned her head and Tanner saw her focus on Cisco as he entered the room.

†

Juliet wondered who the attractive Hispanic man striding confidently into the room was.

"Man, I can't leave you alone for one second. A bonk on the head, huh? Maybe that will improve your nasty disposition."

"Hey, Cisco, meet my lovely girlfriend, Juliet."

"Okay, that last comment just got you a free 'get out of jail' card, but if you ever refer to me as your housewife again, I'll personally smack the other side of your head to give you a matching bump."

"Ooh, I just love it when you talk all tough and commanding." Tanner grinned.

Cough, cough. Cisco held out his hand to Juliet. "I offer my condolences."

"Huh?"

"Oh, I just want to say how sorry I am that Tanner got her meaty claws in you. If you ever come over to the other side, I'm single."

"Stop hitting on my girlfriend, you jackass. So what brings you to Vicksburg and why didn't you answer my calls?"

"Sorry I was out of touch. I needed to be off the grid for a bit, and it sounds like the shit hit the fan while I was taking care of some business."

"It's okay, Cisco. Juliet knows everything, and I mean everything, about me. You don't have to talk in code. How'd you hear about our adventure?"

"Good news travels fast, and to think I didn't even have to lend a hand. You already owe me. Sorry, bud, a debt is a debt."

"I know, I know, but give a gal a break here. I'm a bit banged up at the moment. Just a little breathing room, please."

"So...I caught a little bit of your conversation with the sheriff. You already know they rounded up Miguel. He's not too happy. They seriously clipped his wings, but word on the street is that if he gets out of this mess, he's gunning for you. Personally, my prediction is that the snake will be out in less than three hours. Your paranoia may just be your saving grace, my friend. Look, all joking aside—if you need a place to crash until some of the heat blows over, I got your back. I won't even count that as another favor," Cisco offered.

Tanner frowned. "I don't like the sound of that."

"I didn't think you would. That's why I came all the way over here to give you the news in person and to provide you a personal escort to my lair."

"I'm gonna take you up on that offer, because I'm not risking one beautiful hair on Juliet's head."

"Wow, I never thought I'd see this day again. Tanner Sullivan is in luuuv. It's kinda cute," Cisco taunted.

"Listen, I do need another favor from you. I'm not sure if Miguel has had any time to regroup, but I'm not taking any chances. Do you think you can get us some vests and maybe a few guns? They took the rifle and my personal firearm. Juliet, can you let the doc know that suddenly I'm not doing so well and have agreed to stay a few more hours? There's no way that bastard is going to catch me flat-footed and unaware," Tanner pronounced.

"Consider it done. I got a guy watching out to make sure nobody gets in to see you while you're temporarily laid up. He's discreet, but good. Give me a couple of hours and I'll be back with your gear."

After Cisco left, Juliet asked, "Is all this really necessary? I mean they arrested the guy, didn't they?"

Tanner's face lost any amount of humor. "Guys like Miguel don't ever let things go. Now do you understand why my brand of justice is the only real option?"

"You're going to go after him, aren't you?"

The single nod scared Juliet more than hiding out in the forest had.

Chapter Twenty-one

Miguel didn't feel any sense of satisfaction that his lawyer had managed to get him released in under two hours. The heels of his shoes clipped across the tile in an angry staccato. He waved at his right-hand man to follow as he rushed to get into the waiting car.

He slammed the door shut and reached for his cellphone. The time for finesse had long passed. This was gang warfare. He would revert to his roots. An old-fashioned drive-by shooting might be messy, but it did the trick.

"Hello, Steven. Yeah, I need a special job done. Round up the boys and take a quick trip to Vicksburg for me. You need to do this today. I'll tell you when and where as soon as I get more information.... I think in front of the hospital might be best once my problem is released. Oh, and I have one more job for you in that little shithole. That double-crossing bitch will get what's coming to her. I never should have trusted her.... Yeah, Barbara made a deal with the cops.... I'll be in touch, so stay by your phone," Miguel barked.

"Where to, Boss?" the driver asked.

"I think maybe an early dinner at that little Italian place across from the club, and then we can head there afterward. I need to blow off a little steam tonight."

"You got it, Boss."

Once the boys dealt with the women, he could relax. Most of the time his business ran very smoothly, but today everything seemed to be imploding in his face. He didn't have the patience to take his time seeking vengeance. He had a reputation to maintain. Once all this blew over, he would resume his business, because there was never a shortage of sick fucks who wanted to see the kind of pornography he produced, and they paid top dollar for it. This time he'd be more careful choosing his business partners.

In some ways, getting to Barbara would be easier than snuffing out Tanner, because Barbara was in Seattle. A car full of Hispanics driving down the street wouldn't stick out like a sore thumb in a much bigger city. He had connections in the Seattle Police Department, and the minute she finished with the cops, she was a dead woman.

†

Barbara had spent three hours straight talking with the special task force. She gave them as much information as she could, and they had promised to take care of her. Using Riverville and S-Ville as their base of operations was Miguel's idea. She needed a legitimate reason to move there, so she'd seduced both Old Man Garrison and Nick. Nick was the perfect choice to throw off any potential suspicions. Aiden had been tasked with taking care of moving around the filming to the vacant houses he found through Margie. It had been a perfect setup until Aiden took the mayor's daughter and created the need for Barbara to hide her away until they could resolve the problem.

She hadn't really considered that her life might be in danger. She'd only wanted to avoid jail time. She hadn't even contacted her husband. The look in Nick's eyes told her that he wouldn't be much help to her with her legal difficulties. The marriage was a farce anyway, a means to an end. At least she had enjoyed her time with Nick.

They'd advised her that she might be a candidate for the witness protection program. When they presented that option, she didn't even consider asking Garrison to join her, and Nick certainly wouldn't be interested. It would be just her starting a new life somewhere else. She wasn't even sure she would call her husband. She'd let the marshals take care of that for her. They'd looked at her strangely when she'd suggested that, but she didn't care if they judged her. Maybe the program would find somewhere warm for her and she'd get her little slice of heaven with a pristine, white, sandy beach after all.

The special agent at her side led her by her elbow toward the waiting car. Just as she was about to get into the vehicle that would take her to a safe house and then on to wherever they intended to relocate her, she heard tires screeching and looked up just in time to see and hear the buzz of the passenger-side, tinted windows of the approaching car come down slowly. She almost didn't register what she was seeing as the long barrels of two automatic weapons pointed in her direction. Her last thought before she died was, *I wonder if I'll see Miguel in hell.*

Barbara never made it to the car, and neither did Special Agent Noles, who'd accompanied her to Seattle after he'd picked up Darla. He was a casualty of a war he'd had no hand in starting.

†

200

Tanner was restless. Her head was killing her, and Cisco seemed to be taking his sweet time getting back to the hospital. She knew she was being an ingrate, but she couldn't help feeling agitated. As sure as she knew the sun would come up the next day, she knew Miguel was planning her demise, and he wouldn't want to bring in another hit man. This time the attempt on their lives would be messy and disorganized, but not less dangerous. Brute force and a spray of bullets worked as well as finesse and in-depth planning.

Miguel was pissed and would come at them hard and fast, using inner-city guerilla warfare. Tanner thought there was a good chance they would strike as soon as she walked out of the hospital, which was why she wanted an extra layer of protection. The vests might not protect their head or limbs, but at least they would give the three of them a fighting chance at survival.

But Miguel didn't know that Tanner was also a predator and that she planned to hunt the bastard down that evening. She wouldn't let the grass grow on this job. She had her own pipeline of intelligence and always marveled at the information Cisco was able to obtain so quickly.

Cisco was all smiles when he entered the hospital room carrying a large duffel bag. "Hello, lovely ladies. I've got early Christmas presents for y'all."

"'Bout bloody time, you hack," Tanner joked.

"Now, now, now, is that any way to talk to your benefactor?" Cisco asked.

"Benefactor, my ass. I'll be paying for this favor until I'm ninety-nine."

"Do you two always needle each other?" Juliet asked.

"Yep," Cisco and Tanner said in stereo.

Tanner reached out and wiggled her fingers. "Gimme, gimme. I hope you brought the good stuff."

Cisco glared. "Of course I brought the good stuff, you ingrate." He tossed the bag on the bed. "Take a look."

Tanner unzipped the bag and began pawing through it. Her grin widened. "Holy shit, Cisco, how did you get ahold of three Armor Express vests? These are expensive, over three K, and three Glock G43s. My favorite weapon. You done good, my friend."

Cisco shrugged. "Did you really think I wouldn't get the best for you?" He narrowed his gaze. "I have one condition."

"Oh crap, I knew there would be strings," Tanner complained.

"I'm coming with you tonight to hunt that piece of crap down. Can your girlfriend handle a Glock?"

"How hard can it be? Granny taught me how to shoot a rifle, so I think I can handle a little handgun." Juliet jutted out her chest.

Tanner groaned. "Um, a Glock is not a little handgun and they're kinda different, babe. You wouldn't happen to have an extra rifle in that duffle? You know, like Mary Poppins and her magic bag or something?" Tanner asked.

"I can give her a few pointers today before we head out. I've got a safe place to take both of you until things cool down. I don't think she'll really need it after we do cleanup tonight, but just in case Miguel has multiple teams on this, I'll make sure she's prepared," Cisco assured.

Tanner took a deep breath. "I'm not sure I like leaving her alone, but I guess having your assistance might ensure we end this thing once and for all. You're sure we can get her to a safe place? Maybe one of your pals can lend a hand."

"Consider it done." Cisco waved his hand in the air.

"So what's the word on the street?" Tanner asked.

"Miguel called for a drive-by. Be ready, because there's a car a few blocks away. If I thought I could clip their wings before they made their move, I would have. I have the utmost confidence the two of us can eliminate the threat before any real damage is done, but you have to be ready. That hit to the noggin hasn't slowed you down, has it?"

Tanner didn't want to admit that her head was pounding. Cisco was watching her carefully, and she could tell he would be skeptical no matter what she said.

"I got this. I promise. I wouldn't risk Juliet's life without feeling confident about the additional preparations that tip the scales in our favor. Can your guy lend a hand?" Tanner asked.

"Maybe, but he didn't really sign up for that. I'll take out the driver, and then you gotta be prepared to take out as many of the backseat passengers as you can. You ready? The bullets will likely spray all over, but they could get lucky. You sure you don't want to involve law enforcement?"

Tanner shook her head. "Juliet, I think it's time for the doc to release me. I'm suddenly feeling so much better. Look, I want you to put on this vest even though I don't want you coming out of the hospital until I return and get you after their attack is neutralized."

"I want one of those guns and quick instructions on how to use it. I'm coming with you," Juliet insisted.

"Please, Juliet. I can't concentrate on taking them out if I have to worry about you. Trust me on this. You coming with us puts me in greater danger than if Cisco and I take care of this on our own. Will you do this for me?" Tanner pleaded.

"You don't play fair," Juliet grumbled.

"The important question is, did I win this tiny disagreement?" Tanner asked.

Juliet nodded. "I'll do it your way, but don't expect me to be happy."

Tanner pulled off her flimsy hospital gown and grabbed the T-shirt sitting on the chair after insisting that the nurse "better not fucking remove my clothes from the room."

Juliet raised her eyebrow when Tanner finished putting on her first layer of clothing and added the vest.

Tanner pointed at the vest that was in the duffle and motioned for Juliet to follow suit.

Cisco smiled as he unbuttoned his shirt, donned the third vest, and finished dressing.

Tanner checked the clip on the Glock and grinned at him. "I hope we don't rattle the doc, on second thought, maybe we ought to just sneak out. She was ready to discharge me several hours ago, so I think it'll be fine. You never know who they have watching the hospital. Another element of surprise can't hurt."

Tanner jumped up, turned to Juliet, and gave her a quick kiss on the lips. "Wish us luck, babe."

Juliet crossed her arms over her bulletproof vest and grunted.

Tanner and Cisco emerged from the room and nearly ran into the doctor.

"Where do you think you're going, and how the hell did you get those guns into the room? The hospital is a no-gun zone." She held her hand out. "Gimme those. Please don't tell me that you're wearing bulletproof vests. If you turn my ED into a war zone, I swear I will hunt you down and have you both restrained."

Tanner danced around the doc and Cisco quickly followed. "Gotta fly, Doc. Keep your staff clear from any doors and you'll be fine."

Tanner heard the doc call out, "Hey, I haven't completed your discharge papers yet."

"Mail them to me." Tanner stepped onto the rubber mat in front of the automated ED doors, and they swept open as she activated them.

†

Juliet had watched Tanner activate the Glock and decided it wouldn't be that hard to sneak out and play backup. If Tanner didn't know she was following in her footsteps, she wouldn't worry and Juliet could lend a hand without distracting her. She waited a couple of minutes and crept out of the room. When Dr. Bridges glared at her, she pressed her finger to her lips and whispered, "Sshh, don't yell. I need to catch up with Tanner without her realizing I'm following."

"You people are crazy. I have the amateur SWAT team swarming my ED and I don't like that one bit. If as much as one bullet enters my hallowed space...."

Juliet didn't hear the rest as several things bombarded her senses when she stepped outside.

The pungent smell of burning rubber assaulted her nostrils. Squealing tires brought her head around to see a black sedan careening down the street. Gunfire erupted as the shattering front windshield exploded. A spider-web pattern formed on it, and Juliet wondered why that mesmerized her as she took her focus away from the pandemonium unraveling before her. Bullets pinged around her, and she swiveled her head to watch Tanner get off several rounds at the out-of-control car. Cisco seemed to be firing into the backseat as well.

Juliet felt a sharp pain in her chest and looked down in horror. She realized the vest didn't completely protect her from harm as she fell back on her ass and heard her gun clatter on the cement.

Finally, the car zigzagged and smashed into the column holding up the overhang above the Emergency Department entrance.

Tanner and Cisco ran to the car, guns pointed at the backseat, but silence greeted them. Juliet lay back on the ground, holding her bruised chest. She should probably feel sorrow for the dead gang members, but she wasn't able to muster that emotion. She felt relief, not regret or sadness that they were all probably dead. Neither Tanner nor Cisco appeared to have taken any bullets to their vests or any other parts of their bodies.

"Clear," Cisco shouted.

With her weapon still drawn, Tanner yanked the door open and leaned inside. Juliet saw her shake her head.

The screaming of sirens jolted Juliet from watching Cisco and Tanner secure the area. She listened to the swish of the electric doors and came face-to-face with a very pissed-off Dr. Bridges.

The doctor leaned down, looking Juliet straight in the eye. "Jesus H. Christ. I knew you all were going to send more patients my way when you walked out in your military garb. I see you took a direct hit to your chest, so I'm ordering an x-ray. Are you hurt anywhere else?"

Juliet shook her head. "I don't think so."

Dr. Bridges narrowed her eyes. "Blood on your arm suggests otherwise. Come on, Rambo, let's get you inside. The other two bozos look okay, and I don't hear any more bullets pinging outside my ED, so I suppose those sirens will help clean up the mess your friends started. Hey, amateur SWAT team, your teammate is injured, so get your butts back inside after you finish with the police. I need to take her to a room and check her out."

Juliet looked down, saw the blood on her arm, and promptly passed out.

†

Tanner almost hadn't needed to check the car out because she already knew she'd hit her mark with two of them and Cisco had incapacitated the driver with a clean shot to the head. They were fortunate Miguel had only sent three people. The automatic weapons were a real danger, but fortunately, they were able to stop the barrage of bullets relatively quickly.

After checking to make sure all three were dead, Tanner was pleased with herself until she heard the doctor yell out. She looked back and saw Juliet sitting on the ground with the doc, and then she slumped as Dr. Bridges caught her and kept her from hitting her head on the concrete.

"Son of a bitch," Tanner muttered.

"What?" Cisco asked.

"Look, the cavalry will arrive in a few seconds because I hear the sirens, but something's wrong with Juliet." Tanner began to run to the door. "Can you fill them in while I go with her?" she called over her shoulder.

"Sure thing, leave me to explain everything. You owe me big," Cisco yelled.

"Yeah, yeah, put it on my tab." Tanner waved her hand in the air.

When Tanner reached Juliet and Dr. Bridges, she squatted and grabbed Juliet's hand. Panic rose in her throat as her breathing increased. It felt like déjà vu. She couldn't lose Juliet, not like she'd lost Faith. She couldn't understand why she always escaped without harm and the crossfire seemed to catch gentle souls like Faith and Juliet.

"She was hit, wasn't she?"

"She's going to be fine, just help me get her into a room. I'm not sure which injury I'm more concerned about right now, the bruise on her chest or the bullet in her arm. I'll know soon enough."

Tanner put one arm under Juliet's neck and the other in the crook of her knees. "You go get things ready. I got her."

"All right."

As the doctor rushed inside, Tanner lifted Juliet and followed her. A man with a gurney met her at the door. She gently laid Juliet on it. When Juliet's eyes fluttered open, Tanner felt a great sense of relief.

"Tanner?"

"I'm right here, honey, and the doc is going to take great care of you. I promise." Tanner kissed Juliet's forehead. "You're my girl, right? Don't forget that."

Juliet smiled. "I wanted to help. I'm sorry I'm not very good at following directions."

"Sshh. We'll talk about this later."

"Take her down to X-ray and I'll meet you there. I'll look at her arm while we're waiting for the tech," Dr. Bridges commanded the young man who'd brought the gurney. "You stay out here. I'll come get you when I know more."

Tanner nodded. She didn't want to rile the doctor any further than she already had. She slumped into one of the chairs in the waiting room and waited for the rest of her terrible, horrible, no good, very bad day to end, just like Alexander in her favorite children's book. She wasn't sure if moving to Australia was the answer, but maybe S-Ville was bad for their health and they should consider living somewhere else.

Tanner cringed as Cisco made a beeline for her with four police officers in tow. Their grim faces told the story. She would be lucky if they made it out of Vicksburg by midnight. She had to find a way to zip over to Seattle and strike while the iron was hot. She needed to end this once and for all.

Tanner had started to reach into her vest pocket to pull out her badge when two of the officers pulled their weapons and pointed them in her direction.

"Easy. I'm just getting out my ID and badge. South Riverville Police Department." Tanner held up her ID.

One of the officers smirked. "There's a police department in S-Ville?"

"Yes, there is, you pompous ass, and if I'm not mistaken, the three dead guys are employees of one very bad dude that some incredibly important people want locked up. Seems we've stumbled upon a kiddie pornography ring in S-ville, and as a result, an FBI unit that's been watching this group for years now just got a huge break. We, on the other hand, are on the receiving end of an unhappy douche bag. I guess we poked a huge hornet's nest. Since drive-bys aren't that common here in Vicksburg, I imagine your department might require some additional assistance. Don't look a gift horse in the mouth, boys. Cisco is a top-notch law enforcement man from a special unit, and I'm sure he'll help you unravel everything while I go check on my girlfriend." Tanner winked at Cisco as she slinked down the hall looking for Juliet.

She poked her head in all the rooms but didn't find Juliet. She kept walking down the hall and saw the sign for radiology.

"Bingo. I'll bet she's still in X-ray."

Tanner cautiously opened the door and saw Juliet wincing as the tech positioned her on the table. She didn't think the heavy lead vest was helping. She slipped inside and flattened herself against the back wall so she wouldn't be in the way but could lend Juliet some moral support. She gave Juliet a tiny wave, put her finger to her lips, and grinned.

"I see you slithering against the wall. You must be the girlfriend the doc was complaining about. When I activate the machine, you need to step out, but while I'm getting her into position, you might as well hold her hand," the tech stated.

Tanner frowned when she saw the large bandage on Juliet's arm. "How come you're here in X-ray instead of them taking care of your arm?"

Juliet sounded like she was having a hard time breathing when she answered. "They want to make sure I haven't broken a rib and punctured a lung in the process. That took precedence over the relatively minor flesh wound on my arm. I'm still gonna get some stitches, but they aren't too worried about it."

"Time to step out into the hall now. Extra radiation is the last thing you need. You're already a crazy woman," the tech joked.

Tanner was worried about Juliet's heavy breathing and hoped it was due to the pain from the bruising and not a punctured lung. She wanted to stay by Juliet's side to make sure she was no longer in danger, but she needed to get to Seattle and take out Miguel. That was the only way to end this mini war.

Reluctantly she returned to the waiting room, where the police were quietly talking with Cisco. Something seemed off, as the group was huddled together, whispering among themselves and Cisco looked concerned.

Tanner approached them. "Hey, what's going on?"

"They took out Barbara and Special Agent Noles. Some agents are on their way, and they want to talk with us," Cisco relayed.

"Tomorrow. I'll go wherever they want me to go and provide whatever information they require. I need to stay with Juliet right now. If they force me to do this tonight, then they can kiss any information Juliet or I have good-bye because I'm not saying shit."

"You heard the lady. Better run that up the flagpole. Tanner is the most stubborn person I know. If she says she's not talking until tomorrow, then either arrest her or connect back with us when she's ready." He turned to Tanner. "So I guess they're going to admit her?"

"I think so. Probably has a punctured lung."

"Damn. I thought the vests would do a better job."

"Well, it did save her life. I guess we should be thankful for that."

"I suppose," Cisco admitted.

"We'll be back in the morning, and then we can wrap this up. Thank you for your cooperation," the tall officer stated.

After the police officers left, Tanner asked, "So can you get any more intel? I'd really like to know where Miguel is hanging out tonight."

"Already know that. He has a club he frequents. I think it's a safe bet he'll be there for a while. How are you planning on being in two places at once? Aren't you staying here with Juliet?"

Tanner looked at her feet. "You know I gotta do this, right? I can't let him get to her. I won't let what happened to Faith happen to Juliet."

"Do you want me to stay here with her?" Cisco asked.

"I can't ask you to do that."

"You're not asking, I'm offering. It's a special I'm running. Buy two favors and get the third free."

"Thanks, Cisco. I'd feel better if someone trained that I trust was watching over her. I don't think I can look her in the eyes and leave tonight. Will you explain it to her? I'll be back as soon as I can."

"How are you going to establish an alibi if you leave now?" Cisco asked.

"Shit, good question. I guess I'll have to slip out a little later. It'll be a good thing if a lot of the medical personnel see me here by Juliet's side. I'll need to leave soon if I have any hope of catching him tonight."

"You've got plenty of time. He usually stays out until after midnight."

"If we both stay with Juliet, then I can slip out and you can keep the nurses from coming into the room and noticing I'm not there. If they're busy, they'll be more likely to agree to you letting them know if she needs anything," Tanner suggested.

"Yeah, I think that might just work."

†

Juliet wasn't happy about needing to stay in the hospital for observation, but at least Tanner and Cisco were there for entertainment. When the doctor told her how serious her two cracked ribs and the resulting collapsed lung might be, Juliet decided not to fight her. Her chest hurt every time she took a breath, and she just wanted to get some good drugs and fall asleep. She also thought it would be a good idea if Tanner took the other bed so they could observe her as well, but Tanner adamantly refused. The doctor did a nice job of stitching Juliet up and was pleased the bullet had merely grazed her arm, though she shook her head and tsked the entire time.

Tanner was pinching her nose, and Juliet suspected her head was killing her as she sat in the chair next to Juliet's bed holding her hand while Cisco scrolled through his smartphone. Juliet thought he looked especially bored but didn't want to leave his friend in case something happened.

She couldn't imagine what else that might be. The men who shot at them were all dead. Weren't they safe now? Tanner didn't act like they were safe, though, and that concerned her.

"Why don't you ask the nurse if you can get something for your head? I know it's killing you," Juliet suggested.

"I'm fine. You should worry about your own level of pain because you're not fooling me. I see you wincing."

"Oh, for Christ's sake, I'm going out to the nurses' station and getting someone to give you both something. I fucking hate martyrs," Cisco grumbled.

After he left, Tanner laughed. "I guess he told us. Look, I have no intention of lecturing you while you're in pain, but we do need to talk about your inability to follow the simplest direction. Are you always this noncompliant?"

Juliet noted Tanner's smile, which took the sting out of the gentle chastising. "Yeah, kinda. I'm a rebel with obsessive-compulsive disorder. I used to ignore any cautions—like the ones on my chemistry set warning which chemicals you weren't supposed to combine. It was like a neon sign leading me down a bad path. Some people call me nosy; I'd say I'm excessively curious."

Tanner brought Juliet's hand to her mouth and feathered it with kisses. "I didn't even get to say good-bye to Faith, but it would have been far worse to see her die in my arms. I don't want to lose you because you're too curious for your own good. Remember that curiosity killed the cat."

"Yeah, but satisfaction brought him back," Juliet quipped.

"I'll keep you plenty satisfied, so can you please not put yourself in front of flying bullets again?"

Juliet shifted in her bed and felt a sharp pain in her ribs. "Damn that hurts." She looked up and saw a nurse and Cisco enter her hospital room.

"It would be better if you didn't move around a lot. How about if I give you something to help you sleep? Doc said I can give the hardheaded one some Tylenol for her headache." The nurse chuckled. "Those were her words, not mine." She opened her hand to reveal a medication cup with two small, white pills. "Here, take these and use that recliner if you insist on staying in the room with your partner. I really shouldn't let you both stay, but I'm in a generous mood tonight."

Tanner took the pills, and Juliet didn't quite understand the look that passed between her and Cisco.

The nurse shuffled over to Juliet's IV and injected something into the line. "There, that should help with the pain and also allow you to get some rest. Hey, big guy, go sit in that other chair and try not to keep these two women from getting the rest they need. I'll check back in a few hours to make sure everything is okay."

"Hey, no need, that's what I'm here for. I'll watch over them, and if they need something I'll come get you. All right?" he offered.

The nurse nodded once and walked out.

"Before I nod off to dreamland, what was that look I saw? You two have something up your sleeve, and I want to know what it is," Juliet demanded.

"It's better not to know. Just trust me, okay?" Tanner responded.

"Do I have a choice?" Juliet asked.

"No," Cisco and Tanner answered together.

Juliet couldn't believe how tired she felt, and her eyes started to droop from the effects of the medication the nurse had just administered into her IV. Injected drugs always worked so much quicker.

She soon lost the battle to stay awake, but just before she nodded off, she vaguely heard some murmuring between Cisco and Tanner. All she caught was "dead man," and then it was lights out. That seemed to happen to her a lot ever since she got involved with Tanner.

Chapter Twenty-two

Miguel sprawled out in a booth, legs spread, sipping his drink. He had a female companion on his left and his arm draped loosely over her shoulder. Raoul, his right-hand man, stood off to the side, waiting for Miguel to decide to call it a night.

Miguel watched as Raoul answered his cell phone and furrowed his brow. That could only mean something had not gone as planned this evening.

After Raoul ended the call, he whispered into Miguel's ear, "Barbara and the agent are taken care of, but the cop and snoop are still alive. Our men are dead, and the cops are swarming around the hospital now."

Miguel didn't react, but he was seething inside. Perhaps he should just let it all go because Barbara was dead and she was their key witness. Without her testimony, there wasn't much that would tie this mess back to him. He knew he should consider the matter all wrapped up, but he hated the notion that any potential loose end was out there. He would have to meditate on this and decide his course of action.

"Thank you, Raoul. We'll stay another hour, and then we'll head home. I'll decide later on how to take care of that business you informed me of, but right now I have the company of a lovely lady and I don't intend to abandon her." Miguel turned his head toward his companion and kissed her.

Although Miguel was a ruthless bastard, in public he displayed impeccable manners and treated women with the utmost respect. The strong influence from his Hispanic mother was responsible for that dichotomy. He tried to ignore the fact she would be very disappointed in what he had chosen to do with his life. *God rest her soul.*

†

Tanner broke every speed limit after she'd snuck out of the hospital undetected by the police or hospital personnel. She'd almost run into Dr. Bridges but managed to duck into an empty room at the very last moment where she waited until the doctor rushed past. An incoming trauma had distracted the staff, and that worked to her advantage.

Cisco had provided her keys to his car and given her a slim jim, which she had used to open Miguel's car. She was losing patience as she waited for him and his bodyguard. She'd arrived around half past midnight and had only been there for ten minutes, but she was anxious to finish this.

Either incapacitating both of them at the same time or one shortly after the other would be tricky. She didn't want to kill the bodyguard. He didn't meet the *code*. The syringes Cisco had prepared were critical to her success. Cisco really was a good friend.

He had provided her with detailed intel on Miguel and his habits. From what she'd learned, Miguel always sat in the front passenger's seat. His bodyguard always drove and opened the door for him. It was unusual for someone like

Miguel to forego the more traditional chauffeuring approach, but Cisco had told her Miguel had started as a driver and never wanted his bodyguard not to feel like an equal. He preferred to treat his employees with respect. She counted on the fact the bodyguard had parked the car in a dark location and they wouldn't see her hiding in the back until it was too late. A needle to the neck of the bodyguard to incapacitate him and then her pronouncement of Miguel's sentence was the plan. She would put a gun to the back of Miguel's head, and if necessary she would shoot him, but she preferred to use the needle first and then a quick tightening of the rope around his neck. After taking care of business she would be on her way back to the hospital and Juliet.

Tanner watched as Miguel swaggered out into the parking lot, unaware that he only had minutes to live. She crouched low behind the seats, waiting to pounce on the unsuspecting targets. The door creaked open, and Tanner's heart pounded loudly as she forced herself to wait for the driver to slide into his seat.

The click of the seat belts and the start of the engine signaled her cue to make her move. Tanner popped up from the backseat like a jack-in-the-box and plunged the syringe into the bodyguard's neck. She thanked whatever higher power existed she'd been born ambidextrous and had equally fine motor skills in both hands. She pressed her gun firmly against Miguel's head.

"What the fuck…!" he exclaimed.

"Hello, Miguel. Make one move and I'll blow your brains out. If your friend here makes a move, I'll blow your brains out, but I suspect he'll be in dreamland soon."

As if her words triggered the reaction, the driver slumped forward.

"Who the hell are you?" Miguel asked.

"I am your judge, jury, and executioner. Your first fatal mistake was hiring that piece of shit Aiden, who killed a very special person in my life. That was strike one," Tanner calmly explained.

"So you were the one who took out Aiden," Miguel stated.

Tanner ignored him. "Strike two was when you sent the hit man after Juliet, and strike three was your failed attempt to eliminate both Juliet and myself outside the hospital. I really want your family to bury a decent-looking corpse, so I would prefer if you didn't make any sudden moves."

"I sincerely regret my decision to send my men to eliminate you. I should have decided things were resolved after taking care of the others who were more directly involved. Perhaps we can come to an amiable agreement— one that will satisfy both our needs. I will ensure your safety and the safety of Juliet. I will also compensate you for your previous loss. I would like to clarify that Aiden acted on his own and I did not give the order of execution on the police officer."

"Too late, Miguel. My judgment is final and your sentence is death."

Tanner plunged the second syringe into the muscle, lassoed his neck with the rope, and tightened it against his Adam's apple. She knew how long it would take to complete the sentence she'd imposed on Miguel. Putting continuous pressure on a person's neck for two to three minutes seemed like an unusually long amount of time, but that was what it would take to ensure his death. She thought about how Hollywood tended to get this all wrong by reducing murder to a dramatic five to ten second video clip. She supposed the gruesome reality that death wouldn't occur for several minutes wouldn't necessarily appeal to the masses, but it was a clean method of killing nonetheless. Perhaps another tidy approach was chemical injection, but she didn't know enough about the correct dosage of drugs to ensure death and wasn't about to take any chances.

Tanner had deviated from her usual method with Aiden, but that was very personal to her, and her rage overtook her reason. She didn't want to make tying the two executions together easy by killing both men in the same manner.

Her gloved hands began to cramp after five minutes, which she determined was more than enough time. She pressed two fingers against Miguel's neck to make sure he was dead and slipped out of the car. A quick look around reassured her no witnesses were present who might cause issues for her later.

†

Tanner spotted the police car in the median well before she made the grave error of speeding past. Slowing to the speed limit, she breathed a sigh of relief as she bypassed the semi-hidden vehicle and continued down the highway. She knew she needed to return to the hospital and Juliet's bedside before the nurse made her rounds and insisted on double-checking her patient. Nurses were like that. No matter what the family said, they always wanted to make sure the patient was doing well.

Tanner wondered what Juliet might think if she woke up and Tanner wasn't resting by her side with their hands clasped. *Would she worry?* If Tanner were in her place, she would be concerned. She didn't want to worry Juliet unnecessarily, but if she had to do it all over again, she'd make the same choice.

The dull thud of her headache became an increasing annoyance. She would be glad to stretch out in the reclining chair the hospital staff had provided for her. It wasn't the most comfortable bed, but at this point she was beyond exhausted and anything would do.

Finally, the sign announcing the exit to Vicksburg flashed in her headlights and she was five minutes away. She glanced at her watch. It was only two o'clock. She'd made good time.

She pulled back into the parking space Cisco had initially chosen. It was far enough away from the entrance that no one had parked there while she was away on her mission. She hoped no one had noticed the missing car.

Tanner needed to get back into the hospital without anyone spotting her. This was the tricky part, because at this time of night, there wasn't much activity. A person walking into the emergency department entrance was something the sole admitting representative would readily notice.

Tanner peeked at the woman sitting at the desk and willed her to have an urgent need for a bathroom break. As the woman stood and left the room, Tanner nearly did a happy dance on the other side of the door. She rushed through the doors and quickly walked down the hall, praying she wouldn't run into any hospital personnel.

She turned a corner and nearly collided with two potential witnesses, but she had heard their laughter and ducked into a supply closet to avoid detection. She listened carefully until she was satisfied they'd passed by and headed in the opposite direction from where she needed to go. Ten more minutes of this cat-and-mouse game was working on her last nerve. Her headache was intensifying as she navigated her way back to Juliet.

Tanner heard a commotion just outside of Juliet's room and hung back, straining to listen.

†

Cisco heard the door click and jumped to his feet. He knew the nurse would attempt to check on Juliet and Tanner again.

He rushed to the door and caught it before the nurse managed to open it all the way, then sent the short, rotund older woman his most charming smile and placed his finger to his lips.

"Sshh. They're both sleeping now. I know you would agree that rest is the best thing for both of them. I really would hate for you to wake them after the day they both had. I promise I'll come get you or use the Call button if anything changes, but can you please let them sleep?" he pleaded.

"I really should at least check on them," she waffled.

"Honestly, I would prefer it if you didn't. I know you have other patients that probably need your attention. Go ahead and attend to them. I've got this."

"Well, if you're sure. Please use the Call button if anything changes."

"I will. I feel better knowing there's such a dedicated nurse working this shift and taking care of my friends," Cisco gushed.

The nurse blushed. "Thank you."

He slipped back into the room and sat down in the chair. He tried to remain quiet, but when the chair scratched against the floor as he repositioned himself, Juliet's eyes fluttered open.

"Cisco? Where's Tanner?" Her groggy voice filled the quiet room.

"Here, I'm right here, honey," Tanner whispered.

Cisco turned his head and saw Tanner as she slipped into the room. He mouthed to her, "Perfect timing."

Tanner leaned over the bed and kissed Juliet's forehead. The look in Tanner's eyes was the same one she used to give Faith. He was happy his friend had allowed herself to fall in love again.

✝

Tanner skulked around the corner, waiting for the interchange between Cisco and the nurse to end. He was such a good friend. In the last week, she'd racked up enough favors to fill a truck. She knew he was both kidding and serious about the fact she would owe him. Fortunately, Cisco's favors involved something she didn't mind helping him with—taking care of the scum of the earth. He had his own list of individuals he wanted erased from existence.

When Cisco went back into the room and the nurse scurried down the hallway to answer the Call light for a man moaning loudly, Tanner snuck back into the room.

When she heard Juliet's voice, it broke her heart. She worried Juliet had called for her when she was gone, but a quick glance at Cisco allayed her fears. He gave her the thumbs-up sign, and she stepped forward to reassure Juliet.

Tanner thought an angel must have been looking out for her because her mission to take care of Miguel went more smoothly than she'd envisioned. Every time police or hospital personnel were ready to catch her, something or someone intervened to alert her and she'd managed to dodge detection. Tanner wasn't a religious sort of person and didn't necessarily buy into all that higher-power crap, but in this case, she looked up at the ceiling and sent a small thank-you to Faith. If anyone had been elevated to angel status, it would be her former lover.

She was convinced Faith was watching over her and approved of Juliet. Faith would have liked Juliet. She suddenly realized that while she would never forget Faith, her mourning period had ended. She was ready to move on, and she wanted to include Juliet in whatever future unfolded for her.

The big question Tanner still had was if Juliet could tolerate her darkness and her need to hunt down and execute whomever she determined deserved that final sentence of justice. She didn't want to think about what might happen if Juliet was unable to understand this fundamental part of who she was. She didn't think she could give that up even for someone she had fallen deeply in love with. Time would tell though. Faith had struggled with this but eventually came to accept her, warts and all.

Juliet moaned and broke Tanner from her reverie.

She looked into Juliet's pain-filled eyes. "Cisco, can you get the nurse? Juliet is in pain again."

Cisco jumped up and rushed out of the room.

Tanner smoothed Juliet's furrowed brow. "We'll get you some more of the good stuff."

"No, it's okay, I just forgot and moved. Not the brightest thing. How come you're not sleeping? I'll bet your head is killing you again."

"Stop worrying about me; you have the bigger war wound. Pretty impressive. I guess I'll need to start calling you the badass in our relationship," Tanner teased.

"Um, yeah, right. I'm not sure getting shot without firing a single round constitutes being a badass. I'm talented like that. I can snoop out trouble a mile away and manage to land smack-dab in the middle of it."

"Hey, don't be too hard on yourself. You did come to my rescue twice. I suppose it's the thought that counts, but no offense, you need to stop thinking like that." Tanner chuckled.

The nurse briskly entered the room. "I thought for sure you'd sleep through the night. Did you wake her up, and why are you out of the chair? No wonder the doc was complaining about you two. The only person who has any sense at all is your friend, Cisco, who managed to keep me from waking you earlier, which I can see was for naught because the one with the hard head managed to wake you anyway."

Cisco laughed.

"Hey, I did not wake her up. She moved, and the pain from her broken ribs and collapsed lung was the culprit, not me," Tanner defended and stuck her tongue out at Cisco.

The nurse shook her head. "If you continue to refuse a regular bed, at least get your butt back in the chair and stop pestering your friend." She injected something into Juliet's IV and glared at Tanner.

"Girlfriend," Tanner corrected.

"Okay, girlfriend." The nurse pointed to the recliner.

Tanner slumped back into it, pulled the blanket over her body, grabbed Juliet's hand, and threaded their fingers together.

Shaking her head again, the nurse left with the parting comment, "Call me if your pain continues beyond a level two or three." She pointed to the pain chart hanging on the wall with the cartoon faces next to the numbers one through ten.

"Cheery little thing. She was probably a nurse in the Army. They're usually crusty like that," Tanner remarked. She closed her eyes and finally allowed her body to relax and let sleep overcome her.

Chapter Twenty-three

Raoul woke up and was confused for a minute, and then it all came flooding back. It felt like a woodpecker was hammering on his head as he rotated to the right and looked at Miguel's immobile body. His face had a blotchy, blueish tint, and Raoul recognized strangulation as the cause of death.

He tried not to panic and wondered which option was better for him. Should he walk away and leave Miguel's body in the car? Maybe he could make an anonymous phone call and that would expedite the discovery. He wondered if he called the police and reported the death while waiting for them to come if they would finger him as the murderer. He knew he'd been drugged, probably by that cop, and suspected he could prove that because some of the substance was probably still in his bloodstream. But he knew he couldn't prove who'd drugged him, and honestly he didn't care that she killed Miguel; he just didn't want to do time for a murder he didn't commit.

In Raoul's mind, Miguel got what he deserved. He'd never liked the fact Miguel was a kiddie pornographer—

Raoul had a twelve-year-old daughter. But the money was too good to pass up, and Raoul didn't have too many skills he could fall back on.

In the end, he decided the better option would be to call the police and tell them what he knew, and he hoped that would be enough. Too many people had seen him with Miguel, so walking away was probably a poor choice.

Raoul pulled out his phone and made the call. "I've been drugged and my employer is dead.... Yeah, we're outside of...."

†

The sun filtered into the room, and Juliet felt the warmth settle on her cheek. She opened her eyes, and when they focused, she felt a sense of tranquility as she looked at Tanner sleeping peacefully on the chair—their hands still intertwined.

She couldn't prove it because she'd been asleep, but she was sure Tanner had departed from the room and was missing for several hours. She'd just sensed Tanner was absent during part of the night.

Juliet had a good idea where Tanner may have gone, but she wouldn't ask.

A commotion in the hallway caused Tanner to stir and mumble something that Juliet couldn't quite understand. She watched as Tanner's bloodshot eyes opened.

"Mmm, what time is it?" Tanner murmured.

"I don't know, but it's probably breakfast time. I hear activity in the corridor," Juliet answered.

Tanner tossed the blanket to the side and grinned at her as she glanced at the blanket crumpled on the floor. "Don't worry, I'll fold it up right now. I know it'll drive you crazy if I don't," she teased. Then she raised her hands above her head and looked as if she were reaching for the stars as she stretched. It was a very sensual move, and Juliet enjoyed the view.

The muffled voices in the hallway caused Cisco, Juliet, and Tanner to turn their heads.

Juliet heard the nurse's clipped voice. "No, you will not go into the room and disturb my patients. You can just wait until they awaken, and then I'll come get you."

She strained her ears to hear the response, but it sounded like the teacher in a Charlie Brown special, only with a deeper, distinctively male voice. Juliet chuckled as she remembered the "Mwah, wah, wah, wah, wah" of the teacher's muffled voice and how it used to crack her up as a kid.

She wondered if the nurse had escorted the man down the hall, because the voices sounded farther away now. She smiled as she envisioned the feisty nurse yanking a large man by the ear into the waiting room. Juliet knew this was probably not what had occurred, but the visual tickled her funny bone.

Cisco and Tanner shared a look, and Cisco nodded before standing and quietly exiting the room.

"You were here all night long—right by my side like any good girlfriend would be when their lover is recovering from a gunshot wound." Juliet bored a hole into Tanner's eyes with her gaze. She wanted Tanner to know that even though she knew what Tanner had done, it was okay with her and she would swear on a stack of Bibles if she needed to that Tanner had been there all night.

Tanner squeezed her hand, and with that, Juliet knew her message had gotten through loud and clear.

The door to the room cautiously opened, and the rectangle of light it created on the wall was the only reason

Juliet knew someone had entered. She watched the nurse scan the room. They locked eyes.

"I'm sorry, did that idiot police officer wake you?" the nurse asked.

"No, we'd already managed to wake up on our own. When I felt Juliet stir, I woke up," Tanner responded.

"Are you in pain again, hon?" the nurse asked.

Juliet shook her head. "No, the sun is shining and I could feel the warmth. It was a nice way to wake up."

"There is a very insistent police officer out here who wants to talk with…" the nurse motioned her head toward Tanner "…this one."

"How come you're all lollipops and rainbows with Juliet and vinegar and lemons with me?" Tanner asked.

"'Cause you threatened to leave against medical advice. Stupid people irritate me, but I suppose your dedication to your girlfriend is commendable. Sorry. I'll stop giving you a hard time." The nurse chuckled. "But you know it has been kinda fun to tease you. Do you want me to get rid of the officer? Because I will. Just say the word."

"Naw. It'll just irritate him, and an aggravated officer is no fun," Tanner replied.

†

Tanner clasped her hands in her lap and looked expectantly at the officer she'd met in the waiting room. "Well, what is so freakin' important that you just had to bust into the hospital and disturb me first thing in the morning? I haven't even had the wonderful institutional breakfast yet. I told your colleague I would come in today and make a full statement about yesterday."

"Ms. Sullivan, this morning Miguel Cortez was found dead in his vehicle. We understand you were in the middle of an ongoing investigation into Mr. Cortez. Dead bodies keep turning up around you. You wouldn't happen to know anything about his death, would you?"

"Hmm…let me see. Here's what I know. Apparently, Miguel sent a man after my girlfriend and me, and in self-defense I killed him. Yesterday a car full of gangbangers shot at us, and again we fired our weapons in self-defense. If your department were more on the ball, then perhaps it wouldn't take a small-town cop to do your job, mister…I'm sorry, I didn't catch your name, *Officer*.

"Detective Johnson, Ms. Sullivan."

"Okay, *Detective* Johnson. Through my sources, I learned Miguel managed a successful strike on Barbara and Special Agent Noles. I wasn't about to let his men get to Juliet or me. I'm a girl scout, Detective. I am always prepared. If you expect me to be unhappy that Miguel is dead, then you would be wrong, but you're looking in the wrong place, because I was here all night with my girlfriend and my friend Cisco. I'm sure the hospital personnel will confirm this. Just what is it you think I've done?"

"We have to follow all possible leads." Detective Johnson narrowed his eyes.

"Why do you even care? He was a low-life kiddie pornographer. If you ask me, he got what he deserved. Are we done here?"

"For now. Just so we're clear, I don't like kiddie pornographers any more than you do. I also don't like vigilantes who think they're entitled to do anything they want in the name of justice."

"Noted. For the record, if I knew who did this, vigilante or not, I'd pin a medal on his or her chest." Tanner grinned.

"What about your friend, Cisco. Was he in the room all night long as well?"

"Yes, he was, as a matter of fact. Once again, check with hospital personnel. I'm sure they'll confirm that for you."

"Oh, I plan to, Ms. Sullivan." Detective Johnson glared at her.

I can play the power name-game just as well as you, dickwad. "You do that, *Officer* Johnson. Now if you don't mind, my head is still killing me from the concussion Barbara gave me when she smashed her gun against my head. I think it's time I found out about getting out of the hospital and resting in my own bed."

Tanner slowly rose from the padded chair in the waiting room and walked back down the hallway to Juliet's room.

†

Juliet looked closely at Tanner's expression. She thought she knew Tanner well enough to judge how she was feeling, and Tanner looked perturbed.

Cisco glanced in Tanner's direction. "Everything copasetic?"

"Yeah. I just had some detective try to crawl up my ass. It was particularly fun. I told him I don't swing that way, and he wasn't amused."

Juliet raised her eyebrow. "Can you be a little more specific, please?"

"Apparently, Miguel Cortez was found dead this morning. Imagine that? It couldn't have happened to a nicer guy." Tanner smirked.

Juliet was nervous. She had a good idea who was responsible for Miguel's death, and she hoped the police weren't able to make a case against Tanner. "So what does that have to do with you?" she cautiously asked.

Tanner shrugged. "I think I was their primary subject until I mentioned I was here at the hospital all night long, dutifully sitting right beside my girlfriend. I suggested he check with the hospital personnel, you, and Cisco here. Of course, you can only testify to what you saw, and I don't want you to lie. I know you were sleeping for a portion of the evening, and if they dig and pursue that line of questioning, you need to tell the truth."

"You know I don't exactly know how long I was asleep and when, that's the truth," Juliet declared.

Tanner nodded.

"Well, I wasn't asleep and I can confirm your presence all night long." Cisco winked and held up three fingers.

"I know, I know, the favors keep piling up." Tanner chuckled.

"Seriously, Tanner, how much trouble are you in?" Juliet asked.

"Don't worry your beautiful little head. I'm fine. I'm not at all worried. They're just pissed that this local-yokel cop managed to successfully take out a hit man and three gangbangers with limited assistance. They were all clean shots and they know it. They're also pissed that Special Agent Noles wasn't able to protect their star witness and lost his life in the line of duty. I imagine someone up above is chewing a bunch of them a new asshole. It'll all die down. I think this detective is a lone cowboy on a crusade. Probably a homophobe and a misogynist. The fact a mere woman was able to protect her girlfriend and herself without the big bad men is a stick in his craw."

Cisco chuckled. "You just can't help leaving a wake of destruction, can you? So...are you two planning to stick around, or could I possibly interest you in a move to the big city? You know you always have a job waiting if you want it, Tanner."

Tanner smiled at Juliet. "I don't know. S-ville has something that Seattle doesn't. I'd only consider moving if Juliet decided she wants to leave. I kinda like the slower pace, and small-town folk are a lot more interesting to watch."

"You really want to stay in S-ville?" Juliet asked with hope tinging her voice.

"I said it before and I'll say it again—whither thou goest, I will go." Tanner leaned in and placed a gentle kiss on Juliet's lips.

"Can I be the best man at your wedding?" Cisco asked.

A dopey smile flashed across Tanner's face. "Yeah, I love her. She's a quirky little thing, but I'm madly in love with her."

"Who knew? The badass city cop has a softer, gentler side. Love looks good on you, Tanner. Juliet's an odd one, but she's good people. I think you two are really good for each other."

"All right, I suppose you can be the best man," Tanner responded.

Juliet didn't hear any hint of a joke in Tanner's tone, and her heart skipped a beat at the possibility that Tanner was serious. Marriage was a foreign concept to Juliet, but she was definitely warming to the idea. "I love you, too, but I think you need to ask me before the two of you start making wedding plans."

"Duly noted." Tanner winked.

Epilogue

Tanner and Juliet walked down Main Street with their fingers intertwined. Their lazy smiles revealed their relaxed mood. Since the sun was shining, most of the Riverville residents were finding excuses to pop outside and enjoy the balmy weather. It was a typical day in the geographical wind tunnel that seemed to capture the weather patterns and blow them around. Wind turbines kept popping up and dotting the landscape because the area had such a consistent wind pattern.

Tanner had evolved to the point where she smiled at most of the locals and talked amiably with them about nothing in particular. They'd come to see a different side to the recalcitrant police officer from S-Ville. Tanner wasn't under any illusion that this transformation had happened organically—it was all Juliet's influence.

Harley had managed to avoid jail time and moved on— *Good riddance.* S-ville had hired Paul, the reserve officer, as their other full-time staff member. Tanner liked the young kid even though he followed her around like a little puppy dog and hung on her every word. Someday he might make a fine officer, but for now the small town was aptly suited to his inexperience.

Darla did not fare as well as her brother and got seven years for her role in the kidnapping of the mayor's daughter. All of the mayor's fury had landed smack dab on top of her since no one else was alive to direct the blame at.

Tanner had heard a big butch at the women's prison had taken a special shine to her and Darla hadn't seemed to mind one bit. Tanner supposed love developed in the strangest places and between the oddest people.

Her mom had always told her that every pot had a lid. Tanner had found her lid with Juliet. She speculated the town thought they were an odd couple, but everyone seemed to embrace their relationship with the normal live-and-let-live philosophy so deeply ingrained in both Riverville and S-ville.

Clark, the town lush and quirky grocery store owner, whose high-school good looks were long gone, stuck his head out of his store and began frantically waving his arms. "Hey, Tanner, hey, Juliet. Enjoying our fine weather today?"

She remembered Juliet filling her in on how he'd ruined his marriage to Nancy and was in the middle of a hot-and-heavy affair with Scarlet, the preacher's wife. Tanner still chuckled on occasion regarding Juliet's in-depth knowledge of various citizens in the two small towns. She supposed that was all part of her charm. Yes, Juliet was a snoop, but her eagerness to learn about everyone wasn't malicious. Tanner suspected Juliet would write a book not intended to harm anyone, but to entertain people about the quirky characters in their small corner of the world.

"Hey, Clark." Juliet waved back. Her impish grin began to take form. "I heard the preacher's wife is getting a divorce?"

Clark blushed. "Yeah, Scarlet mentioned that to me."

"I'll just bet she did." Juliet laughed.

"Oh, for crying out loud. Clark, you gonna make an honest woman of her or what?" Tanner asked.

"Um...uh...I don't know what you're talking about," Clark stuttered.

"You're not still pining after Nancy, are you? She finally moved to Seattle with that big-time computer executive," Tanner needled.

One evening Juliet had confided in Tanner that she'd discovered Nancy's big secret. Margie, of all people, had relayed this particular piece of gossip. Tanner had begun to realize Juliet wasn't the biggest snoop in town after all. Apparently, Nancy had gotten herself linked up with one of the online dating sites and started dating a rich executive who lived on Lake Washington. Nancy's fancy car was a gift, and her frequent trips out of town were compliments of "Mr. Big."

"I heard they're getting married in the fall," Tanner poked.

She didn't really care for Clark and thought he was an egotistical blowhard. Juliet gave him a bit more grace, and she was sure Juliet would represent him more kindly than he deserved in her novel.

"I know that," Clark replied defensively. "I don't care one bit about Nancy. Scarlet and I are just friends."

"Yeah, right. Clark, everyone in this town knows about you two, so you might as well fess up to it. The preacher finally snagged a new trophy wife, and I don't think he ever cared much about you two anyway. Time to man up and make it official," Tanner declared.

"Mind your own business, Tanner. I'll get married again when you woman up and ask Juliet to be your wife. It's legal now, you know," Clark rebutted.

Juliet turned her head and smiled. "Guess he shut you up, huh?"

Tanner just grinned back at Juliet. She had a secret and wasn't about to reveal it in front of Clark or Margie, who waddled up to the small group.

"Wow, Margie, you're looking very pregnant all of a sudden. When's the baby due?" Juliet asked.

"Not soon enough. God, my dogs are killing me, and Harold is about as much help as a trapdoor on a canoe. Getting pregnant at forty-two wasn't the brightest thing I've ever done, but at least it brought Harold and I closer together. I can almost stand being in the same room with him now." Margie laughed.

Tanner wasn't fooled by her unkind words about her husband, since Margie had confided in Juliet that after Aiden's death, she'd realized what a sweet man Harold really was and that she needed to invest more in their relationship. She'd opened up to him and talked more about her needs, and he'd loved her enough to listen and make changes. Apparently, whatever changes he'd made resulted in Margie finally getting pregnant. She hadn't slowed down from the real estate business, but Tanner suspected that under that tough exterior, Margie was over the moon about her pregnancy.

"Be nice, Margie. Harold would do just about anything for you and you know it. Be happy for what you have, because he's a special guy," Juliet chastised.

Margie placed her hands on her stomach. "Yeah, he is. Who knew he could take such good direction. The man is a really quick learner. Well, y'all, take care. I need to waddle my ass home and see what Harold made me for lunch."

"You know, Harold is looking a lot less creepy lately. Did you take him for some kind of makeover? If I didn't know, I wouldn't guess he was the local undertaker," Tanner joked.

Margie smiled. "I decided I needed a makeover, and Harold insisted on coming along. I think he wanted to make himself more attractive after…well, I'm not exactly proud of my past behavior with Aiden. God, if I'd only known what a horrible person he really was, I never would have started that affair. I'm glad Harold gave me a second chance. I really do love the big lug."

"Love is a good thing." Juliet grinned and kissed Tanner's cheek.

Tanner blushed and then quirked her head at Juliet, sending her the signal that she'd had enough of the neighborly-good-will chat and wanted to get home to their big night. It was their anniversary and Tanner had plans for Juliet. Tanner chuckled as she thought what a strange date they'd picked to celebrate. September twentieth was the day she'd kidnapped Juliet, but Juliet insisted it should be the day to honor as the start of their relationship.

†

Juliet smoothed Tanner's shirt and kissed her on the nose. Tanner had on a nearly identical outfit to Juliet. The only difference was her blue T-shirt under the black hoodie and matching blue, high-top sneakers. Tanner filled out the T-shirt much better than Juliet, and she noticed every sculpted muscle.

She had purchased the blue tennis shoes and various spy items attached to Tanner's belt, as well as the T-shirt that matched Tanner's bright blue eyes. Juliet was a sucker for a woman with blue eyes, but Tanner's would turn any woman's head.

"I look ridiculous," Tanner lamented.

238

"No, you don't, you look sexy. You promised you would go out with me tonight. I need just a little more information for my book. I figured we could hit up the casino again. You have better observational skills than I do. Come on, please, I need your expertise," Juliet begged.

"You know you took advantage of me when I promised you. What a clever little minx you are. I would have agreed to just about anything, when you...uh...you know...had your head between my legs and I begged you not to stop."

Juliet grinned. "A promise is a promise—no matter what the circumstances were regarding the timing of the agreement you made."

"I don't know, Juliet. Your snooping seems to get you in trouble, and now you want to drag me into it. Can't we just go out to dinner, then dancing at a club, and have hot, wild sex like any other normal couple?" Tanner asked.

Juliet pouted. "It'll be like the perfect anniversary date. Don't you remember that it was my snooping that got you interested in me?"

"Um...that's a very generous way to describe how we got together. I still can't believe you forgave me for drugging you and then putting a gun to your forehead."

"We're unconventional. I like that we don't follow normal societal patterns. You certainly made an impression on me."

Tanner chuckled. "Okay, Juliet the Spy, lead the way. Whither thou goest, I will go. By the way...." She dropped to one knee and, from a pouch on her tool belt, removed a dark green ring box. "This is one thing I insist on doing the normal way. Will you marry me, Juliet Lewis, and make me the happiest woman in the world?"

Juliet dropped down to Tanner's level and threw her arms around Tanner's neck. "I thought you'd never ask, and to think all I needed to do was take you out on a snooping mission. I love you and can't wait to get married. Hey, we should call Cisco. He'll be so happy to know you're going to have him be your best man. Does this constitute another favor you owe him?"

"Nuh-uh. I'm planning on telling him he needs to reduce the count by one for the privilege of being my best man."

"You know, whenever you go off on your secret missions to pay back a favor, you start whistling. I think you enjoy helping him out. You get to do what you're best at since I'm sure staying on as one of S-ville's finest can't be very exciting."

"It's really kinda fun. Small-town politics aside, there are interesting people in both towns. I think getting to know the locals a little better has been a good thing. Ever since they heard about me taking care of the hit man, my badassery is legendary," Tanner boasted.

"Hmmm, that humility doesn't seem to go well with the spy outfit you're wearing. Wrong color, I guess. Oh, and I'm not marrying you unless I get to clean whatever place we decide to reserve for the wedding and reception. You can't trust anyone to make sure those places are clean."

"No, you certainly can't...." Tanner brought their lips together and gave Juliet a searing kiss.

About the Author

Annette Mori

Annette is an award-winning author who lives in the beautiful Pacific Northwest with her wife and their five furry kids. With eight published novels and one Goldie Award for her fourth novel, *Locked Inside*, she finally feels like a real author. Annette is as much a reader as a writer and always looking for the next lesfic novel to queue up. She came up with the One Fan at a Time tagline because it rolled off the tongue much better than One Reader at a Time. After pondering who she was at her core, it was all about connecting to each reader on a personal level. She would be the first to admit she doesn't do well with the masses. If someone picks up her book and it touches them, she believes she has achieved what she wants with her writing by reaching each reader. It is who she is at her core. Drop her a line; she loves to hear from readers: annettemori0859@gmail.com You can also catch her latest blogs at: https://annettemori0859.wordpress.com/.

Annette Mori

Other Affinity Press Books

Pausing by Renee MacKenzie
Jordy Chapman is the Emergency Service Coordinator at Cypress Haven mental health facility in Naples, FL. Keira Yeager's family owns an upscale furniture store in Naples and orchestrates a generous donation of furniture to Cypress Haven. When the two meet, they hit it off immediately. Will a Yeager family's anguish and misunderstanding threaten their new relationship?

Breaking the Silence by JM Dragon
Still grieving five years after the death of her father, Dilana Sterling is a shadow of the woman she once was…a successful author with a string of best sellers, and a longer string of women. Rachael Alderman, a teacher at the local orphanage, lives a quiet, yet satisfying life. When Dilana and Rachael meet, they develop a friendship that leads them on personal journeys of self-discovery. Will their memories of the past prevent them from moving towards each other, or

will they find a path that leads to each other so they can experience life together?

The Termination by Annette Mori
Codee is having a bad day and it's only going to get worse. Sawyer, a compassionate young woman, is resigned to her fate. Her only question is what fate is that? After slipping on ice, Codee wonders if she is hallucinating and fallen into an Alice type rabbit hole. The only thing she knows is that she needs to save Sawyer. Enjoy this satirical romance, with all of its twists and turns, that just might make you go hmm...

The Next Time by Erin O'Reilly
What if you had the chance to make history stop repeating itself? Would you sacrifice today for a chance at a better tomorrow? There is a moment in everyone's life that defines their future. For Jac and Carol, that time is now. Jump ahead twenty-five years and meet Carol's granddaughter Livvy. She is ready for a challenge and is fleeing the nest and getting on with her life. Read this wonderful love story that spans several lifetimes.

Open Your Heart a Sensual Collection by Ali Spooner
Excite your senses, rejuvenate your memories and best of all flirt with the edge of eroticism. Allow us to help you relive that first kiss, flirting with young love, your dream come true, surprise encounters, and your wildest desires... Enjoy these stories of love, sweet seduction, and steamy encounters. Open Your Heart...a sensual collection.

Secret of Stone Creek by Natalie London
Jennifer Cameron arrives in Stone Creek, Wisconsin to sell her grandparents' large Victorian home. While there she is intrigued by a twenty-four-year-old never solved murder. Her

attraction to the lovely and mysterious librarian, Diana vies for her attention. Follow this suspenseful whodunit to its conclusion.

The Promise by JM Dragon
An accidental meeting with Melissa Grant, leads to an unexpected offer for Kris Lake—refurbishing a beach cottage, with the help of Melissa's granddaughter Claire. Do outer imperfections prevent them from reaching the beauty that lives inside and the chance of a happy new life? Find out in this lovely romance that will fill you with heart-warming sensations throughout the story.

Christmas at Winterbourne by Jen Silver
The Christmas festivities for the guests booked into Winterbourne House has all the goings-on of a traditional holiday. The only difference is that this guesthouse is run by lesbians, for lesbians. Join the guests and staff at Winterbourne for a Christmas you'll not soon forget.

The Review by Annette Mori
Silver Lining, a successful lesbian romance writer, has the crazy idea to sponsor a contest where the first reader who posts a review wins a home-cooked meal with an offer to fly the winner to Washington State. Jasmine, the winner, has engaged in subtle flirtations with Silver. Bizarre messages from the unknown fan has Silver questioning the wisdom of a relationship with Jasmine.

South of Heaven by Ali Spooner
Kendra Drake has taken over as Captain of her father's shrimp boat. As a favor to her father, Kendra has agreed to

give fellow shrimper, Lindsey Bowen, a chance to work on the boat but first must prove herself to Kendra and her crew. Lindsey finds a way into Kendra's heart. Will it only last for the summer?

Catch to Release by Lacey Schmidt
On the verge of success, lesbian folk-rock star, Shay Greenaura, finds herself caught up in more than just her music. Threats have her manager hiring a security firm for protection. Addison Weller, a former Diplomatic Security Services agent is called in to assess the threats against Shay. Their undeniable attraction, brewing silently between them, could prove to be a fatal distraction. Follow this fast-paced adventure to its surprising romantic conclusion.

Ready for Love by Erin O'Reilly
Kylie Wilcox's life dramatically changed with the death of her husband. Dr. LJ Evans, a renowned archaeologist, needed and wanted nothing but her work for her happiness. Their worlds are about to collide and lives will be altered forever.

Neptune's Ring by Ali Spooner
In the sequel to *Venus Rising*, Nat and Liz, owners of Venus Rising, invite Levi and Vanessa to join them in a venture for a new club on another island. They find the perfect place in an unfinished resort, Neptune's Ring. While on the island, Levi is drawn into a mystery involving secret compartments and a murder. Join the characters in this page-turning adventure, filled with steamy romance, intrigue, and an unsolved murder.

The Ultimate Betrayal by Annette Mori
Lara is a successful, beautiful, charming, financier. She is also a total control freak, so whatever Lara wants, Lara

makes sure she gets. Rachel is Lara's fun-loving, charming, irresistible wife. Sophia's surprise visit to see Lara sets in motion a number of life changing events for them all. Hell has no fury as a woman scorned.

Keeping Faith by TJ Vertigo
You loved them in the previous novels, Private Dancer, Reece's Faith, and Reece's Star, now join the antics of Reece, Faith, Cori, Vi, and even The Animal, one last time in *Keeping Faith*.

Bound by Ali Spooner
A rogue, master vampire threatens the existence of the New Orleans vampire clan. Lord Jordan enlists Devin Benoit, sister of the Baton Rouge Alpha, and her witch lover, Tia, to assist with cleansing the city from potential disaster.

The Circle Dance by Jen Silver
Jamie Steele has moved to another town, trying to forget the heartbreak of losing her lover of six years. Sasha Fairfield finds her thoughts taken up with her ex-lover and thinks she wants Jamie back. Follow this captivating romance as love dances through the lives of these women to its surprising conclusion.

Anywhere, Everywhere by Renee MacKenzie
Gwen Martin's life in the Ten Thousand Islands area changes irrevocably when Piper Jackson comes into her life. Without trust, can the budding relationship between Gwen and Piper survive? Or will the answers to the questions continue to haunt them?

E-Books, Print, Free e-books

Visit our website for more publications available online.

www.affinityebooks.com

Published by Affinity E-Book Press NZ LTD
Canterbury, New Zealand

Registered Company 2517228

CPSIA information can be obtained
at www.ICGtesting.com
Printed in the USA
LVHW04s1450290818
588519LV00012B/597/P